The Prodigal Parents
Sinclair Lewis

Harry Sinclair Lewis (1885 – 1951) was an American novelist, short-story writer, and playwright. In 1930, he became the first writer from the United States to receive the Nobel Prize in Literature, which was awarded "for his vigorous and graphic art of description and his ability to create, with wit and humor, new types of characters." His works are known for their insightful and critical views of American capitalism and materialism between the wars. He is also respected for his strong characterizations of modern working women.

The Prodigal Parents

CHAPTER I

In the darkness of the country road after midnight the car was speeding, but the three young men jammed together in the one seat did not worry. They were exhilarated by the violence of the speeches they had heard at the strikers' mass meeting in the factory town of Cathay. When the car skidded slightly on a turn and the left-hand wheels crunched on the gravelled shoulder, the driver yelped, 'Hey, whoa-up!' But she did not whoa-up.

They were not drunk, except with high spirits. They had had a few bottles of beer, but what intoxicated them was the drama of thick-necked, bright-eyed strike leaders denouncing the tyranny of the bosses, the press, the taxpayers and all other oppressors. Two of the young men were juniors in Truxon College, and as they considered themselves to have been frequently and ludicrously misjudged by their own bosses, their parents and professors, they would (they told themselves) have stayed on in Cathay, joined the picket line, brave with bricks and pick handles, and probably have been gloriously killed, had it not been for a critically important fraternity dance at Truxon next evening.

As a substitute for thus entering the martyrs' profession, they now howled a song which stated that Labour was a Mighty Giant which was going to smash all its foemen immediately.

The third young man did not sing with them. He was a radical agitator; his name was Eugene Silga; he was slim and taut, with skin the colour of a cigar; and he had had quite enough singing in Cathay County Jail, a month ago. When the students stopped for breath, he protested, in the easy voice of a professional speaker, 'You seem to think it's going to be a cinch to overthrow the exploiting capitalist class--your own class, remember, you cursed sons of aristocrats. It's not! It'll take a lot more than singing to make Wall Street apologize to the Proletariat and go crawl in a hole.'

'Hurray! Wall Street in a hole! Lez go dig the hole!' bawled the driver.

This driver was a tall, wide young man, with wavy hair of red gold, a Norse god with eyes like the Baltic Sea in summer, and a face handsome as a magazine cover and stupid as a domesticated carp. His name was Howard Cornplow, and he was an adept in football, in golf, and in finding reasons why, at any particular recitation hour, he knew nothing whatever about the epistemology of Plato's *Meno*. He did know a great deal about the crawl stroke, however, which may have been just as well.

Howard Cornplow was a hearty young man, and he loved to argue. Accelerating a little, occasionally looking away from the road toward the agitator Silga, who sat in the dimness over beside the right-hand door, he shouted, 'Oh, rats, Gene! Don't you think if all us educated guys gang up on our folks, they'll snap out of their fool ex-up-expropriating attitude?'

'I do not!'

'Now look here. You take my dad. Old Fred. I can argue him down till he skips out and slams the door.'

As Howard continued, it was revealed that this 'dad', motor dealer in the city of Sachem Falls, N.Y., was an acceptable fellow, and that he was chronically overcome by his son's eloquence. Just to clarify it, Howard gave samples of the eloquence, and during the spirited recital he forgot that he was driving an automobile, and at sixty-five miles an hour.

The other student, Guy Staybridge, scrawny, big-nosed, spectacled, eager, wailed, 'Hey, watch what you're doing, will you, young Cornplow?'

'Don't you worry. I'm a careful driver,' clucked the Norse god, as he happily developed his theme that, in order to be converted to loving communism, the stuffy, prosperous, middle-class merchants like Fred Cornplow needed nothing more than friendly tips from such up-to-date examples of the Youth Movement as Howard Cornplow, Eugene Silga, and Guy Staybridge, with a few explanations about how the economic system really worked.

The car swayed on an abrupt turning. Howard kept it snugly to the right. But this was an S-curve, and as Howard looked away from the road towards Eugene, accelerating a little in his triumphant high spirits, the car, in a hundredth of a second, in a madness of speed that had nothing to do with time by the watch, bolted across the ditch, bounded on turf, twisted--crushing the three young men closer together--half swung around, grazed a birch tree, smashed a fender and a headlight and half the hood, and came up short, while the huddle of three were jerked sidewise, then hurled toward the windshield.

Instantly, an incredible silence of night. The car's lights were gone. Stillness and darkness clothed them in unreality. Nothing had happened. They were dead, worried Eugene Silga, as slowly he came to believe that he was not dead.

He was on his hands and knees on the wet turf of early winter; his cheek seemed to be bleeding, and his left shoulder stung; he could feel that his sleeves had been slashed to rags. But Gene Silga had been through riots, through club and paving-stone battles between strikers and policemen; he had been beaten by deputies; he was a veteran; and for all the reeking ache of his shoulder, he was not hysterical as he decided that the right-hand door must have burst open and himself been hurled out. He crawled to his feet, more conscious of the cold grass than of his pain, and sloped toward the car. No sound save hoarse breathing in this obscene silence.

He lit a cigar lighter--it was a trinket of gold--foppish and expensive for an agitator like Gene Silga; and the wife of a cement manufacturer had given it to him when he was abetting a strike against her husband. He saw that Howard Cornplow and Guy Staybridge were bleeding from cut foreheads, both of them unconscious, both alive.

He felt them over. He quietly set the flaming cigar lighter in a crevice of the crumpled dashboard, and with his handkerchief and others from the boys' pockets, bound their heads. He tugged Howard out of the car and laid him on the earth, his own coat under the Norse god's head. He propped up Guy in the seat. He stepped down from the running board, wincing as, to his sick fancy, his shoulder seemed to howl with pain. He staggered into the road and looked methodically back and ahead.

He made out a tiny light back along the road and went swaying toward it, his thin hand pressed tight to his shoulder. As he plodded, he hummed the 'Internationale', though it was punctuated with small groans.

The source of the light was a farmhouse, a bulk of darkness--and instantly there was a hateful dog pattering toward him, snarling. Gene kicked to right and left, felt a stone with his toe, stooped, cringing with pain, to pick up the stone, and marched on to meet the coming dog . . . For more than a year, once, Gene had been a hobo and learned the harsh wisdom of outfacing dangers: deppities and railroad dicks and their relatives, the savage dogs. He gushed, in the tone of a spinster lady addressing her Pekinese: 'Why Towser I'm tho ashamed of you! Don't oo remember oo's old friend Gene, oo sweet dirty son of a so and so, darling?'

The dog was puzzled. In a truce, but a truce still armed, it sniffed at Gene and followed him to the farmhouse door, from which an old man was peering.

Gene droned, 'Motor accident--smash-up--got a telephone I can use?'

'Guess so. Thought I heard a crash. Come in, boy.'

Gene telephoned on to Truxon village, site of the college, for an ambulance, a doctor. When he turned, the farmer called from an adjoining room, 'Be right with you, soon 's I dress.'

'Thanks, sir. I'll go ahead.'

'Want a flashlight?'

The question seemed to stir in Gene Silga some startling thought, and he sounded doubtful as he muttered, 'Oh. Oh, sure, you bet. Thanks.'

He was too reflective, as he trembled out of the house, to pay much heed to the still grumbling dog; he absently patted its head, while its tail wagged as finally it recognized a fellow killer.

On his way to the car, Gene thought angrily: 'Well, why not? Why shouldn't I? These snobs like Howard--oh, they'll buy you a dinner, yes, with beer and highballs, if they've recently gouged any money out of their slave-drivers of dads. That's so they can show off how liberal and brave they are. But do they care a hoot whether an organizer has one cent for breakfast--whether you sleep in a lousy lodging house--whether you have to hitch-hike to the next town? They do not! They've got to be *made* to care, and to pay. It's not for me personally. It's for the Revolution . . . Stealing? . . . Nothing but a word. One of my last holdovers from bourgeois morals . . . Didn't Stalin himself,' and mentally, Gene crossed himself, 'didn't he rob banks, as a youngster, to get money for the Cause? . . . Of course I'll do it.'

He had reached the wrecked car.

He ran the glow of the flashlight over Howard and Guy Staybridge. They were still out. With fingers sensitive as those of a miniature painter, or even a pickpocket, he searched them. From inside Howard's coat he took a billfold which contained three ten-dollar bills, six ones and a five. He removed one ten and three ones; with precise care he folded them small and tucked them into his shoe; and more delicately than ever he slid the billfold back into the pocket where (but only according to outmoded bourgeois ethics, of course) it belonged.

He examined Howard's bandage, straightened it a little, and sat on the running board till the farmer and the ambulance should come. He had already forgotten the pleasant addition to his war chest. He was thinking of the editorial on the flimsiness of college courses in economics which he was going to write as soon as he succeeded in founding a communist magazine.

The farmer loomed up, grunted, looked, exhibited the proper pleasure at seeing a real accident so near his hearthstone, made sure that he got his flashlight back from Gene and went away after, surprisingly, asking no questions beyond: Who were these three young men? Their occupations? Their parentage? Dates of birth? Place of birth? Their opinions of Franklin D. Roosevelt? And where had they been going, and why were they going so fast, considering that the farmer himself never drove over 30 m.p.h.--though, course, it was true that he didn't have no car like this Triumph Special, a dandy job that Special was, and how many m.p.h. did Gene, upon reasoned opinion, think a Triumph could do?

The coming ambulance smashed the grateful peace after the farmer had gone his ways, provided with new breakfast conversation.

The doctor in the Truxon ambulance found that there was among the three young men no mortal injury: Howard Cornplow had a superficial frontal cut and two ribs cracked against the steering wheel; Guy Staybridge, a fractured arm and a contusion probably not serious; Gene Silga, a broken shoulder-blade.

'Of course you young college geniuses . . .' began the interne, on the front seat with Gene and the driver.

'I'm no young college genius. I got kicked out of City College of New York six years ago, when I was twenty, for insubordination: to wit, telling a prof that he was a fat-headed grafter and beating up a tin soldier who tried to stop a pacifist parade,' said Gene, in the gentlest of purrs.

'Well anyway, you young hell-raisers think you've got more zip than four thousand pounds of steel and petrol. Anybody that ever drives over forty miles an hour is a fool,' said the interne--as the ambulance accelerated to fifty. Fretfully he added, to the driver, 'Step on it, can't you? I got to get back to my poker game. I need a little sleep, but, as I was telling you, what could I do when I had a full house, and Doc Brady lays for me, and seems he has four kinks, cold, and so I kep' raising him and he raised back . . . What's the matter with this bus, anyway? Crawls along like a steam-roller.'

CHAPTER II

To Frederick William Cornplow, this day was as another. The round little man, district agent for Triumph and Houndtooth automobiles in the Sachem Falls territory, had finished his cornflakes and bacon and poached eggs, in the scarlet-and-canary-yellow breakfast porch, which was not a porch, when he was called to the telephone and learned that his son, Howard, was in the hospital with injuries from a motor accident.

'I'll be there right away,' answered Fred Cornplow evenly.

He told neither his good wife, Hazel, nor his daughter, Sara, of the accident. For Hazel, who always drifted down to breakfast late, a soft and smiling sleepyhead, he left a note, 'Had to hustle office to see a man. F.'

The distance from his brick Colonial house, on the corner of Fenimore Cooper Boulevard and Tuke Street, Sachem Falls, N.Y., to the William Jackson Belch Infirmary, Truxon College, was seventy and a half miles, with a good deal of factory trucking traffic. He drove it in two hours flat. He got up to seventy on stretches, but through villages he dropped to twenty-five. He was a veteran driver and rigidly careful. He decidedly did not sing about Labour being a giant or anything else. He did not think much of Labour anyway. He employed it.

Through the drive, never taking his eyes from the road, he alternately decided that Howard could not be badly hurt, therefore Howard was a young fool and ought to have his car taken away from him, and that Howard was nigh unto death, in which case he was a superb driver whose accident was due to some double-damned garage mechanic's carelessness with steering gear or brakes . . . and that, in either case, the Norse god, with his kinky copper hair and his easy smile, was his father's heart and soul and means of immortality.

Fred jumped out at the Truxon infirmary, just back of the white and pillared official residence of the college president, and ran up the steps, but to the reception girl he said with gravity, 'My name is Cornplow. I believe my son was injured in a smash.'

'Oh yes. He's not badly hurt. The doctor isn't here, but I think you can go in and see Mr. Cornplow--he's in Room E, with some other stoodents.'

As Fred clumped up the linoleum-shining stairs, he reflected that it was startling to hear Howard called 'Mr. Cornplow'. He, Fredk Wm, was Mr. Cornplow. Howard--heck!--he was *Howard!*

He peeped into Room E, where, sunk on their pillows or sitting on the edges of their beds, were six young men, all bandaged, all pale, and all--in Fred's opinion--crazy as ticks, for they were screaming their opinions (or the opinions of whichever newspaper they happened to read) of Russia, Roosevelt,

Manchuria, backgammon, biochemistry, and the ham and cabbage at the college dining hall.

Howard was on his back. As Fred walked between the rows of beds, shy in the presence of these gilded young strangers, irritated that he had been so yearningly sentimental all the way from Sachem, Howard saw him and bellowed, 'Hello, Dad! Swell of you to come. I'm O.K. Couple of ribs K.O.'d. They don't hurt much, but gosh almighty, the doc insisted on putting a big, thick adhesive-tape bandage on me, it's like a double-strength corset, and wow, does it itch, ask me, *does* it, and the bandage so thick you can't scratch through it, and say, I figure there's a whole war manoeuvres going on underneath it--there's six regiments of fleas and a troop of light-mounted lice and . . .'

Fred sat on a chair by the bed and he, the round, the cheery, the jesting salesman, was solemn, feeling that the other crocks were inspecting this phenomenon, a Visiting Father. He interrupted:

'How'd it happen?'

'Happen? Nobody could've avoided it. Car jumped the road and hit a tree. And I was cold sober, and tending strictly to business . . .'

'How fast?'

'Fast? You mean how fast was I going?'

'I do.'

'Oh, I dunno--not more 'n forty . . .'

'Or maybe sixty?'

'Well, you know--just a fair cruising speed. There was an S-curve there-- absolutely a disgrace--entirely the fault of the county authorities--simply a crime--and when I get out of this, I'm going to sue the county. Oh say, Dad, you know Guy Staybridge, from Sachem, don't you--old hawkface, there in the next bed?'

Fred bowed. Guy waggled a melancholy fingertip. 'Oh, yes--the son of Putnam Staybridge?' Fred murmured.

'I--I understand so,' said Guy.

Fred was almost reverent. Like most Americans, he was perfectly democratic, except, perhaps, as regards social standing, wealth, political power, and club membership; but was not Mr. Putnam Staybridge believed to be a descendant of the *Mayflower?* Was he not the chief aristocrat of Sachem Falls?

Howard was volleying on: 'Yessir, absolutely county supervisors' fault, and they ought to be shown up. Just like all governments, except in Russia--oppress the people and kill 'em by tyranny and darn careless sloppiness. Dad, did you realize that in the past year--and the Americans thinking *they're* so efficient--the growth in production in heavy industry in the Ural section of Russia has been two hundred and seventeen per cent?'

'So? What is this "heavy industry"?'

'Heavy industry? Oh, you know. Darn it, I guess Gene Silga--say, now I think of it, I wonder where they took Gene when they brought us here, Guy?--but anyway, I don't believe Gene said anything about what heavy industry does cover. It's machines and so on, isn't it? What d'you think, Dad?'

Fred Cornplow, in the manner of a Roman candle on Fourth of July evening, suddenly flowered and flamed in parental rage. But he spoke so softly that not even Guy, in the next bed, could overhear.

'Think? Think? I think you're a conceited, inconsiderate young pup! I think you're so self-centred and so dog*gone* satisfied with yourself that it never occurs to you to remember how you might scare your mother and Sara and me, or how you hurt our feelings! I think it would be a bright idea to keep your scholarship marks from dropping about two hundred and seventeen per cent per each and every doggone annum, instead of going around feeling good because you've personally whooped up Soviet production so doggone much. And finally, I suppose you'll expect me to pay for having your car fixed after you've deliberately been and gone and driven so carelessly that I know doggone well you weren't keeping your eyes on the road and you ran off it! And of course, pass the buck to the county--and to me, to get it fixed!'

Howard's blue eyes of a young Balder, Norse godling of the summer radiance, looked hurt.

'But gee, Dad, it won't cost so much, will it, if you have it done in your own repair shop, at the agency?'

Fred was glaring now, and Howard begged, 'Gosh, honest, I wasn't driving fast, Dad. I don't *think* I was. I'm awfully sorry.'

'Grrrrr!' said Fredk Wm. For this was the third calamitous accident Howard had achieved in two years, and each time Fred had determined that it was his duty, finally, to say 'Grrrrr!'

CHAPTER III

'It might have been something I ate. That's what it was. Prob'ly something I ate,' said Fred. 'Or maybe it was the snow glare. Made me dizzy. Or prob'ly that cold I had last week. But chances are,' and he spoke with solidity and conviction, 'it was something I ate.'

He crawled from under the mountain range of bedclothes, he rubbed his forehead, he scratched his ruddy moustache, which resembled half a doughnut, he flapped his tongue in an interested and speculative manner, he took a romantic position, eyes closed and forefinger to temple, as befitted one who was importantly ill, and he croaked, 'I'll bet it was the pie.'

'If you know just what you're talking about, dear, I'd be glad of a tip on the subject,' sighed his wife, from the other twin bed in their pink and creamy chamber.

'If I--if I *know*--what I'm talking about!' He was moved to light a cigarette, though normally he was not one to sit in his nightshirt, upon the edges of beds, after midnight, and toy with cigarettes. 'Of course--of course. Man dying of pneumonia or malaria or something--just dying, that's all--and all his family is interested in is: "Does he know what he's talking about?"'

'Dear, I just meant. . . What is it, really?'

'I've got a fever.'

'You? A fever?'

'Yes, me. Not Sara, nor Howard, nor the cat, nor the maid's second cousin's brother-in-law, but me! F-e-v-e-r!'

Hazel Cornplow, plump little wife of the plump little man, climbed out of the misty layers of sleep in which she had been nestling, out of the downy strata of the very best poplin and blankets and foamy pink comforter, appropriate to this February night, drowsily wrapped herself in something that was a cross between, a feather boa and a Persian rug ($31.98 at Swazey & Lindbeck's, this past Christmas), and laid her plump, kind hand on his forehead.

'My! It does seem hot!' she exulted, with the pleasure all right-thinking persons feel in discovering that the best-beloved is helpless and that we shall be allowed to manage him.

'Something I ate. Lunch at the Elks' Club,' he croaked, ignorant of how fondly, in what he believed to be a grand and impressive tantrum, he was looking at her.

'What did you have?'

'Well--you know--just an ordinary lunch--I was lunching with Walter Lindbeck and Doc Kamerkink--we were talking about coddling the unemployed. I said to the doc, "Where's this business going to end, that's what I want to know;" and Walter says . . .'

'But what did you eat, dear?'

'Oh. Eat? Well, zy remember it, I had some corn soup, and I wish to thunder you'd try to coax that hired girl to make it for me oftener, no better soup made than a good corn soup with *corn* in it, and I had couple pork chops and some pickled beets and pickled watermelon rind and some cucumbers and some pie *a la mode*--raisin pie it was, with orange ice on it. . .'

Over Hazel's face--after slumber she looked not her fifty-three, but a fresh thirty--quivered a grin.

Fred held up his hand like a traffic policeman and protested:

'No! Wait! I know! I guess maybe it wasn't an entirely sensible lunch. But still, I don't rate this awful fever just from mixing up my grub a little. Are you going to sit there and gabble while I'm practically dying, you might say?'

'Oh, I know, Fred. Listen. Sara's got a clinical thermometer up in her room-- she used it for something or other when she was doing charity work in New York. It'll tell if you really feel bad.'

'I don't need any clinical thermometer to tell me how I feel! I just listen to the voice of my inner conscience, and it tells me I feel like the wrath of God!'

'I'm not,' she said, with that power of ignoring chatter which a professional wife develops after thirty years, 'I'm not sure I can read the thermometer right. Isn't it funny how we brought up two children without thermometers or bran or psychology or any of those new inventions! But I'll try it.'

She paddled into the wide hall with its landscape wallpaper. She did not seem oppressively worried. When she returned with the thermometer, which she held as though it were composed of dynamite, she spoke not of woe and mortalities, but gossiped, 'Almost one o'clock, and Sara not in yet.'

'Where the dickens that young woman goes . . . These modern girls. Sit *around*. Drink gin and try to talk politics! Discuss Conditions and Situations. Never get any sleep. They'll never have our pep at our age. When I was twenty-eight, like Sara . . . Brugluph!'

Hazel, with the rapture of an amateur nurse, had taken advantage of him by jamming the thermometer under his tongue. He sat slowly wobbling it with his lips, trying to continue his look of brave suffering, though by now he had almost forgotten from what he suffered. The sight of the black-rubber thermometer case in Hazel's hand recalled to him a new grievance, and as soon as she had slid the glass tube out of his mouth, he exploded:

'And another thing! You been using my fountain pen again! Oh, I can tell! The cap was on loose.'

She did not listen to this entirely justified charge. Like any other sound wife, she intended to go right on using his pen, as well as his razor and even his portable typewriter.

Studying the thermometer, she worried:

'Fred! Darling! You *have* got a fever!'

'Whadie tell you!'

'But it seems quite bad. If I make this thing out correctly, your temperature is a hundred and twenty degrees!'

'You're crazy! Gimme that thing! Hundred and twenty! If I had that, I'd be dead. I'll show you.'

He sucked the thermometer again, removed it, glanced at it with the careless mastery of a veteran salesman, and howled, 'Good heavens, girl, I *have* got a temperature of a hundred and twenty! I'm dead as a doornail!'

Side by side, hands clinging, they sat worrying.

His lament had covered a sound of footsteps in the hall, and neither of them was conscious of their daughter till she stood in the door, demanding, like an inspector out raiding, 'Why the wailing, Dad? What may all the trouble be?'

Pitifully, like a child showing a broken toy, Fred held up the thermometer, protesting, 'I've got a temperature of a hundred and twenty!'

'Oh, stuff!' Sara was, at twenty-eight, a perfect Queen Elizabeth. (Her name had been Sarah until, as a junior in high school, she had decapitated it.) 'You can't even read a thermometer. A fine lot of good you'd be if you were over in China now, fighting. Couldn't even care for the wounded. As untrained as Howard.'

'I don't intend to be over in China now, fighting, nor any other time, neither. The home talent there takes plenty care of that.'

'Huh! Here, open your mouth, Dad.'

She stood regally tall, silver cape about her seal-brown evening frock, while Fred, not the meekest of little men, had his temperature taken for the third time within ten minutes.

The lady Storm Trooper firmly removed the thermometer, and crowed, 'You haven't even half a degree of temperature. What you need is more sleep--at your age. G' night.'

She was gone, trailing behind her that magnificent intolerance.

Hazel looked at Fred, just looked, understandingly, and he trembled into speech:

'"At your age". And me only fifty-five! I ask you, is fifty-five any "your age"? It is not! And here I'd intended to find out what she means, staying out till all hours. That's where I lost out--when I first gave her a latchkey without a struggle.

'And . . . I suppose a fellow always loves his own daughter, don't he?' Fred pondered.

'Why, of course!'

'You do read in these novels and stories and everything where sons and daughters don't always love their parents, though, don't you?'

'Yes, I . . . I guess maybe you do.'

'Think their folks are just cranks and stuffed shirts?'

'Yes, but--oh, she's young, Fred.'

'Her? I'd been married three years, at her age.'

'Sara is so clever and educated and all. And she does look exactly like Diana. So tall and elegant. . .'

'Diana who?'

'The goddess--you know--in that green book.'

And, indeed, Hazel did not exaggerate. The supple, grey-eyed, neat-nosed, swift-moving Miss Sara Cornplow did look exactly like Diana--not that anybody knows how Diana looked.

'That don't excuse her for being so superior,' complained Fred. 'It beats the dickens how smart she is at making a fellow feel guilty all the time about things that aren't any of his business. Conditions and Situations! Inhibitions and Hormones! Russia! Share croppers! Miners' wages! Rats!'

Always Fred would mix the literacy of his college days with the colloquialisms of repair shop and junction lunchroom, till a foreigner would be puzzled as to whether he might be a scholar or a comedian.

'Doggone it, I don't own any mines! I'm not underpaying any miners! I don't have to feel guilty! I've always treated my family O.K., haven't I?'

'Of course.'

'Ain't a man in the motor game that can say Fred Cornplow ever done them, not even in the second-hand business. Why, say, I don't suppose I've pepped up some old plug with ether, not more'n half a dozen times in my life. But Sara--say, she even says, just because I like a good healthy nightshirt better 'n I do pyjamas, that I belong to the horse-and-buggy era--me that invented an oil filter that almost got taken up by Ford--and prob'ly she thinks you're a secret tobacco-chewer.

'And now that Howard seems to have gone and become a Red, guess it's from some brain injury he got in that last accident, him and Sara will gang up on me. I could always count on their bucking each other. When she come out of Vassar and first got noble and humanitarian on me, and had that six-months' charity job in New York, Howard was all for athletics; and when she managed to hitch up socialism and high sassiety, me having about an equal grouch on both of 'em, Howard decided he was a hairy pioneer and liked camping. But if they work together, what a run they'll give us.

'Still, maybe I am hard on Sara. She don't know yet what she wants to do--sits around waiting for Santa Claus--can't decide will she get married or be a missionary or raise wire-haired terriers. Poor kid, she's kind of lost, don't you think so?'

'Of course, dear.'

Hazel was wide asleep. But so wrathful was he that, though he had principles about 'getting your beauty sleep', he opened his current detective story and found happiness again: the delights of Chinese daggers, robbers' castles on the Yorkshire moors, baronets bleeding in rooms with locked doors and no windows.

He sighed happily as he came to the end of the tale:

'". . . that whatever you say will be taken down in writing and may be used against you", said Superintendent McCleaver.

'The professor coughed and raised a delicate hand to his pallid lips.

'"Seize him, men!" shouted the superintendent, lumbering out of the unwieldy Tudor chair. Sergeant McBeaver sprang at the professor, then stood appalled as that slim febrile body, all steel and rubber, slumped in the chair, and his head fell sidewise.

'P.C. McDeaver growled, "He must 've had potassium cyanide (KCN) concealed in his hand."

'The superintendent and Dr. Rosecliff exchanged slight smiles, and the Doctor murmured, "Oh no, that wouldn't be, would it? Or would it?"'

Fred Cornplow joined them in the slight smiles. This was fine. He was glad that they had captured the professor; a really dangerous, anti-social gent, given to murdering with fishhooks the spinster aunts of rural deans; but the poor maniac had been helpful to the soya-bean farmers of West Wiltshire. Fred looked tenderly at Hazel and turned off the light, and not till 8 a.m. did he think again of the slings and arrows of outrageous Sara, the sea of troubles that was certain to lave the golden feet of Howard.

CHAPTER IV

Frederick William Cornplow was in his office, at the Triumph agency, and he was busy. He had perceived that it was time to add an agency for trailers to his business, and he had sent his foreman and assistant manager, Paul Popple, out to Chicago to look into the matter of the Duplex Trailer, a new make, only just now in production but promising well.

That left Fred shorthanded. He had no one to sell cars except salesmen, and they had one fault: they could not endure just selling a car; they had to go through their little pieces about the Triumph which, with such agony, they had learned from Fred, and if a customer should attempt to buy a car off the floor, without letting the salesman lift the bonnet and point out that those funny jiggers there were the spark plugs, the salesman would go to pieces.

Fred had finished the morning mail. He had dictated to his secretary his decisions that he wouldn't really care to donate a free car to the Navaho, New Hampshire, Orphanage; nor serve as a committeeman for the Chamber of Commerce annual banquet in honour of Commodore Perry; nor contribute a hundred dollars to the Truxon College badminton association. Pleased that this morning he had been satisfactorily hardhearted, Fred lighted his first cigar of the day (the cigarettes began just after the cornflakes), and clucked, as into the office was ushered his sub-agent, Bert Whizzle, Triumph representative at Enigmaville.

'Well, well, well, Bert, how's the boy?' he said.

'Fine, fine! How's everything by you, Fred?'

'Swell! Couldn't be better! The new Houndtooth station wagon is simply wiping all the other boys off the map. You bet. Well, how's the little woman, Bert?'

'Fine, fine! Just fine and dandy.'

'Fine! And how's the three young uns, Bert?'

'Fine and dandy. Just fine. Say,' and Mr. Whizzle laughed a good deal, 'here was the funniest thing. Here couple nights ago we had the kids' grandma over for supper, and I let Peggy--she's the youngest--only six but bright's a dollar--I let her stay up to say howdy to the old dame, and what d' you think she said to her?'

'What was it? Tell me!' Fred's enthusiasm was as untarnished as on the day, twenty-nine years ago, when, a cadet travelling man in hardware, he had sold his first glamorous order of sixteen tack hammers and one three-tined manure fork.

'Well sir, believe me or not, the little tyke took one look at her grandmother and she pipes up and says, "Say, Gramma, does oo smoke cigarettes?" Well, sir, I thought I'd die! What d' you think of Roosevelt's New Deal, Fred?'

Fred meditated swiftly. Confound it, he couldn't remember whether Mr. Whizzle was a Democrat or a Republican. (It may be added that there were times when Fred could not remember whether he himself was a Sterling Republican or a Loyal Democrat.) He said weightily, 'Way I see it: now you take F.D.R. I'm perfectly certain there ain't a more humanitarian politician in the country--and what a voice on the radio! But same time, the needs and aspirations of the Republicans have got to be given every consideration. Way I see it!'

'You bet! You're dead right,' said Mr. Whizzle feelingly. 'Well say, Fred, got any interest in a couple 'r three orders this morning? Like to make a little dough?'

'Oh, I guess I could stand up under the foul blow--or fell blow, whichever it is. But the fact is . . . Now I don't know whether you'll believe this or not, but I'm not half as interested in the cash as I am in the fun of the game.' He did not believe that Mr. Whizzle believed that he believed anything of the sort, but it made a nice, refined atmosphere.

'Sure. Same way myself, Fred. Well, I've got orders for a Houndtooth convertible coop, de luxe, Persian green; a Triumph two-ton truck, closed body; and a Triumph special four-door sedan, Garden of Allah sand colour.'

'Have 'em for you by to-morrow, if they aren't already in stock,' chuckled Fred, as into the office charged his assistant, Paul Popple, bawling, 'Mr. Cornplow, we've got hold of the biggest thing . . .!'

'Just a minute! Just a minute, Paul! Can't you see I'm busy? You know Mr. Whizzle?'

'Oh--oh sure,' said Popple, as vaguely as a bridegroom. When Mr. Whizzle was gone, Fred turned on Popple with, 'Look here, son! Am I never going to learn you that it's these sub-agents that push off most of the cars we sell? Who do you think you are, anyway?'

'Oh, I'm sorry, but I was all excited. You will be, too.'

'How'd you get back from Chicago so quick? Didn't expect you till to-morrow.'

'Flew, sir.'

'Flew?'

'You bet.'

'In an aeroplane?'

'Nothing less.'

'Well, I'll be doggoned! I've flown, couple of times. But don't know's I liked it so much. Kept wanting to pull up beside the road and rest a little and maybe chew the rag with a filling-station attendant, and then I'd look down and there wasn't any road--just spider webs, down there. I felt like a toad in a cyclone.' His recollections were interrupted by the realization that Popple was jittery with a grandiose impatience, and he complained, 'But what was the idea? What was all the rush?'

'Mr. Cornplow, I think we've gotten hold of a whale of a proposition. I've brought with me a contract giving us not just a district agency but the whole of northern New York State for the Duplex Trailer! I looked it up, and there are six million people in the territory, and if we can't sell fifty thousand Duplexes in the next five years--'

'Take it easy! Get down to brass tacks, Paul. What is this machine for counterfeiting money that you think you've discovered?'

'Honest, Mr. Cornplow, the Duplex is a natural! It's got everything. On the road, it looks like an ordinary high-class passenger trailer, except that it's about eighteen inches higher--which still gives it as much clearance for railroad underpasses as any big furniture truck. Well, in that extra eighteen inches, there's an entire extra story to the trailer, collapsed like a bellows when you're driving.

'The roof of the second story--it's of aeroplane linen, with ribs of ribbon steel-- drops right down on the flat roof of the first story, with room between them for collapsible aluminum-alloy beds and chairs, and even collapsible washstands. The sides of the second story are of tarpaulin, and they cave in like an accordion.'

Fred was not interrupting. Fred was a lively enough chatterer when the customers wanted encouragement, but he had trained himself to utter stillness of listening when it should be useful.

'When you make camp, you raise the top roof with compressed air worked from the engine--in two minutes you can raise it, and you've added three separate bedrooms, with tarpaulin partitions and a gangway. And that leaves you a really comfortable big living room and kitchen downstairs. So Pop and Mom and two-three kids can all travel together with some privacy. It's a real moving home! It's a knockout! Look at these photos!'

Fred did look and felt like the first time he had put on radio earphones, heard Philadelphia talking, and guessed that someday he would listen from afar to presidents and kings. Fred had always found business a diverting struggle; he could not understand these superior people who considered trade mechanical and witless; and in the Duplex Trailer he smelled a new adventure.

'I kind of trust your mechanical sense, and you seem to think this Duplex is O.K., Paul. I'll think it over.'

'But I'm afraid you'll have to jump. They can only keep it open for us a few days. Honestly! You'll have to put up ten thousand cash for a start. All they need is that and your signature on the contract.'

And Fred signed. And the bookkeeper notarized. And the office-boy galloped off to the post-office to catch the air mail. And just as Fred leaned back, fretting a little, the Norse god Howard glowed into the office.

'Hello, Dad. H'are you, h'are you?'

'Fine and dandy, Howard. Ribs all right?'

'Grand!'

'What you doing in town?'

'Li'l' party with the Staybridges--Guy's going to introduce Sara and me to his Dad, you know, old Putnam, and his sister Annabel. Course I've met Annabel, dances and so on, but I don't really know her. And a friend of mine, a labour leader--Eugene Silga, his name is--is coming along.'

(It is true that, with 125,000 inhabitants in Sachem Falls, sound burghers like the Cornplows would not, save by accident, be intimate with the proud Staybridges.)

'All right, son. Staying at the house to-night?'

'No, got to buzz back to Truxon and . . . No, no, now wait, Dad. I'll drive like an old lady.'

'You will not! And if you want to break your neck, that's your business, but I'm getting good and tired of paying fines and repair bills, while you loaf through college!'

'But,' with wide, glad innocence, 'that's just what I came to see you about! Dad, I'm not getting anything out of college. The professors are the darnedest lot of crabs and bookworms. What good does it do me to learn about the--the--well, all these things they teach you? Couldn't you give me a job here in the agency?'

'Son, someday I hope you do really settle down and look at things seriously and want to come in with me. Someday I'll be thinking about retiring.'

'You? Never! You like your hand on the steering wheel too well! You'll be shoving off Triumphs on the sub-agents when you're eighty. But how about me starting in here . . .'

'Howard, I don't want to be any crankier than the law allows, but I certainly don't want you here, filling this place up with a lot of your fancy college friends, Guy Staybridge and God knows who all else, smoking and singing and playing contract.'

'Dad, you don't understand! Eugene has shown both Guy and me where . . . We've cut out being aristocrats.'

'Don't tell me!'

'We have. We see now that there's got to be a new world. Youth has got to take charge. Gene and Guy and me have been thinking about starting a cell of the Workers' International Cohesion in Sachem--the "Coheeze" they call it--you know, to make a United Front of all socialists and democrats and liberals and the whole bloomin' lot. I don't intend to have anything more to do with all those snobs and idlers. I'm going to go to work for you, and Guy and me are going to just associate with the intellectuals.'

'D'you think I'd be so crazy to have *them* make this shop a hangout? It wouldn't be any very big help to my business to have Reds and Bolsheviks and these new Coheezers of yours making speeches from running boards in the showroom, all day long. No, I'm sorry, but you can't come in here till you really want to sell cars because you want to sell cars, if I'm making it clear.'

'You're not, Dad, but . . . Lookit: course I don't want to be a fanatic about these revolutionary activities. Fact, I'd just soon chuck Eugene--you know: I mean, not let him have too much of an undue influence on me. How about me quitting school and taking up aviation? You know what a good driver I am . . .'

'Eh?'

'. . . and I'm dead certain I'd be a good aviator--you know, cross the ocean and everything. Or what do you think of starting a silver fox farm?'

'Or grow frogs' legs?'

It was Fred's supposition that he was being bitter, but the Norse god answered with bright gladness:

'Oh, there'd probably be a lot of money in that, too, but I don't believe frogs would be as much fun to raise as foxes--*or* aviation. How about it? Do something useful.'

A little wearily, a little savagely, altogether patiently, Fred explained, 'Howard, two years ago you wanted to quit and go to Hollywood. A year ago, when you had that piece about your fraternity dance in your college paper, you were ready to quit and take up your burden as London correspondent for the Associated Press. Listen! I don't necessarily think so much of college. But you've only got a year and a half to go before you get your degree, and if you can't stick that out, you'll have to get along on your own. My guess is that you'd make a first-rate coat holder for some posthole digger on a WPA project that ain't started yet!'

'Why Dad!' It was clear that Howard was hurt. Shocked, surprised, wounded in his filial piety. 'You mean, if I quit college and tried to really make something of myself, say wanted to buy an interest in one of these small broadcasting agencies, you wouldn't back me up?'

'Exactly!'

'Then, gosh, it's all true what Silga says about the Youth Movement: the older generation is trying to crush our aspirations and throttle us economically . . . Oh say, Dad, this Gene is a grand guy, and awfully hard up. Could you let me have twenty-five bucks to lend him?'

'I could not!'

'Well--well--see you again soon.'

Howard departed in complete cheerfulness.

In the heart of Fred, sitting motionless, there was considerably less cheer. He glanced irritably about his office. Yesterday it had been a sparkling gem of efficiency; now it seemed drearily commonplace: merely a desk, a couple of filing cabinets, a tableful of bright catalogues; the inner walls half wood and half clouded glass; the outer windows looking on a cemented yard full of dejected turn-ins with one horrible wreck that confessed a windshield jagged and stained. The only sounds were the rasping screech of valve-grinding, and from the sales floor, just outside, the voice of a salesman: 'Not a chance of your shimmying with a job like this. You can drive over cobblestones like you were in your cradle.'

'Dumb place. Never anything new,' Fred grunted.

It was running smoothly, it was his own machine, but suddenly he did not care whether it ran or not. Was that all that Howard and Sara wanted from him, just to 'back them up'?

This Duplex business: It might be too successful.

He might be caught up again in a delirium of business. Why wasn't it possible, just possibly possible, for Hazel and him to take a little time off, to flee from the pleasant padded servitude of the office, of their home, and see the world? Do a few crazy things like learning to ride horseback--gambling not more'n once or twice at Monte Carlo--trying to play the piano--seeing the Midnight Sun--building furniture--sitting at a small table in the piazza of Venice?

As a voice from beyond the clouds came the thought that, actually, they could do some of those things--do all of them! He was not rich, but he had money enough; the agency was not perfect but, under Paul Popple (not under Howard, by jiminy!), it would get along.

Almost frightened, he ran from the heretical inspiration; jammed on his hat and heavy overcoat; fled to the Sachem Club and the comforting dull talk of Doc Kamerkink and Walter Lindbeck and Ed Appletree.

For--he put it to himself in protest against himself--what the dickens would happen to the world if people ever did what they wanted to?

CHAPTER V

The present house of the Frederick Cornplows was a good brick Georgian house, on a good street, with a good little lawn and a good big maple tree, and it proved to their world that they were successful. But it was like fifty other residences on Fenimore Cooper Boulevard, which was like five hundred and fifty other handsome boulevards in America.

The residence of Mr. Putnam Staybridge--he who with seeming indifference bore the honour of being the father of Guy--was a museum piece: a square, white, frame object, with a cupola. It seemed to have been built of ice and icily to have defied the common sun. Every piece of furniture, to the last console table and damask-seated chair, belonged rigidly to the period--had in fact been created by one of the most eminent fakers of antiques.

This was fitting, because Mr. Staybridge was what is technically known as of a 'better family' than Fred Cornplow.

A better family is one that has had money or land longer than most; there is nothing more to the trick, and titles and armorial bearings are merely to fool the eye. Nor is it always good taste to ask where the family got the land and money in the first place. The truth about the Norman families of England is that William the Conqueror, a folio edition of Al Capone, stole the country from the

Saxons (who had stolen it from the Early English) and divided it among his gang, not yesterday, which would make it criminal, but back around 1100, which is aristocratic, and renders Norman lineage even more important than your golf handicap.

If it had been the Eskimos who had seized England and picked out pretty titles as earls eight hundred years ago, then the Best Families, both British and American, would to-day be claiming descent from Oley the Blubber.

Just so, a Staybridge ancestor, in Salem in the early 1700's, a pious man, fond of sermons about hell-fire, was a shipowner who from the West Indies brought molasses which he distilled into rum, which he shipped to Africa, where it was exchanged for kidnapped Negroes, who were taken as slaves to the West Indies, to be exchanged for molasses, with a profit at every corner of the triangle. So his descendants were able to become college founders, cabinet members, and Putnam Staybridges.

Putnam was so aristocratic that he dared, even in 1936, to wear a small beard. Perhaps he had slid down a little from the family standard, in that he was merely a clock manufacturer and a bank director, but he was first or second cousin to an ambassador, a Harvard professor, an Episcopalian bishop, and to the spouse of a Neapolitan duke; and his stamp collection contained a unique hexagonal black Swiss-Guiana specimen.

When Howard Cornplow lumberingly, Sara tensely, and the black-enamel-eyed organizer, Eugene Silga, placidly, came roaring with Guy into the Staybridge mansion, Putnam was artistically seated in the library, holding an Elzevir Apuleius in his lap and tapping the walnut chair arm with his eyeglasses . . . He had owned the Apuleius for ten years and had not, to date, read ten words beyond the title page. And he had been arranged here, tapping the glasses, for half an hour, ever since Guy had telephoned to announce this dreadful visitation.

He arose, for the purpose of bowing to Sara, looking quizzically at Howard, and snubbing Gene Silga, and went back to sitting, to tapping, and to glancing at his book.

Behind him was his daughter, Annabel, and Annabel was, to be brief, a darling. She was a tousled, smiling, shy, sloppy, brown-haired, easygoing, very pretty, happily cynical darling of nineteen or twenty, and Howard looked upon her--she looked upon the Norse god--with young rapture. Years ago they had met, at dances, but since she had been chased off to school at Farmington, they had never said anything more ardent than 'Mave nexdance?'

Howard was jarred out of his adoration by Mr. Putnam Staybridge's answer to whatever it was Guy had been babbling:

'So you intend to inaugurate in Sachem Falls a chapter of the Workers' International Cohesion--the Coheeze? Delightful name; so suitable to a young man like yourself, Guy, who was brought up to the traditions of Henry Adams. You purpose to start a monthly called *Protest & Progress,* nicknamed "P. & P.", to be cheaply printed and to unite the underprivileged of the entire world--no mean feat for three young men, even when abetted by so charming a young lady as Miss Sara Cornplow, considering that all the revolutionists in the world, including the accomplished Mr. Lenin, have hitherto failed to achieve this. And you wish me to contribute a sum which, I should judge from your slightly hysterical exposition, Guy, would be approximately a hundred dollars? . . . Now, Mr. Silga, will you be so good as to tell me whether this *Protest & Progress* will be definitely communistic?'

'Not in the least, sir.' Gene was calm, and Gene's smile was tender.

'It will not be under the eventual control of the Party, or whatever you may call the organization that receives orders from Moscow?'

'Oh no. The purpose of the "P. & P.", Mr. Staybridge, will be to unite people of all political faiths who believe in scientific control of politics, whether they are Republicans or Reds--except that, I'm sure, the Reds will denounce us as wishy-washy.'

Mr. Staybridge arose quietly. He murmured, 'In that case, I shall give Guy a cheque for one hundred dollars for your enterprise, on *condition* that no copy of the blasted sheet shall ever be brought into this house!'

He went beautifully up to his bedroom and read the same detective story that Fred Cornplow was, just then, reading at home.

When his father was safely gone, Guy fretted:

'But lookit, Gene, of course "P. & P." *will* be pro-communist.'

'Of course.'

'But you told Father it wouldn't be.'

'Of course I did.'

'But that's a lie.'

'Of course it is. Do you intend to go down to police headquarters and pin up posters announcing we're going to take over the constabulary, soon as we get the strength?'

Howard intruded, while the thrushlike Annabel Staybridge admired his copper-shining nobleness:

'Thunder, no, Guy, you certainly wouldn't do that?'

'No, maybe not,' said Guy, rubbing his large Staybridge nose, wiping his spectacles, in a jittery manner. It was only of late that he had gone from poetry into the lusher fields of communism and Holy Russia.

Gene exulted, 'With the seven-fifty the New York Coheeze has promised us, that makes eleven hundred and fifty dollars we've raised to start *Protest & Progress.* Think you can get a hundred out of your father, Howard--Sara?'

'Well, the old man is pretty down on the Reds, but he's a kindhearted old skate, if you're patient and let him get his bellyaching over,' rejoiced Howard.

'Even without it, we'll be able to get out one number, anyway--and what a terrible printing job *that's* going to be!' said Gene.

Eugene was a year or two younger than the Dianic Sara, a quarter of an inch shorter, and not having, like Sara, studied French at Vassar, he could not speak it. (Neither could Sara.) But so easy was he, so understandingly did those bright dark eyes look into her, that Sara was flattered to be called by her first name, was captivated by Gene's power--the result of his excellent endocrine glands--and interpreted it as her conversion to communism. She had done a little communism, just as she had done a little tennis, Thomas Wolfe, golf, Bach diving, William Faulkner, biochemistry, Buddhism, vegetarianism, and Buchmanism. Now she plunged deep, and at one end of Putnam Staybridge's chaste drawing-room Guy and Eugene and she happily agreed that within five years Putnam would be set by the American Soviets to digging canals.

But Annabel and Howard were at the other end of the apartment, and nothing like so revolutionary.

'Gosh, Miss Staybridge, I'm sorry I never really had a chance to get acquainted with you. You must of been just a kid when you went off to school.'

'Yes, I was--just a skinny awkward kid. But then I guess I still am, Mr. Cornplow.'

'You are not! Say, gosh, Miss Staybridge, you got more darn gracefulness and the loveliest lips I ever did see.'

'Oh, now you're flattering me, Mr. Cornplow. You college pundits! I'm just another young female, where you're a regular movie star. You play football at Truxon, don't you?'

'Well--that is--course I'm on the scrub team. The captain and the coach ganged up on me. They claim I'm lazy, just because they said I had to live on prunes and bran and go to bed at nine, and I told 'em where they got off! "I'm not going to bed at any nine o'clock and I'm not going to eat any prunes", I told 'em. No sir! Prunes! Don't you think so?'

'Oh, absolutely, Mr. Cornplow . . . Prunes!'

'I bet you love to dance, Miss Staybridge.'

'Oh, I adore it, but not with any of these little shrimps--only with tall men--and I've noticed that all you golden-haired boys, I don't know *why* it is, but somehow, you always dance so well.'

'Me? Golden-haired? It's just plain, dumb *red*--tray ordinary.'

'Oh, it is not red! It's gold.'

'It's red!'

'Gold!'

They dived into laughter--Romeo and Juliet, Tristan and Isolde, Mrs. Nickleby and the vegetable marrows.

At the other end of the room, Gene Silga explaining that in Russia--to which he had never been nearer than Fall River--the least skilful workman has a better time than any Detroit foreman: free lectures and a chance to do parachute jumping.

The revolutionary conspirators, the two lovers, could hear from above them an irritable pacing.

'That's Father, registering indignation,' sighed Guy. 'Don't it beat the Dutch how unsympathetic all fathers are!'

This beginning of the open season on parents drew the romantics back to the general hunting party, as Sara observed, 'Doesn't it! My father, old Freddie, wants to do the right thing by his offspring, sometimes dismayingly so, but he has no imagination; he can't understand that young people aren't altogether content to play bridge every evening and go to bed at ten-thirty. Why--why--he still wears a nightshirt instead of pyjamas!'

'No!' marvelled Guy.

'He's lucky. I usually don't have on anything at night except an undershirt,' said Gene.

'I'll bet Mr. Cornplow does so have imagination,' protested Annabel. 'I mean, I don't really know your father very well, but I talked to him once about getting a new car--Mr. Putnam Staybridge sure quenched *that* maiden's dream--and I thought your father was swell. He was so kind and he joked so . . .'

'Naturally, if he thought he could sell you a car!' said Sara. 'Oh, Dad really is kind, or means to be, but he hasn't got the imagination to see that the younger generation wants something more than being a respected resident of Cooper Boulevard. It's impossible for him to conceive that we, that Youth, no longer wants anything merely for itself, but demands that the whole world be freed of the bonds of capitalism.' She looked to Eugene for approval, and got it, from his well-trained professional smile. 'Why . . . Look, Annabel--I may call you Annabel, mayn't I?--doesn't your father travel a lot?'

'Sure. Comrade Putnam is even worse than the kind of globe-trotter that shows you his snapshots--he's the kind that sneaks off to Vienna and Rio and then gloats at you and won't even tell you what he's seen.'

Sara was relentless: 'Well, Dad won't travel one bit. Doesn't want to travel. And he can perfectly well afford to, the rest of his life. Why, time and again I've offered to take him to Paris--think of it, I've never been there myself!--and he always says, "We'll see", and sneaks out of it. Positively, Freddie *enjoys* being an old horse in a treadmill. I believe, no matter how he kicks about it, he's secretly pleased when we sponge on him. Shows what a noble, stalwart pillar of society he is! We must see to it that he contributes to the Coheeze.'

'Yes, we must see to that,' said Gene.

'Anyway, this whole business of parents,' began Guy, the poet, philosopher and pal, 'is a funny--well, it's a funny business. I think they ought to appreciate their children for taking the trouble to represent them in the new social movements, the socialization of education and the extension of labour unionism, since they're too old-fashioned to do it themselves. But say, speaking of your dad, how's to skip down to your house? There's Putnam making unfriendly noises upstairs again.'

'Grand! Come along! It's only ten-forty. Dad will be glad to see us.'

Howard was buoyant, and Annabel followed him in demure obedience. And Sara hinted no opposition after she had looked at Eugene and found him ready, and after she covered all points by explaining:

'Well . . . All right.'

CHAPTER VI

Fred had wound his watch, he had listened to the broadcaster's opinion that tomorrow it would rain in Omaha and parts of West Virginia, and he had proffered to Hazel his nightly observation, 'How about turning in and getting a little sleep?' The front door crashed, and in, like a flock of sheep with the voices of crows, tumbled Sara, Howard, Eugene, Guy, Annabel.

But when Fred had been presented to Annabel, he was sweet to her--too sweet, thought Hazel.

Sara purred, 'Father, Mother, this is Eugene Silga of the Workers' International Cohesion. I think you've heard Howard speak of him.'

'Oh yes, yes, sure, you bet!' crowed Fred, shaking hands.

Gene's thin hands were hard, and his eyes half friendly, half shrewd, altogether cynical. The comedian Fred, who all day long shouted stories, became cautious and dead quiet.

'Sara has been telling me about your two-story trailer,' said Eugene to him.

'Yes?'

'I'll remember it, next time I have anything to do with a demonstration in Union Square. Speech from the second story might go over big. I'm not sure you approve, but I'm interested in radical labour unions, Mr. Cornplow.'

Sara flared, 'Oh, why don't you *tell* 'em you're a communist and a party member, Mr. Silga--Eugene? It won't hurt 'em!'

Fred was more cautious than ever. 'No, it won't hurt us at all. I heard you were a communist, Mr. Silga, when you were mixed up in the Pragg glass-works strike. But here's something even stranger than that. Me, I'm a Republican and go to church!'

From Hazel there was a faint squawk that sounded like, *'When?'* as Fred went on selling:

'I'm glad to meet you, I won't pretend I like communism, but I much prefer you out-and-out advocates to the limousine socialists, like Sara here, who say, No, it wasn't the communism, it was something they ate; who cuss out capitalism and go right on living on it.'

'I don't know, Mr. Cornplow. An agitator finds limousines awfully useful sometimes, for escaping from the cops.'

'Hm. Yes. Glad meet you. I've been reading where it's become the fashion for the Reds to shave and bathe and leave the bombs home . . .'

'Sorry, never seen a bomb.'

'. . . in the bottom bureau drawer, and I'm interested to see that it's true, Gene.'

With warm-hearted aid from Guy and Howard, derisiveness from Annabel, and watchful silence from Eugene, Sara portrayed for Fred and Hazel the future of the Coheeze, and of the monthly *Protest & Progress,* which was to bring to far-flung workers in byre and grange and speak-easy the surprising news that, if they were real toilers and not parasites, like Fred, all Irishmen, Chinese, Japanese, Germans, Frenchmen, Spanish leftists, Spanish rightists, Negroes, Californians, Floridians, New York garment workers, Vermont apple growers, and pearl divers in Borneo loved one another to death.

'What do I do about it?' weaseled Fred.

'Why, you contribute!' Sara laughed heartily.

'Not me. I laid off loving the workers when the last automobile strike prevented my getting any cars to sell for couple of months, right at the height of the season.'

Sara protested, 'Guy's father, Mr. Staybridge, has given us a hundred dollars. Are you going to let him beat you?'

'Absolutely! Guy, you tell your father I'll let him contribute the whole doggone fund, if he wants to.'

'Oh, Dad!' (That was Sara again.)

Hazel spoiled everything:

'Fred, if Sara is enjoying this so much, and I'm sure Mr. Silga could tell us such interesting things about Russia, sex and divorces and how much the servants get and all--I do hope he'll be willing to lecture before the Egeria Club, it's my turn next month to get a speaker--and if Sara is having a good time out of it, I'm going to donate fifty dollars myself! Out of my own money, I mean!'

Fred goggled, remembering that Hazel's 'own money', from the estate of an unexpected uncle, had last year brought in $786.10, of which, to his knowledge, she had spent over nine hundred. While Hazel was being thanked, Fred craftily led Annabel apart and fished:

'Didn't know you knew my boy, Miss Staybridge.'

'Oh, I don't, really. I've just met him at dances.'

'That's probably the best place to meet him. I'd steer clear of him in the classroom.'

'Don't you guarantee him?'

'Well, he uses an awful lot of oil and gas and he backfires going uphill, not down, and his brakes are slipping. But he's got a nice three-coat finish, and I kind of like him.'

'So do I!'

Everyone else was lounging; everyone was chattering; Hazel was explaining to Gene Silga what a wonderful time they had had at the Egeria Club when they had entertained a pupil of Dale Carnegie, who had informed them that the ability to express one's self on one's feet was as important to a clubwoman as it was even to a senator or a lubricant salesman. But Annabel sat straight, her hands folded in her lap, her eyes straight ahead, in a trance. Her lips seemed very soft; Fred thought that they would tremble, if she was hurt. She seemed to him made not of patches of prejudice and unimportant informations, like the rest, but to be all of one piece, clear and sure and kind.

'She'll fall in love with Howard because he looks like a movie star, and then keep it up because she'll be sorry for him,' sighed Fred to himself. 'He'll wear her out. Here, quit it! Don't crab about your own son. Way Annabel's looking round, guess she likes it here--kind of free and easy--or would be if Sara wasn't so doggone high-minded--in comparison with Staybridge, that old stiff. But Annabel--got the friendliest eyes I ever saw--friendly 's a pup--I'd like to have Howard safely married to a good loyal girl like her, but do I want to see *her* married to a loafer? Duties of parents? Someday I'll chuck the lot of 'em . . . I won't!'

By request of Sara, Eugene Silga outstayed Annabel and Guy. After ten minutes' discussion of the fact that, if he started in five minutes, he could be in Truxon at a fair hour, Howard went up to bed; and Eugene and Fred, with the Cornplow women for gallery, circled about each other.

Let us be clear about the political activities of Eugene Silga. He was not at all like the melodramatic Bolsheviks of British detective stories; he had no secret gang with an abbey crypt for hideout, no beautiful phoney countess (in black with a platinum dog collar) for spy. Fred suspected that Sara's radical toying, suddenly become so active this evening, meant nothing more than a desire to be important, to be Different, and to associate with romantic young men. But Gene's purpose was clear. He had hated the bland and rich ever since his infanthood in a riverside slum in Brooklyn. Making his way at City College of New York by pressing clothes had not improved his benevolence. He wanted power and revenge; he was willing to risk death in the hope of smashing the entire democratic system and winding up with the factory workers dictatorially running the country, and himself running the workers.

Both Sara and he did love humanity. Whether either of them loved a single individual human being was less certain.

Eugene did not come out of the comic papers. He was neither dirty-necked nor bellowing, nor had he any especial tropism for soapboxes. He was neat and quiet-voiced; he smiled affectionately; and he was, to the world of Fred Cornplow--to the world of Franklin and Emerson and Mark Twain, of Willa Cather and William Allen White--as dangerous as a rattlesnake.

There is a vulgar error about rattlesnakes. Hordes of sensible people assume that it is treacherous in a rattlesnake to bite the tourists, but to himself a rattlesnake is an honest, kind-hearted family man who believes that human beings treacherously kill a lot more rattlesnakes than snakes kill humans.

Eugene was telling Fred about the Youth Movement.

'It's not purely a communist doctrine. We're willing to make a United Front with the liberals and even lukewarm socialists. I've just been out at a Youth Convention in Cincinnati. We're demanding of Congress . . .'

'Demanding?'

'Certainly! Demanding that all young people up to twenty-five--oh, I'm a year beyond that limit, so it's not personal--be granted college educations with all expenses paid, free cigarettes, free movies twice a week, and jobs at union wages guaranteed after college.'

Fred was gulping, but Sara stopped him with, 'Now, Dad, please don't tell us again how you waited on table at college, and then went to work at seven dollars a week.'

It was Hazel who, surprisingly, led the attack: 'I never could quite understand the Youth Movement. I know; so many of the boys and girls are having a dreadful time getting started, nowadays. But is it any harder on them when they can't find a job than it is on a man of forty-five, with a sick wife and three children?'

'That's scarcely an answer,' condescended Eugene, while inwardly Fred began to rage that, 'Doggone it, this Silga fellow acts like he owned the house. Pretty soon he'll give us lessons in how to drive a car, if we'll just pay strict attention.'

'That's scarcely an answer. Naturally, I believe in guaranteeing work, with a maximum week's labour of thirty hours and a minimum wage of fifty dollars, for all workers, whether they are twenty-five or sixty-five. But our chief concern is with Youth, because it has a chance to be educated: it isn't blinded by the American myth that this is a democracy and that everybody still has a chance.'

While Fred tried to look relaxed and impartial, and did look as relaxed and impartial as a cat on flypaper, Eugene informed him that all automobile workers' wages could easily be doubled if the manufacturers would get rid of the middleman (such as Fred Cornplow); that it was a good thought that Great Britain would soon lose India and Egypt, France lose Indo-China, and Holland lose Java; that it was an even better thought that during the first three months of the Next War, Russia would take over Alaska, western Canada, China, Scandinavia and Poland, and make their inhabitants as joyous as the Russian peasants. So, by easy stages, they came to Spain, where, everyone said, there would be a dangerous right revolution before long.

Eugene announced, and quite politely, 'I've talked it all over with Sara, Mr. Cornplow and--I hope you won't think it's impertinent of us, but we find that the only way to get proper contributions for the Spanish government is to figure out quotas for different contributors, and let them know.'

'But I'm not a con . . .'

'And Sara and I feel that you could show that you really do believe in democracy and popular rule by contributing five hundred dollars to the Spanish government and . . .'

'Five hun . . .'

'Certainly! Heaven knows I can't give anything, with my wretched income,' snarled Sara.

Fredk Wm, who gave her that income, didn't think it was at all wretched, considering his own resources. A thousand a year and all found? So that was wretched, was it? He spoke with spirit and wrath:

'Look here, you young people, I'm getting tired of being badgered. I know I'm just a millionaire capitalist--just a multi-millionaire, that's all, nothing but a face grinder and an orphan robber, just a foe of the oppressed. Sure, I understand that horny-handed proletarians like you two have got to destroy capitalists like me--certainly--just take us out and destroy us--put us up against a wall and destroy us--take away my steam yacht and my French château and my wife's ruby necklace--just take 'em away and stick us up against a wall and fill us full of holes. That's the proper caper, just destroy us. Only, I don't expect to contribute for the privilege of being destroyed! I'll be content with just being shot; let the other fellow pay for the bullets.

'No, wait now, Sara. I know, when you open your mouth like a fish, I'm going to get hell. But you listen to me first, for a while.

'I do read the newspapers. Seriously, I do know there's a lot of things wrong in this world; mining is dangerous and badly paid; Tom Mooney was rail-roaded and ought to be released; the Southern share croppers have a terrible time--*and* so do most of the plantation owners!--a lot of priests and college professors get sent to prison in Europe for telling the truth; the Negroes get an awful deal; a lot of farmers just work to feed their mortgages.

'But unlike you communists, I don't feel that I'm Almighty God. I can't do everything in the world at once. I'm the president of the Mind Your Own Business Association. I'm just not rich enough and not smart enough to rebuild the New York slums and stop all war at one and the same time. I don't think I've done so bad with my own job. My workmen and my customers both seem pretty well satisfied. I get along all right with my own family . . .'

'Do you?' breathed Sara.

That hurt. It seemed to Fred equally pertinent and impertinent. He went on less confidently.

'I mean . . . And so . . . Well, as I was trying to say: I don't pretend to be a Rockefeller. I'm just a plain ordinary citizen of Sachem Falls, N.Y., and you highbrows, who love to talk so much about realism and seeing clearly, ought to appreciate the fact that I know what I am.'

Hazel had looked at Fred sympathetically, and she charged up with reinforcements. With the most restful prosiness, she told Eugene about the Spreadeagle Little Theatre of Sachem, about Howard's remarkable success in baseball, as a boy, and about her cousins in California. This warm bath soothed them all, and Eugene eased out, with an abstracted farewell which said that he would never come back.

'Did you really have to go out of your way to be insulting?' demanded Sara.

'Not very far! I never could understand why it was that thirty years ago we were supposed to be apologetic to all the visiting firemen from France and England for being American, and now we're expected to apologize to Russia. When this young pup hits me in a tender spot . . .'

'Your pocket-book, Father!'

'You bet! It's what you've always lived on, isn't it, young lady, if you want me to be vulgar?'

'I don't!'

'Well, when he sashays in here and tells me my duty . . .'

'I wonder you didn't spring on him something refreshing like, "If you don't like it here, why don't you go back where you came from?"'

'Well, I did think of taking that up, but I wasn't sure he came from some country I disliked enough to wish him off on it! But I respect him more than I do you. He has the decency to be openly a threat to every doggone thing I stand for, and risk his life in strikes, and prob'ly he lives on fifteen-twenty bucks a week, while the young folks like you sponge on your parents for all you can get, and are ashamed of yourselves for it, and take it out on us!'

'Father!'

'Absolutely. Maybe you're not to blame personally. Whole country's full of smart young people whose folks have sent 'em to school and done all they could to help 'em socially and financially, and the kids despise 'em for being so soft, and don't for one second hesitate to correct their parents' manners and historical dates! But I don't intend to have any of those intellectual snobs in my house, not if I know it! Young lady, after children get to be eighteen or so, they have no more claim on their parents' affection than anybody else. They've got to earn it!'

Sara rushed from the room, sobbing.

Fred paced a good deal.

'Oh, hang it, I didn't mean . . . But that girl, Sara, she got me so riled up, just when I'd laid myself out to be so polite to her and that dark-eyed comrade, that Bolshevik gigolo! Why can't they be nice, like Annabel? There's *my* daughter. Not sure I'll let her marry Howard, the stuffed sweater! But Sara . . . All right, all *right!* Shall I wait and apologize to her to-morrow, or go up and get it over now?'

CHAPTER VII

The renowned Old Home Week of Sachem Falls was held in March, however inclement, because that month marked the birthday of the city's one revolutionary hero, General Abram Pough, of whom no one knew anything except that he had been a hero, that he had almost certainly been born, that he had been born in March, and that he had not been born at the celebrated Pough Birthplace, on Beecher Street. The annual Home Week parade was, by custom, the occasion for the first outdoor showing of the new automobile models, an attraction altogether more interesting than General Pough to the citizenry.

It was in this parade that Fred exhibited the first Duplex Trailers beheld in Sachem. His assistant, Paul Popple, had fretted, 'Say, Chief, I've got the low-down on what the Conqueror people are going to do. They're showing six models, all decorated with hot-house flowers. What say we have ours tied up with gold ribbons?'

'I'm not selling ribbons. Nor gold. Nor flowers. I'm selling automobiles. I'll work out our display,' snorted Fred.

Paul Popple was doubtful, Hazel was doubtful, and Sara was shocked when, in the Old Home Week parade, after floats showing the Dutch first settlers making cheese and consequently being scalped by the Iroquois, after the American Legion and the Sons of Sweden and the pickle-works exhibit and the Woodmen of America, rich in axes and badges, after the elegant display of the rival Conqueror Motor Company, ornate with roses and daffodils, came the eccentric display arranged by Fred. Leading it was a Triumph town car, and in that car was the mayor of Sachem, who owed Fred three hundred dollars. The spectators, packed in like baled hay and encouraged by dollar-a-day clappers hired by Fred, applauded with an apparent feeling that this was official and the Triumph must, therefore, be a very good car indeed. Following was a Houndtooth Six, and, to Sara's wan disapproval, it lacked not only flowers and ribbons, but even a decent body. There was only the chassis, without fenders and with the driver on a greasy wooden box. But the crowd was stirred by seeing the wheels go round, and jammed in close to the Houndtooth, crying, 'Look, Bill, the way them brakes work!'

After it rolled six Duplex Trailers, and this was the first time that any outsider in Sachem had seen a Duplex.

The trailers were in busy action. The extra second story of each was being raised or taken down. The crowd gasped and gurgled, and Hazel patted Fred's cheek in wonder, as she saw three bedrooms magically created out of air.

The news stories about the parade, later, in all three papers, could not ignore this innovation--particularly as Fred had promised each of them a full-page Duplex advertisement. In each news story was a paragraph to the effect: 'The surprise of the show, however, was a fleet of Duplex Trailers, which unfold to provide a second story.'

Fred had sold six Duplexes before twilight the next day.

But at home, quiet beside Hazel on the couch, listening to a nostalgic Hawaiian radio quartette (from the Bronx), Fred pondered, 'Yuh, it was a good show. I'm a swell salesman *and* a good showman. But--funny--the kick don't seem to last. I felt kind of naked out there, watching the Duplexes dress and undress in public. Am I getting tired of just being a showman, honey? Then what 'll I *do?*

He did not speak to Hazel, he didn't even speak to himself, about the important occurrence of the Old Home Week parade.

During the passing of the Duplexes, Fred had wandered away from Hazel, to greet possible customers, and in the crowd had come upon Putnam Staybridge and Annabel.

But for the treachery of George Washington, Mr. Staybridge would now be Gen. the Rt. Hon. Sir Putnam Staybridge, P.C., D.S.O., K.C.M.G., and though he had been robbed of this rightful label, yet in the precision of his little beard, the quiet intolerance of his grey eyes, the erectness of his frail shoulders, Mr. Staybridge showed his private knightliness. He was devoting it now to sneering at the Duplex demonstration, and it did not help Fred to know that Mr. Staybridge had some unacknowledged interest in the opposition Conqueror Motor Company.

'How d'you do, Mr . . . Cornplow,' said Mr. Staybridge. But Fred felt that he didn't really much care how he did, or whether he did at all. Putnam was already ignoring him while he acknowledged the passing of a woman acquaintance by pinching the top of his hat and slightly widening his lips, like the stretching of a rubber band.

But Annabel was beaming. Fred flagrantly winked at her.

Five minutes later, while Fred was watching the passing of the Boy Scouts, someone plucked at his sleeve, and he looked down--not very far down--on a shy Annabel.

He comprehensively remarked, 'Well, well!'

'Father's gone and . . .'

'You stay with me. I'll guard you. I used to be a G-man.'

'Honestly?'

'Absolutely. I captured Jesse James.'

'Jesse James wasn't captured. He was shot in the back by a member of his gang.'

Fred looked on Annabel with favour. How rare it was, he thought, to find anyone under thirty these days who was not dazzled by the movies and aviation, but knew such sanctities of American history as the James Boys. 'Good girl,' he said. He could not treat her like a Staybridge. She really seemed human. He grumbled, 'Afraid your father didn't care much for my trick trailers, Miss Staybridge.'

'I'm afraid he enjoys not caring for much of anything. Uh . . . uh . . .' Annabel twisted a button of his coat. 'Have you seen Howard?'

'Not for a few days. He's coming down for my birthday party, at the house, week from next Tuesday. Look! Why don't you come?'

'I'd love to, Mr. Cornplow!'

He envied the clear light of Annabel in a foggy, complicated world.

'By golly,' he swore, 'if Howard don't fall properly in love with her, I'll--well, I'll do the worst thing to him I possibly can: I'll let him do what he thinks he wants to do--leave college and go to work!'

CHAPTER VIII

The house of Frederick William Cornplow was filled with openly secret preparations for his fifty-sixth birthday, next day. He sat in plump contentment, awaiting dinner and snorting over the evening paper, and all life seemed secure.

The doorbell rang then, and all the forgotten sorrows of life trooped in.

Hilda, the maid, announced, 'There's some folks here, name of Tillery, Enos Tillery and his folks; they say they want to see you.'

'Tillery? Never heard . . . Oh, wait.'

With creeping horror Fred remembered that he did have some second-hand cousins of that ominous name. One Joe Tillery, from back yonder. Not since boyhood had he seen any of the tribe, but he remembered them, in a paintless farm shanty, unbathed, uncombed, insolvent and full of jolly music; he remembered his father giving Joe a tenth of the ten dollars which Joe had modestly solicited. This Enos Tillery would be Joe's faithful son.

Fred stalked into the hall. With touching trustfulness he hoped that the Tillerys would get no farther.

By the door, looked appallingly friendly, was a man of Fred's own age--Enos, presumably--whose hair had not been cut for two months nor his cheeks shaven for four days, but who displayed checked plus-fours, golf stockings purple and leaf-green, and a moth-eaten red sweater. Enos was reinforced by his wife, in a tweed coat with a fur collar which needed combing, as did her greasy black hair, and by two lumps of grown sons and a small boy and a small girl.

Now Fred had resolutely freed himself of the heresy, held by his father and his father's friends, that there was disgrace in poverty and evil in the poor. On the other hand, he had not slipped into the new credo that poverty and bad luck and dirt are always and necessarily superior to thrift and good fortune and soap . . . And perhaps he wouldn't have cared a hang, one way or the other, but he was that most shrewdly disciplined of beings, a Good Family Man, and as the Tillerys broke out in a rash of smiles that to the experienced tradesman meant cases of the helping-themselves hand, Fred was itchily conscious that Hazel might be peeping around a corner and refusing to forgive him for having brought these relatives into the world.

Enos was shouting, 'Well, well, it's fat little Freddie Cornplow, the old thief! Remember how you used to pinch apples, at our farm, and Dad walloped the daylights out of you? Remember how you were scared to go swimming in the crick? Oh, those were the great days!'

From the blue distances of jocund Youth, there seemed to float past Fred a delicate odour of the Tillery pigpen. But he got out shakily:

'Oh, yuh, sure--yuh, that's right. So this is the family.'

'Yes, here's Edna, the wife, and Mac and Cal, the big fellows, and little Tom and Sagittaria.'

Fred did not understand it, but somehow they were no longer in the hall; they were in the living-room, seated, and Cal had helped himself to a cigarette, Mrs. Tillery to candy, while Tom and Sagittaria were bouncing gleefully on the couch, whose springs were none too hale.

(But you couldn't turn down your relatives, your own cousins, now could you? Blood thicker than--thicker 'n glue, this time . . . But golly, if Sara came in!)

Enos was caroling, 'Well, sir, we're kind of driving down towards West Virginia--fellow told us there was some kind of Rural Resettlement project down there where we could get a farm free, and all the tools. I noticed we was right near here, and I says to Edna, that's the wife, "We'll just drop in on fat little Freddie--not make any trouble--maybe he's got engagements--not give him and his woman . . ." Eglantine, that's your wife's name, ain't it?'

'Hazel.'

'Hazel? Kind of a hick name. She just a plain farmer, too, like you and me, Fred? Well, anyway, Edna says no--says it's almost forty years since you and me have seen each other--you wouldn't want to entertain us, she says, but I says "Of course he'll want to see a *cousin!*" I says. "Wouldn't I be tickled to death to give *him* a shakedown if I had a house and if him and his family come along?" . . . How many kids you got, Fred?'

'Two.'

'Oh well, you never were much good. Six, I've got--these four, and another one that's got a fine job selling patent medicines, and the other--well, he had kind of bad luck, and 's matter of fact, he was innocent, but he's in the reformatory, and . . . Anyway, "No," I says to Edna, "of course he'll be glad to see us. What's relatives for?" I says. "Fred may have gone and got rich, but I'll bet he don't think he's too good for his own people--I'll bet that at heart he's just a dumb, plain rube like the rest of us." Is that steak I smell?'

Fred was by now in a simple state of dementia. Beyond question he knew that if he invited his kin, and perhaps kind, to dinner, Hazel would kill him and Sara cremate him. He stuttered:

'H-had your supper, E-Enos?'

'Not yet! Ready to eat an ox!'

'How you fixed for money?'

Enos laughed. His wife laughed. His young laughed. Enos giggled, 'You wouldn't kid me, would you? You always were a great little kidder.' He arose to run at Fred and jab him in the ribs--unnecessarily, Fred thought. 'Between us, we've got about a dollar and a half.'

'Well, you let this be my treat. Here's five dollars, Enos.'

Enos took the bill not at all reluctantly; the only reluctance was in his yearning venture, 'But wouldn't it maybe be cheaper to feed us here, Freddie? Not but what I could take the five bucks too, if you insist!'

Enos laughed. His wife laughed. His young . . .

Reduced already to the state of a pitiful liar, and not a very good liar, Fred implored, 'We've got some folks coming in for dinner . . .'

'That's all right with me, if it is with you. I could run down to the store and get couple cans of beans . . .'

Desperately, 'No, guess we better have it this way.'

'Well, look, Freddie, I don't want to be a nuisance. No man living can say I've ever been a bother to nobody. I've often said, "I may not have much of this world's goods, but I've worked and worked hard for what I've got, and one thing I always been proud of is, I've been independent." Neither a borrower be nor a lender, like the fellow says. But I was wondering if you happened to have any spare rooms we could stay in, just for to-night--maybe a couple of nights, so the children could look over the town. Educate 'em. We wouldn't be a bit of trouble. The younger kids could just well sleep here in the sitting-room.'

'Uh--uh--afraid our guests will be staying . . .'

Fred's brow was sopping; he wished that he could again try Sara's clinical thermometer.

'Enos!' said his wife.

'Huh?'

'Beat it!' said his wife.

'Me?'

'All of us. Scram!' said his wife.

'All right . . . Now there's just one other thing, Freddie. Happen to know about any jobs for Mac and Cal here? Course I want to grab me that Gov'ment farm, but the boys are real good at fixing cars. Both worked in filling stations, and of course with your big agency . . .'

'What have they done?'

'Cal, he was in the CCC for a while, but he didn't care so much for it, and then he hitched up with the WPA, but say, those WPA bosses are fierce, they expect you to work like it was a real paid job, and then he was kind of a sweeper in a factory and afterwards, he had a couple of days cooking in a lunch wagon when the fellow was sick, but Cal didn't seem to take to that so much, and here lately he hasn't hardly been doing anything, you might say, just travelling with us--we had a real interesting time--most of the winter we was in Florida, but we had kind of a run-in with the authorities. Oh yes, Cal's a good worker, providin' he has a boss that understands he's high-strung and nobody that you can cuss and knock around. But Mac . . . Well, he reads a lot, but he hasn't had Cal's experience. But what the dickens! No use worrying. Gov'ment owes everybody a living, don't it?'

Fred rose. The others didn't. He had to make it severe--at least he tried to make it severe, even in face of Enos's leering remembrance of himself as fat little Freddie Cornplow:

'Enos! Have Cal and Mac come to see me at the Triumph agency to-morrow, between ten and twelve. I'll see if I can't put them to work.'

It took half an hour before the Tillerys oozed out of the house, during which period Hazel peeped in and looked at Fred like the Gorgon sisters; it took five days and a hundred dollars before Fred coaxed them to ooze out of Sachem. As Mac and Cal were only half an hour late in coming to see him the next day, he put both of them at work, washing though rarely cleaning cars.

The brief comedy of the Tillerys affected him as biliously as Sara's conversion to communism or Howard's desire to leave college.

Fred had not hugely differed from Enos Tillery in a simple faith that a man is as chained to his family, even to all of his blessedly lost relatives, as he is to the law and the prophets and his most understanding friends. But the affaire Tillery, coming just a day before the family gathering on his fifty-sixth birthday, left him in a shocking state of tribal infidelity.

'My own bunch are Hazel, and now Annabel, and friends like Doc Kamerkink and Walter Lindbeck--none of them blood relations, thank heaven!' he blasphemed, and, greatly daring, he wondered whether he was compelled to serve the desires of even Howard and Sara, unless they should choose to be his friends as well as his children.

At dinner, Hazel said, 'Did I hear those people say they were cousins of yours? Why didn't you invite them to dinner?'

CHAPTER IX

The living-room was littered with crocuses and daffodils, lilies and hothouse roses, for Fred's birthday party, and he, who hated this clammy reminder of advancing years, grumbled, 'Sure! Getting me used to my funeral by degrees!'

The dining-room was set out with the gold-and-sky-blue Limoges plates, cut-glass dishes of Hazel's celebrated brandied peaches, and gold-rimmed, faintly etched wineglasses, from which they would each drink two doses of champagne, except for Fred, who would have three, and Annabel Staybridge, who would have ginger ale.

The more he disliked birthdays, the more Fred drove himself to be merry and grateful, particularly when they produced the surprise gifts, which he had already viewed, in their hiding-place in the linen closet, with disapproval. The gifts were also a give-away of the donors. Fred had complained that he hadn't a dressing-gown long enough to cover his nervous feet on a winter morning, and from Hazel he had a woolly robe large enough to cover the feet of Jumbo. But it was of a dizzying purple, edged with fiery red cord, and the sash, he was certain, would never stay tied. Howard gave him a framed photograph--of Howard; and from his friends and guests Dr. and Mrs. Kamerkink, he had a pipe. It was the second pipe they had given him, and Fred never smoked a pipe, but the Doc believed that for a gentleman of forty and upwards a pipe was more manly and hygienic than cigarettes.

Fred gabbled, 'Mighty handsome pipe. Imported from England? Golly!'

Sara was responsible for a dreadful bottom-shelf book, *A Statistical Survey of the Diminishing Returns of the Capitalist System,* whose sour cover contrasted with the frock of silver lamé which she wore as the result of capitalist returns. Fred was meanly suspicious about her having really spent three-fifty on a book for him, and later he privily investigated. Sure enough; on the flyleaf there had previously been a pencilled name, now erased.

But from the blessed Annabel was an omnibus of Dorothy Sayers' detective stories, with the promise that for his next birthday he should have a set of Agatha Christie. 'Girl, you're walking out with the wrong generation of Cornplows,' he said, and he kissed her, Howard kissed her, and Hazel, who had watched all this foolishness without applause, kissed her with an entirely different accent.

The dinner was lush but difficult.

The extra maid, brought in temporarily for waiting on table, had been trained in a laundry, so that while she was warm and quick, she did rather slop things, and things you would not have expected to be slopped: not only the soup and champagne, but the currant jelly and the ice cream. Sara, the socialist, was testy with her, as Sara always was with waiters, taxi-drivers and telephone girls. Hazel was bland and forgiving, but then, Sara sniffed, Hazel was still afraid of servants.

With the hors d'oeuvres which Fred called the 'duffers'--there were anchovies and sardines and two kinds of potato salad--they all asked with considerable politeness about the progress of the Duplex Trailer and happily turned to boasting of their own troubles: Howard's fascinating troubles with the Truxon proctor who disliked the melodies of a mouth organ at two a.m.; Sara's troubles with finding a 'half-way human' hairdresser in Sachem; Doc Kamerkink's troubles with a scoundrel who had developed a coronary thrombosis on the day when he had promised to pay his bill.

With the mushroom soup, Howard talked about the probability of his being student commandant of the Truxon R.O.T.C. next year, while Sara informed them that in Russia, though under the Tsar music and dancing had been unknown, the peasantry now spent practically every moment from five p.m. to eight next day in dancing by moonlight.

But with the duck, and continuing through the ice cream and chocolate sauce, Howard really got under way, and every moment, as he became more exhilarated, Miss Annabel Staybridge looked at him more proudly. The glances she telegraphed to Fred indicated that she was not deceived; she considered Howard a good deal of a baby, but adored him nevertheless.

It was a little hard for the others, particularly the Kamerkinks, to understand just what it was that Howard expected to do.

It seemed that he was going to remain in college, thwart his enemies and play in the college football team; yet simultaneously march out of college and do something thrilling and lucrative with rockets, which, he rejoiced, were shortly to replace gasoline motors for flying, and propel a plane from New York to London in five hours. At the same time, apparently, he was going to start a cabaret near Truxon. All he needed was a few thousand dollars--and in the bright buoyancy of youth, he beamed at Fred, who flinched.

'Cal Tillery's cousin, that's who Howard is,' thought Fred.

With the apricot brandy, a drink which Fred considered related to pink silk underwear and rose-tipped cigarettes, Howard had managed to bring off an entirely new victory. Apparently he was now with the Triumph-Houndtooth-Duplex agency, as assistant and future successor to Fred, and was making things not merely hum but yell.

'You've certainly done a grand job, Dad, but there's a lot of new ideas that would quadruple the racket. Pretty soon, I think, we could add television sales to our other junk, and say, I've got some real ideas about the kind of showroom we ought to have--knock the eyes out of every other dealer in town--place right on Chester Avenue, all black glass and mirrors and red leather upholstery, and maybe a private bar for the big shots, and we could keep open evenings in summer and have an orchestra.'

Fred saw, instantly, that so insane is the world that Howard's hysterical plans for the Triumph agency might actually succeed. They really might 'quadruple the racket', and quadruple his work; and if that happened, he wanted to be out of it, hiding in a haystack.

He recalled that for more than thirty years he had been slapping almost unslappable backs, taking buyers to cafés when he had longed for his slippers, enduring more talk about the weather than there had been weather. He saw that it had been with the tension of a crusade that he had engaged himself in loving like a brother anybody who had $1100 for a car. He was suddenly and inexplicably weary. It would be a pleasure to refuse ever to sell anything else to anybody.

'Certainly, Mr. Jones, we have five million television sets, 1943 model, on hand, and I wouldn't sell you one for five million dollars! I don't like your split infinitives!'

Fred heard himself saying, but not in the least believing, 'You better get busy and learn something about motor engineering, Howard, if you're going into my firm, because pretty soon I'm going to sell it and retire.'

The entire company, who had hardened into the affable boredom suitable to a birthday party, sat up.

'You're going . . .'

'You're going . . .'

'To retire?'

'Nonsense!'

'You?'

'When?'

Fred enjoyed it. He had not been so important in his family since he had bought his opera hat. It pleased his vanity to see that his reputation for Being Different was so solid that he had taken in all of them, except perhaps Hazel, and that even she was wondering a little.

'And when would you pull this big hermit-and-monastery act?' Dr. Kamerkink demanded.

'One year from now.'

Howard bleated, 'Dad! You couldn't possibly! Whether I stick it out in college or not, I've got to get started, somehow, and you're the only one that'll help me!'

But it was Annabel's eyes that most pleaded for Howard.

'Good Lord, son, I expect to help you get started. But only started. I don't expect to carry you for years and years, like a lot of parents are doing, nowadays. I guess that's another demand the Youth Movement is making on Congress--let the old folks do it--penalize the folks that like to work by making 'em support the ones that don't.'

Hazel, rather sharply for Hazel: 'Don't tease him, Fred.'

'Me? I'm not teasing.' And Fred wondered if he really had been only teasing.

Howard, shocked at the threat to his one sure lifelong profession, was begging, 'But Dad, if you retired in ten-fifteen years from now, when I had things going . . !'

'No. One year. You can go to work and learn the motor car business from Paul Popple.'

'But Dad, oh, Paul is O.K., but he isn't even a college man!'

It was Sara who cut through the argument; who killed the epigrams which Fred was trying to work out, to the effect that a couple of fellows named Washington and Lincoln and Henry Ford and Thomas Edison had got along without college. She explained, more affectionately than usual:

'Father, of course we know you don't mean it, but please don't dramatize yourself, like a child playing soldiers. You aren't one bit abused; you like the game of selling things to people who don't want them, and you like seeing us dependent on you and turning to you for everything.'

Fred winced.

'I think your Duplex Trailer is absurd; in the very worst taste, and too horribly inconvenient--like those covered wagons of the pioneers, that always seem so romantic, but they must have been beastly uncomfortable to ride in and impossible to sleep in. But I do believe the thing may make a lot of money, and so might these nuisances that Howard raves about: television and nasty airships with rockets in their tails. There'll be a lot of cash, and of course you want to get it while the getting's good!'

'Why, Sara, I thought you were so much against all this doggone capitalistic acquisition of wealth and everything!'

'If I had--if we had the money, I could do such splendid things for *Protest & Progress* and the Workers' International Cohesion, an organization which . . .'

'You mean the Coheeze?'

'I believe it is sometimes so called.'

Believe? reflected Fred. She knew doggone good and well it was so called. He had heard her so-calling it on the telephone, that evening.

She was continuing, in the benign manner of St. Patrick watching the last snake leave Ireland: 'I'm working with Eugene Silga every day now, making plans to start the "P. & P." Of course we're not communists, but we believe the Soviets must have a chance, and we want to expose the beastly libel that the Bolsheviks have ever liquidated one . . .'

'"Liquidate!" That mean "slaughter"?'

'. . . single person unless they were traitors and spies for Trotsky, and trying to wreck the people's state. What would you do, if you were Stalin?'

'Now how the devil do I know what I'd do if I were Stalin? I don't even know what I'd do if I were Max Schmeling or Mae West. I never claimed to be much good on deciding what other people ought to do.'

'And yet you're constantly deciding what Howard and Mother and I ought to do.'

'Ow. You win, girl.' For the first time since his confession of desertion, there were smiles at the table. 'But look here; you're crowding me. You're getting me away from the subject in hand--the fact that I am going to retire in one year, and your mother and I are going to enjoy ourselves. Anybody got any real objections?'

'Yes. I have,' said his wife.

CHAPTER X

'I don't suppose for a minute,' said Hazel, 'that you mean any of this, but what would you do with yourself if you did retire?'

'Prob'ly travel.'

'You remember our one big trip together? Didn't we see everything--Washington, Mount Vernon, Chicago, the Yellowstone, the Grand Canyon? But all I can recall is how sore our feet got.'

'Well, thunder, we went too fast. Day and a half in Washington! Too quick. Why, Washington's a darn interesting town. Worth maybe three days of anybody's time. I'd like to go to Europe, say, and really sit around.'

'Can't we sit around here? Just think, dear, how uncomfortable you'd be in a strange bed. Or having waiters carve the roast beef. No, no! You stay on the job and have the fun of working with Howard and seeing the business expand. You'll never retire! You don't *want* to. You want to see the children get along, and help 'em.'

'Of course. You'd be bored to death travelling,' shouted Howard.

Annabel now burst:

'Please excuse me--I'm a dreadful outsider--but why shouldn't Mr. Cornplow go off bumming if he wants to, after all these years? I think it would be swell if he went and sat under a palm tree and threw rocks at the whales! Instead of teaching you which part of a car the engine's in, Howard!'

All of them stared at her severely, all but Howard, who was bothered, and Fred, who did not see her at all.

For this moment, during a rather pointless talk at a rather pointless birthday party, was suddenly and appallingly the most important in his life.

Whether it was the addition of another year to his age, or the toothaching memory of the cousinly Tillerys' sponging, or Howard's picture of an expanded agency with Fred as leading lunatic, or Sara's explanation that he was useless except as a feeder for communism, or whether it was some hidden impatience that for years he had struggled against recognizing, he knew, in this half-second, and knew terrifyingly, that what he had said as jest was devastating truth. He perceived that he did want to retire and, with Hazel, try to discover what manner of man he was and might become . . . that he *intended* to retire . . . that he might even actually do it.

He looked puzzled. He coughed a little. He scratched his ear. He jiggled his watch chain. The table and the guests came back to him out of the mist. He informed himself that he had returned to his senses, that the retirement notion was fantastic and that no sane fella like himself could be so anarchistic as to do something merely because he wanted and intended to do it.

He was conscious that Howard was finishing what had, apparently, been a lengthy speech:

'. . . and in my opinion, if you care for it, Dad, I think you'd be making a big mistake. But I agree with Mother that you don't mean it. You couldn't possibly retire. In one year--impossible! Because, to be specific, as my history prof says, aside from coupla months travelling in Europe, what could you *do?*'

It was hard for Fred to outface their pity. He waggled his fingers while he fumbled and mumbled:

'Do? Oh. *Do.* There's a lot of things I could do. I've been a good salesman; I've helped spread mechanical conveniences among a lot of stubborn dumb-bells, and I'm glad of it. Sara thinks I've been a pedlar; I think I've been a missionary. But I'd hate to pass out thinking I couldn't do anything else. Do? Travel, like I said, and not just two months in Europe, either. Nosir! Study it thoroughly, every corner; take an entire year! And learn things, like languages and music. And this manual stuff, carpentry and fixing clocks--nice, clean, interesting work. Maybe wind up in the country and have a crossroads store and a small farm, just to have something to fuss with.'

Hazel was worried. Better than any of them she knew that Fred had possibilities of madness, and she said luringly, 'But, dear, you'd be bored, after the city and contacting all these different people--stimulus, you might say.'

'Think I get so much kick out of "contacts" with Bert Whizzle and Paul Popple--and Cal and Mac Tillery, the rubber-boot twins? High-class stimulus that is!'

'But we can't just consider ourselves in this life, Fred. After all, we have got a duty to our family and friends.'

'Duty! Duty! Duty!' Was this the conservative Fred Cornplow? 'I'm sick of hearing about duty. Duty of husbands to come home to their wives every night, when it would be better for everybody's temper if they stayed downtown and had a little poker and liquor with the boys! Duty of wives to stay home instead of going out to the movies, just because Pa has his slippers on! Duty of Howard and Sara here to pretend they think I went to college once, and read a book. Duty of Annabel and the Kamerkinks to pretend they're not embarrassed by this family's undressing in public . . .'

'Not at all,' said Dr. Kamerkink.

'Ought to hear the Staybridges,' said Annabel.

'Duty! I figger life would be a lot better for everybody if more folks did things because it was fun and not because it was their dumb duty! Remember what Chum Frink wrote:

'"Lives of great men all remind us
We can make our lives sublime
If we nag the kids and neighbours
And look noble all the time!"'

'Duty!' said Fred.

'Horrid word,' said Annabel.

'Shut up, dearest,' said Howard.

'O.K.,' said Annabel.

CHAPTER XI

As the Cornplows' family physician, Dr. Kamerkink must have known that there was no use in giving Fred any advice which Fred was not, beforehand, prepared to hear and pay for. But the Doc had recently begun a book which showed that the latest thing in medical practice--true, it was known to the ancient Greeks, but without the sparkling terms which now made it interesting-- was to use psychiatry on the patients: not let an honest citizen develop cramps or colitis because, subconsciously, he didn't like his wife's new green dress. No. Change the dress. Or change the wife.

Unfortunately the Doc hadn't got far enough into the book to learn what, in detail, you did with psychic therapeutics, but he took a shot with what he had:

'Now, Fred, if you'll allow me to give you some advice both as your physician and old golfing companion . . . This idea of yours about retiring and going off and making yourself uncomfortable is just an incipient psychosis. Course, I advise you to cut down your smoking and drinking and eat at regular periods and get a lot of rest.'

'No!'

'Oh yes. I told you that before. But the thing to correct is your--uh--your conditioned reflexes.'

This time it was Annabel who jeered 'No!'--but softly, almost inoffensively, with lips puckered in Fred's direction.

'Just as important as these somatic corrections, however, is the mental hygiene, and in good old cart horses like you and me, Fred, that implies a steady carrying on of your normal occupation. Any man who retires from his natural work before he's finally carted off to the hospital is a sap! None of these high-class psychiatrists, that get a hundred bucks an hour for telling you what you already know, could beat me at advocating plenty of good, juicy vacations and hobbies. Why, I knew one insurance agent with dyspepsia who, on my humble advice, took up archery, with the result that his wife--I want you to listen to this carefully now, Fred; it's quite a sensational case, and I'd of written it up for the *Journal of Psychiatry* if I'd had the time--and the result was that his wife, who was about twenty years younger than he was and who he suspected of sneaking off to dances with younger men, began to join him in archery. . .'

'Archery? Shooting arrows? No! I won't shoot any arrows!'

'Well, she became his real pal. But appetite ticklers like that are just the opposite of retiring. Fellow's got to be an authority on one thing, and stick by it, if he's going to win people's respect. Suppose, say, you were on a steamer and . . .'

'Steamer to where?' demanded Annabel.

'Heavens! Steamer to anywhere! I'm just imagining a case.'

'Oh,' said Annabel.

Fred chuckled, and Dr. Kamerkink looked at both of them suspiciously as he struggled on:

'You're on this steamer, and somebody asks you, "Who's that guy?" Do you answer, "Why, he's the fellow that sang 'Trees' at the ship's concert," or "He's the one that knows the difference between Barbados and Haitian rum." No! What you answer is, "Him? He's the biggest manufacturer of automobile tops west of the Mississippi!" and the other fellow gets interested and says, "Is that a fact! Say, I've got an automobile top! I'd like to get acquainted with him." See how I mean, Fred?'

'I see,' said Fred.

Hadn't Doc Kamerkink been saying something about how to get along well on steamers? He'd like to get along on steamers, well or ill.

Sara finished it--Sara tore it.

'But of course if you ever did retire, actually you wouldn't stay away for more than a month, Father. Impossible!'

'How so?'

'You're too much a creature of habit. You've often laughed and told us about how fussy Grandpa Cornplow was: had to have the wastebasket or his footstool in exactly the same place, and carried on if anybody moved his ruler, which he never used, one inch from its proper place. And of course you're precisely like him!'

'Me? That've always made such fun of him . . .'

'Precisely! If the cleaning woman ever changes the order you always keep your toothbrushes in, you have three fits before breakfast. You're as fixed in your routine as if you were in a plaster cast, and you'd be chilly without it!'

'Wh-why--me--why, I'm known throughout the entire motor business as a lone wolf. Do just what I please . . .'

'But, darling, you're always pleased to do exactly the same thing at exactly the same second every day, and if you went travelling and had to change your habits, you'd go crazy. Please, Father, this isn't any criticism. Since you'd rather play cards than read anything new and discover what's going on in the world, it doesn't matter. Gives you a stability that, maybe, the rest of us do depend on, as you hinted--not awfully politely, I thought. But it does mean you'll never in the world be able to do anything different from selling Triumphs and coming home to hear Lowell Thomas on the radio.'

'Why--why . . .' said Fred.

'Isn't that just what I told you!' crowed Doc Kamerkink, who hadn't.

There was a certain listlessness, as the party broke up, in all of them except Howard and Annabel, who trotted off together.

'Routine? Fixed habits? *Me?'* raged Fred, as he drank a glass of sodium bicarbonate--remembering that it had been his father's habit, also, to think that after every company dinner he needed soda.

Hazel raised her eyes at him and dropped them, silent.

While he worried his undershirt off, even during the pleasure of scratching his back, he studied her, and sighed to himself, 'Hazel's the best woman I know.'

But, he fretted, she was fanatically devoted to possessions, to things. Perhaps she coddled her belongings just to keep from being bored to death, but still . . . She was the cave woman who desired a larger fire, a thicker bearskin, than the lady in the next-door den.

Almost the only jealousy that had ever spotted her life was a small, annoying envy of the possessions of others. In the cottage of her Utica father she had lived meagrely, with any new purchase, a new doormat, a fly net for the horse, a matter to be discussed by the family for days. Yet at fifty-three she believed that she would be miserable if she were deprived of her candle-wick bedspreads, the grand piano she had bought for Sara, her private jar of balsam-scented bath salts.

'You and I really could skip off together and have a handsome time, if you weren't so set on having things just so,' he sighed.

'Fred! If you ever really *want* to travel, or do anything else, anything at all, I'll always be right there with you. But we mustn't fool ourselves. I've always said it would be a great treat to see Europe, but honestly, we wouldn't be happy, trying to get along without our comforts. I suppose in London, or even in Paris, there's hotels modern as anything in Sachem, but how would you like to go back to sleeping on a horrible hard mattress, like you probably had as a boy? Cornhusks! You can say what you want to, but it's awfully important to have an advertised mattress.'

'If I liked the scenery, I wouldn't care if I slept on a board.'

'But you can't very well look at the scenery while you're sleeping.'

'Oh, you know what I mean.'

'And since when did you ever sleep on a board? Not since you were arrested for rioting in college!'

'Arrested? Me? You know doggone good and well I've never been arrested in my life--except maybe ten-twelve times for speeding, and that time when I was a kid and punched the fresh waiter . . . Say, there's a button off this clean shirt, and I was going to wear it to-morrow!'

'Put it there on the chair; I'll sew it on . . .'

'But I was going to wear it . . .'

'Oh, wear another one! And you know, it isn't just *things,* that we've got fixed up so nice now, as we want 'em. It's our children and friends--people you can trust and count on. Course it's pleasant to meet strangers, but you can't understand 'em and feel *safe,* not like with your own folks.'

'Oh--well--thunder--gee--I guess maybe you're right. Don't meet many fellows like Doc Kamerkink, or Walter Lindbeck--even if he is fifteen-sixteen years younger than me, but how he can play poker!' Fred smacked his head on the pillow, turned the pillow over and pulled the blanket up under his chin, 'And Annabel's a peach.'

'And Sara, of course.'

'Except when she says fool things like my being a slave of habit.'

Resolutely he flopped on the pillow again. A truce to all this chatter. He was a man of resolute action, and he was going to sleep. Yes, he'd never be able to get away; he had enough nerve to admit it, when he had taken a licking.

He lay awake watching the shadows move against the yellow window blinds and trying to remember where he had heard a phrase, meaningless to him and exciting and a little sad:

'We take the Golden Road to Samarkand.'

CHAPTER XII

The morning after his birthday, he wondered what it was that had been plaguing his sleep--something confused and risky. He was aghast as he remembered that he had made threats about becoming a Kipling hero.

But slowly, as morning strength flowed into him, he rejoiced. Yes! They hadn't licked him! He would do it! He would see many golden roads beyond the walls of Samarkand . . . Incidentally, where the deuce was Samarkand?

It was a frowsy day, cold for mid-spring, with a meaningless drizzle that seemed more to rise from the sticky brown earth than to drop from the disapproving skies. The rain was as dreary as Sara's charge of last evening that he had been so imprisoned in ruts that he couldn't even look over the edges.

In his shaky zest for freedom, he tried to defy the thought of Sara, but he shrewdly watched himself during the routine of dressing; he really saw himself; and that is, for any man over thirty-five, no joyful sight before breakfast. He stood apart and spied on his own fussing. He noticed that always, on rising, he first looked at the still-sleeping Hazel, to see if she was really there and still alive. On chilly mornings he always completed the first layers of dressing in the warm bathroom. He discovered that he always--but invariably with the prickliest discomfort if he failed to follow the rite--hung his underclothes on the bathroom hooks in the same order, with some fidgety notion of its being easier thus to dress after his bath.

He noticed that, perhaps every morning for a good many years, he had daily protested, 'All nonsense, this daily bath business. As kids we only got bathed once a week, didn't we, and we didn't smell so bad, did we?'

He noticed that he always soaped his feet before soaping his knees, and that it was a struggle to reverse that order. He noticed that it maddened him to find that the maid had left his bottle of mouthwash on the window-sill instead of where, by all the ritual proprieties, it belonged--in the medicine chest, and not just stuck any old where in the medicine chest either, but put away nicely and correctly between the sodium bicarbonate and the aspirin.

Where it *belongs?* he queried, in rebellion against his own pattern. Who passed that law?

He discovered that he always closed his eyes when he brushed his teeth; furiously discovered that he had to close his eyes.

It was distressing to admit that Sara could be right. Then it was time to break the mould of his job and household and tricks of personal habit, do anything, go anywhere, before he was encased in the coffin of routine, a living dead man.

Yes, and he'd do it, too. Wasn't going to permit even the best of habits to be his master. Already, he exulted, as he drew on his coat and started downstairs, he was changing . . . and noticed then that he had, as on every morning these last twenty years, coughed a tiny and perfectly meaningless cough at the exact moment when he tucked his watch into his lower left-hand vest pocket . . . and that if he had inconceivably ever found the watch in any other pocket, he would have felt naked.

So, with his exultations quenched, he went down to breakfast, in the scarlet-and-canary-yellow 'nook' off the butler's pantry, and as he heard himself muttering to the maid, 'I'll have my coffee right with my porridge', he realized that he had said this once a day for decades . . . and realized that if the *Morning Recorder* had not been there, exactly where it 'belonged', six inches to the right of his water glass, he would have felt himself betrayed by his nearest and dearest.

'Looks like I've gotten in such a habit I simply can't start the day without coffee and the baseball news. I better get out of this quick.'

It was rather too bad, because for years he had enjoyed his anecdotes about how ludicrously punctual his father had always been. 'Yessir, neighbours used to set their clocks by him. Made it kind of hard for a wild bunch like us young uns!' . . . How many times, for how many years, had he been saying that? he wondered.

Hazel, as always--and he now perceived that she had her own rigidities of habit--came down to breakfast as he was finishing. She was, as always, drowsily apologetic for being late, but she was so downy, so soft in her grey-and-crimson *négligé,* so like a robin with ruffled feathers, that her comfortableness reassured him. He would achieve freedom, yes; but no concept of freedom that did not include the presence of Hazel was imaginable. He was as married as a cooing dove or an Anglican bishop. Once or twice in his cheery life he may have looked with approval upon a cigar-store wench or a grass-widow customer, but he had never wanted to live on either cream puffs or caviare; and he knew that he would be for ever hungry without the honest bread and butter of Hazel.

'Well, still like to maybe travel a little?' he said.

'Oh, yes,' Hazel babbled. 'I think it would be grand. My, I would like to see this Westminster Cathedral or Monastery or whatever it is where they're going to have the Coronation. It must be a lovely church. Honestly, do you think we could go . . . for a few weeks?'

'Could we? Say, we can do any doggone thing we doggone well want to!' swore Fred.

Sara made her entrance as he was leaving. She was less purposeful and disciplinary this morning; she was, indeed, all one youthful yawn, and she spoke to him tolerantly:

'Say, Dad, I hate most awfully to bother you, but my allowance is nearly overdrawn. I wonder if you could let me have twenty-five dollars? I had to lend twenty-five to a poor fellow that came in to see Gene and me at the Coheeze yesterday.'

'Who? Why?'

'He's been out in Detroit helping organize the automobile workers, and the cops were after him and he had to scram.'

'Scram--cops! What kind of language d'you call that, young lady? Think that's what I sent you to Vassar to learn? Doggone it, I'll be everlastingly doggoned if I'll stand for anybody slinging that kind of slang and colloquialisms around this shack! And just kindly lemme call to your attention the fact that I happen to deal in motor cars, and I'm not any too darn rapturous about sit-down strikes and Lord knows what all darn shenanigans that keep me from getting cars to sell!'

'So you think the poor workers have no right to organize!'

'Sure they have, if they can get away with it. But we poor God-forsaken bourjoyces also got the right to organize against their sitting down on our pocket-books. Why should I hand twenty-five bucks to your little comrade to help him keep me from making a living! Go on and read the *Daily Worker* about people like me, girl. It'll explain that I'm such a dirty dog that it's a waste of time to expect me to dig down and support a revolution against everything I stand for. That's all, just a dirty dog, nothing but a dirty dog, just a bourjoyce bum--go on, read your communist paper, just read it, that's all. Yessir, dirty dog. And your allowance is overdrawn $68.60 already. Good morning!'

Sara stared at the menacing purple aura left behind him when the hall door had closed. Not since she had won the high-school literary medal with an essay on the errors of Thomas Jefferson had her muttonheaded parent dared so to speak to her. Her lips flattened in rage, and she stormed, 'I see that, for your own sake, darling, so you won't make yourself publicly ridiculous, you will have to be taken in hand!'

CHAPTER XIII

Despite streets slippery as a soapy bathtub, grey as a kitchen mop, Fred drove merrily to his office.

Shame to have to jump on poor Sara like that, but he'd had to do it for her own sake, so that she wouldn't make herself publicly ridiculous. And wasn't he already doing something about his chronic routinitis? Hadn't he shown independence in refusing to let the parental Sara nag him any longer?

Retire? Prob'ly not, but he certainly was going to take longer vacations. He was going to study this travel proposition a little more.

He came into the office whistling, with a feeling that it was somehow particularly suitable, 'Columbia, the Gem of the Ocean'. But he was restless. After the mail and the daily balance sheet, he jumped up abruptly and announced to Paul Popple, 'Going out for a breath of fresh air.'

'This time of day?'

'Yes, this time of day. I'm good and sick of being expected to have my breakfast every morning at eight-fifteen, rain, pour or shine, and always be in the office at eight forty-five, and sit here all day and listen to every sub-agent that thinks he can just walk in and waste my time. Don't know when I'll be back. Don't ever get into too much of a rut, Paul. Learn to dominate your habits, way I do.'

Fredk Wm, that man of mechanisms, usually drove, even in the city, and economized on time by taking fifteen minutes to find a parking space in order to avoid an eight-minute walk. But to-day he tramped out into the rain, the collar of his leather jacket high and a handkerchief thrust inside it. His legs had no protection; presently his knees were itching with wetness, his shoes were like sponges soaked in ice water, but he walked sturdily and in bliss.

Everything in this sober inland city was inexplicably transformed; everything was rosy as the hills of Georgia, blue as the Caribbean.

At the window of a hardware shop, a row of dangling new dishpans did not remind this ex-hardware-drummer of wholesale prices on kitchenware, but of an Algerian market square. There would be camels there prob'ly and mouse-coloured asses with tiny bells, white-hooded men with red pointed shoes, and the smell of musk and attar of rose. The blue and yellow dressing-gowns of silk in Swazey & Lindbeck's windows were to Fred nothing so domestic; they belonged to mandarins in porcelain temples where the doomed gongs boomed. The red pumps at a filling station were letter boxes on Piccadilly, and in a 'gents' furnishing store' there were orange bathing suits for Deauville.

He came to a liquor store, and saw vodka from Poland, rice wine from Canton, and Moselle with castles upon the labels.

He sighed, and wilfully, just at the time when the office would be busy and he sorely needed, he turned into the lunchroom of 'Nick from Naples' and ordered coffee and sinkers.

'Ever go back to Naples, Nick?' he demanded.

'Sure. That's a fine place.'

'Can you sure enough see Vesuvius from there?'

'Sure, smoke alla time.'

'You can see smoke coming out of the volcano?'

'Sure. Smoke, coals, fire--ev'thing--shine like hell all night.'

'Well sir, I cer'nly would like to see that. Glows at night, eh? Well sir, that must be mighty interesting.' Fred turned to the amiable, unshaven taxi-driver beside him and chuckled, 'Be kind of nice to travel in Europe, if a fellow could afford it.'

'O.K., I guess. My old man was born in Jugoslavia.'

'Is that a fact! Hear they got old walled cities there--yuh, great, big thick long walls--built by the Romans! I'd like to see 'em.'

'Yuh.'

'By the Romans! Dog*gone!'*

He was now emboldened to risk the implications suggested in actually entering a travel bureau.

The clerk was amused by the excitement of what was to him just a round little business man in a leather driving jacket, a jesting, over-cordial little man, for this clerk was a person who hated his job, who stood behind counters only till it should be time to escape, and dash to the Y.M.C.A. and gloriously race with himself on the rowing machine. He did not know that he was a merchant of adventure; he supposed that he was selling minimum rates, and tariffs on dogs and children, and reservations on steamer chairs, and not the mist of dawn over rosy seas, Norman cathedrals, goat-loud uplands in the Massif Central. But he will have been of some use to civilization, for he enabled Fred to walk out with pamphlets on Why Not Winter in Flowery South Africa, Native Dances in the Island of Celebes, and Ski Haunts in the Tyrol.

Fred could not promise himself that he would ever know his South Africa, or speak whatever it is they do speak in the Island of Celebes, and he professionally loathed skis--with a ski you couldn't just put it in low and grind comfortably uphill. But he liked the idea.

While the mere body of Frederick William Cornplow, plump and sometimes panting, unmagically draped in double-breasted blue suits and startling red and green neckties, went about the office correctly doing the correct things-- delivering selling talks like a phonograph, signing papers, planning a sales-floor addition to house the trailers--the person inside Fred would have astounded the customers, for he was not a man but a credulous child. Fred was nourishing an idea greater than himself. He was like a small boy who has, in a forest, found the entrance to a cave which surely leads to the centre of the earth. He was playing with the concept that there is no law that a man of fifty-six must stop all of living except sleeping and reading the newspapers and going to the bathroom.

Why, he might have another thirty years of vigour and experiment, and that was a journey which lay as far ahead of him as was the journey back to the time when he had been a brat of twenty-six, younger than Sara now! But he had to start his pilgrimage out of hand; he had to undergo the ticklish complications of retiring in a year or of taking a whole year's vacation.

Having made this reasonable decision, in three days he abruptly changed it--and with that the whole world changed. And why not? For who in the world has ever been more important than Fred Cornplow?

He has, at times, been too noisy or too prosy, he has now and then thought more of money than of virtue and music; but he has been the eternal doer; equally depended upon--and equally hated--by the savage mob and by the insolent nobility.

When Fred Cornplow was an Egyptian, it was he who planned the pyramids, conciliated the mad pharaohs, tried to make existence endurable for the sweating slaves. In the days when he was called a Roman Citizen, he was a centurion and he conquered Syria and ruled his small corner of it with as much justice as the day allowed.

As Fr. Abbot Cornplow, in the bright Dark Ages, he developed agriculture and the use of building stone; later, as a captain under Cromwell, he helped tame the political power of the ecclesiastics. The American Civil War was not fought between General Grant and General Lee, but between Private Fred Cornplow of Massachusetts and Private Ed Cornplow of Alabama; and a few years later it was they who created bribery and railroads and gave all their loot to science.

From Fred Cornplow's family, between B.C. 1937 and A.D. 1937, there came, despite an occasional aristocratic Byron or an infrequent proletarian John Bunyan, nearly all the medical researchers, the discoverers of better varieties of wheat, the poets, the builders, the singers, the captains of great ships. Sometimes his name has been pronounced Babbitt; sometimes it has been called Ben Franklin; and once, if Eugene O'Neill may be trusted, he went by the style of Marco Polo and brought back from civilized China to barbaric Europe the sound of camel bells, and the silken tents, scented with sandalwood, which have overshadowed the continent ever since.

He is the eternal bourgeois, the bourjoyce, the burgher, the Middle Class, whom the Bolsheviks hate and imitate, whom the English love and deprecate, and who is most of the population worth considering in France and Germany and these United States.

He is Fred Cornplow; and when he changes his mind that crisis is weightier than Waterloo or Thermopylae.

No, Fred decided, he couldn't either retire or take a year's vacation. Howard, confound him, was right; just now, he had to stay by the ship. But he certainly wouldn't drudge on for another ten or fifteen years. He would retire in five years from now, exactly; he had made up his mind, and dog*gone,* let anybody try to change it! And meantime he would gorgeously 'get in shape.'

He felt absurd in doing it, but Fred was in training for adventure. He stopped smoking before breakfast; he occasionally walked to the office; and once or twice a week, with intense distress and a feeling of being silly, he wabbled dumb-bells in the Elks' gymnasium or joined in the calisthenics of a squad of bankers and brokers and superintendents of schools, worthy gentlemen who as dancers and high kickers resembled a mixed group of turkeys and hippopotami enacting an Andalusian flower song.

But he persisted. He had worked out for himself a principle: 'You'll never make any change in your life that you haven't already begun.'

A fortnight after the beginning of Fred's madness, Howard appeared in the office and croaked, 'Of course all those jokes you pulled at your birthday party about retiring--I know you're too responsible to do anything like that.'

'Well, *you* know, son--fellow sometimes feels like kicking the dashboard.'

'Sure. I didn't take you seriously.'

'No? Well . . . Gosh it's hot for May.' Indeed, Fred was wiping his forehead.

'Sure is. Yessir, actually hot!'

'Guess I'll drop in at Swazey & Lindbeck's, this noon, and pick me out a summer suit.'

'No, no.' Howard was pretty firm. 'They'll sting you. Go to the Gotham Mart.'

'You think so?'

'I know it. And I don't want you to stop carrying a silk muffler yet. Pretty fickle weather.'

'Yuh, I suppose . . . Though I bet your mother is sweating to death, this morning, laying out her sweet peas.'

'And that's another thing. I've told Mother and I've told her, but I just can't get her to listen to me. It's all foolishness, her trying to grow sweet peas. Why don't she put in some good sturdy rose bushes that don't need so much attention? But think she'd pay any attention to me? Oh no!'

When Howard was gone, to drive back to Truxon College at a conservative sixty miles an hour, Fred mused, 'So if the young man should make good, and not always lean on me, fifteen years from now he'd be tying up Hazel and me by the fireplace and telling us when to breathe. Nothing doing! He travels the fastest who travels alone . . . Always providing, of course, he has Hazel with him, you understand.'

CHAPTER XIV

No doubt Sara and Eugene Silga didn't deserve any particular credit for it.

Their office was one stingy room on the third floor of the Stiggis Building, between a photographer of riotous babies and the agency for a platinum mine. They had nothing but two kitchen tables, four kitchen chairs, a wire basket filled with bills, a pile of rival radical magazines which damned one another for lukewarmness in revolution, one window--dirty; and a telephone--in arrears, but no doubt they enjoyed it more than a plush and walnut office with respectful attendants. You can feel more heroic in shirt-sleeves than in ermine.

In this primitive office of the Sachem Falls Cell of the Workers' International Cohesion, and of *Protest & Progress,* Sara was luxuriously misreading proof on the forthcoming first number, while Gene sputtered on the telephone:

'Why, certainly, comrade, we'll provide the speakers . . . Good? Listen! One of 'em's been beaten by the gorillas seven times . . . Sure, all the decorations; I've got a four-by-seven-foot poster of Lenin . . . No. Fifty per cent of the gate . . . No, won't touch it for less . . . All right, you talk to 'em and give me a ring.'

Gene glanced at her with those eyes, daring and amused, that seemed to understand her every foolishness and desire. She didn't *care,* resolved Sara; she would marry Gene even if they had to live in a one-room flat and she do the cooking. Oh yes; that was what she had been trying to remember: she must learn to cook.

She chucked the proofs and swam shyly toward him. She panted as he smiled at her with his especial smile of friendliness, but what he said was:

'Sara!'

'Yes, Gene!'

'I, uh . . . You know these Channing Praggs--the glass manufacturer? Think you could get old lady Pragg to pull a soirée, or whatever she calls it, for me? I'll spiel on birth control in Russia and pass the hat. Isn't it funny, darling!' He patted her hand, which was clenching the edge of his table-desk. 'Nobody comes through with funds for the revolution like the wives of millionaires, even after we've openly announced we intend to overthrow the Democratic State and institute a real, honest-to-God dictatorship of the rednecks like me. How come? You're a capitalist, darling. Why do you guys in the ruling class let us get away with it?'

'I don't think Mr. Frederick W. Cornplow is as keen on our getting away with it as I'd like to see. We'll have to work on him a lot yet, dear.'

Their laughter was a gust that blew away all such featherbrains as Fred. She was certain that Gene was going to show a little more affection now than just the patting of hands which had been his only gesture, and she leaned over the shining blackness of his hair--as Frieda Kitz clumped into the office.

Frieda earned her living in a wall-paper warehouse; she was treasurer of the Coheeze; she never laughed except for a triumphant snort at the thought of a firing squad's converting the Praggs and Cornplows; and though she had a tranquil broad-browed loveliness, she wore her hair tight and never dressed in anything but stiff corduroy suits and flat low shoes.

Sara looked at Frieda with hatred--she at Sara with contempt--while Gene greeted Frieda all too quietly, too understandingly, 'Good morning, comrade.'

Sara felt that she had been sent back to the kitchen. She had been snubbed by amateur snobs like Mrs. Channing Pragg; not till now had she been snubbed by an expert like Comrade Kitz. She crept to her desk and the suddenly hateful proofs.

Gene and the Comrade did not seem to think that she was important enough to hide their secrets from her as they talked softly at his desk of orders from the great lords of communism in New York. Sara was as uncomfortable as she had felt when, at ten, she had blundered into one of her mother's tiny coffee parties and heard those shocking bores, the Grown-up Ladies, confiding, 'Oh, they say he drinks', and 'In October, she told me.'

She was sickened by the easy intimacy with which Gene and Frieda shook hands at parting, needing to say nothing beyond a soft, revealing, 'So long, comrade.' But she made no comment on Frieda, as Gene again pulled toward him the telephone on which, all day long, he placidly forwarded his plans to smash the American government. She buckled to work. She had not learned until now that most banal, most ancient, most weighty truth, that there is refuge in work.

Sara was magnificently playing the role of new broom. She was assistant secretary of the Coheeze, and managing editor (the other editors were Eugene Silga) as well as two-finger stenographer and advertising solicitor of *Protest & Progress*. She wrote the minor editorials, with happy thought of how much they were going to annoy Fred, and in them felt herself a combination of Queen Marie, Emma Goldman, Lady Astor, Virginia Woolf and Charlotte Corday. It was a good job, this profession of being not merely allowed but encouraged to clout every head that rose above the mob, and of actually being paid for doing it--provided she went out and raised funds for the payment.

Into the office exploded their collaborators, Howard Cornplow and Guy Staybridge, with the uncollaborative, the hopelessly*bourgeois* Annabel tagging after them.

'Gene! Gene! I've got a poem for you! Wrote it in biology class!' crowed Guy. "This'll stir up the fakers in Washington. Listen:

"'Here is a dime," the President said,
"If you'll vote for me twice and bow your head.
Red roses rioting North and South--
Think of them buddy, and shut your mouth.

Go buy you a suit of clothes," he said, "But careful, buddy, the coat ain't red!"'

'Fine! Fine!' said Gene easily, and for that ease Sara loved him. He dropped the poem into the pasteboard box which, Sara knew, held the manuscripts he had accepted and would never publish. He gushed, 'Hope you've been able to raise a little dough, Guy. Kind of a crisis with the "P. & P." If our friends will help us to get through this month . . .'

'Yeh, I got fifteen dollars from Dr. Gomber, the professor of drama--he sympathizes with communism--he's got plenty money--his father owns in on the Piping Rock Explosives Corporation.' Guy handed over a wrinkled ten-dollar bill and a five. These did not go into any pasteboard box, but into Gene's vest pocket, and Gene turned on Howard with an affectionate, 'How about you, old man?'

Howard was looking vaguely at the window. 'You ought to have more air in here, Gene. If I had time I could fix it so you'd have more air in here, Gene.'

'I'm sure you could, Howard, but did you manage to raise any funds?'

'Oh, I was going to, but I've been awful busy.'

'Sure, but the world revolution has to be pretty busy, too, Howard.'

'Well now, I'll tell you how I feel about that, Gene. I can't say I'm entirely sold on communism.' Howard looked as handsome as Pike's Peak at sunset and as dumb. 'With my scientific training, Gene, you got to show me the data--show me the data; the thing is . . .'

'The data,' chirped Annabel, sitting on a pile of 'Proletarian Art'.

Howard faced her crossly. 'Well, what about it? Don't *you* think you gotta have the data, Bell?'

'Sure. Data is the goods.'

'You're so frivolous all the time! You got no idea the risks I take, in a conservative dump like Truxon, coming right out for the left wing. Are you with me or aren't you?'

'I'm with you, beautiful, just the same as your mother will be with your father, no matter how much she may kick beforehand, if he ever decides to go and do something sweet and crazy.'

Sara and Howard swapped glances of surprise. It had not occurred to them that anybody, certainly not a flippant young woman, certainly not a superior Staybridge, could speak of their matter-of-fact parents with enthusiastic affection.

'Howard!' Sara demanded. 'Tell me something more about rockets for aerial power. Just exactly how do they work, mechanically?'

'Rockets?'

'Good heavens, don't you remember that the other day you were making a fortune out of them? Come through now; don't hold out all this priceless information on your comrade and sister, stupid. How do the rockets work? I've got to write something about 'em.'

Annabel was helpful: 'The aviator wears an opera hat with the rockets in 'em, and every time he shuts the thing, a rocket goes off.'

'Can it!' said Howard.

'Don't be an idiot,' said Sara.

'Darling!' said Gene.

'Check,' said Annabel.

'Now rockets,' said Howard, 'these rockets--well, if you want a technical explanation, they're affixed to the, I think it's the rear of the fuselage, I think it's the fuselage, and--well, they go off, and the sum of the reaction is equal to the reaction, I mean to the action, and there you are, Sara, can't you see? If you'd only studied physics, instead of all this literature and stuff!'

'My beautiful,' yearned Annabel.

Winnie Weston Blear's Tea Room was to Sachem Falls a combination of all the Greenwich Village restaurants that begin with Ye and all the Broadway restaurants in which legitimate theatrical producers have a farewell drink before catching the train for Hollywood. Mrs. Blear's establishment had caviare once or twice a year, you could get slivovitz if you knew the head waitress, and English muffins were practically obligatory. Here exhibited themselves the featured players of the Spreadeagle Little Theatre, all the violin teachers in town, and the local literary celebrity--the dramatic critic on the *Evening Tidings,* who had written a book on his travels in New Zealand.

Guy took all of the 'P. & P.' conspirators, except Gene, who had a rendezvous with the telephone, over to Mrs. Blear's and went cosmopolitan on them. His father, the bleak Mr. Putnam Staybridge, had once suffered Guy's presence for two weeks in London and one in Paris, and Guy explained now, to the untravelled Howard and Sara and Annabel, how sophisticated were cream cheese with bar le duc, avocado soaked with curaçao, and Stilton with port-- while the nearest they came to these elegances was cinnamon toast with chilly tea.

Annabel paid attention to her brother not with her ears but with her memory. For years she had listened to her father and Guy being airy about European food, and that may explain why she looked so fondly on a Howard who confessed that he knew no more about Stilton (which he seemed to regard as some variety of sponge cake) than a rabbit. Howard warmed handsomely to her stilly gaze, and suddenly, to the disgust of those hard-boiled communist warriors, Sara and Guy, he demanded of Annabel:

'Are you crazy about me?'

'Absolutely.'

'How crazy?'

'Catatonics, catelepsies and cataclysms.'

Sara barked, 'I'm going to the office.'

'And me,' said Guy. 'When do you publish my poem?'

CHAPTER XV

While Fred, with Hazel on the arm of his chair, was reading the first copy of *Protest & Progress,* Sara pretended to be lost in the *Daily Worker,* and over it she watched them with what she hoped was cynical amusement.

On the 'P. & P.' cover, in a technique familiar to Fred from the high-school papers his children had once brought home, was a caricature labelled 'A Dictator of the Auto Industry', depicting a grossly fat man drinking champagne from a magnum. That was fairly easy for Hazel to understand, but she balked at two other caricatures, 'Workers Unite!' and 'The Newest Deal'. In the first, 'Labour' was revealed as an agonized dwarf lashed by a diabolic monster named 'Capital', but in the second Labour was a young and singing giant who laughed at a wizened Capital held in the palm of his brawny hand: a hand worthy of a structural steel worker or even of Litvinoff.

Hazel worried, 'Look, Fred, I don't get that. If Labour is such a shrimp in one place and gets all beat up by Capital, how come he can squeeze Capital so, two pages farther on?'

'Hush, Hazel. That shows how fast the Coheeze is working. Don't be bourjoyce.'

Sara sniffed.

The bourjoyces studied, then, the 'P. & P.'s' news from Russia.

With only nineteen years since the revolution, it appeared, the Soviets had built factories, railroads, playgrounds and a twelve-story hotel.

'Hm. Pretty good. Still, that's the same period as from 1865 to 1884, when America built up the entire West, after having had the stuffin's knocked out of her in the Civil War,' said Fred.

To his delight, that did draw Sara. 'Entirely different,' she proclaimed. 'How?' said Fred. 'Any number of ways,' said Sara.

He was not so well pleased when he read Eugene Silga's interview with the executive vice-president of the Colonial Motor Car Company, which presented the executive as a languider, pouchier and more mulish version of George III, ignorant alike of motor engineering and of the living conditions of the workers. This demon Fred had met in Detroit; he knew that he was the son of a blacksmith, an engineer who was equally interested in rear-end motors, in mountain climbing and in hospitals. 'We are not amused,' felt Fred.

'Huh. Oh, Hazel--jus' second--almost forgot--phone the Kamerkinks about Sunday--c'mon, jus' second,' he blurted. As Hazel opened her mouth, he pinched her arm in caution, and she followed him into the hall. He led her not to the telephone but to the coat closet.

'Eh?' she wondered.

'Hush. Take a swig of this. Maybe it'll get us through the intelligence test without our kicking Sara.'

He had taken from the inside pocket of an aged raincoat a bottle of gin; he gargled at it and handed it over.

'Oh, so that's where you keep it! No. I can't drink the beastly stuff . . . Straight? I never heard--I never heard of . . . My, that has got a kick . . . I do feel better!'

They read through the editorials, two of which began:

So-called modern ingenuity is producing a wealth of mechanical gadgets which, if they were conceived of as serving the Proletariat and as vehicles for sound Propaganda, would be triumphs of popular achievement. Such innovations as trailers, easily transported and opening out into four- or five-room houses, television, and the probable future of propulsion of airships by rockets, so that one could go from New York State to Moscow in six or eight hours, should institute a new civilization, but to the dull, greedy, cruel and unimaginative mind of the American 'business man' they are nothing but future sources of profit wherewith he can the better contribute to the funds of the Fascist armies threatening Russia.

And:

A sardonically amusing revelation of the mind of the American 'business man' is found in the fact that as soon as he can pile up the swag, he betrays his real lack of interest in his calling by hoping to retire. Naturally! He has none of the deep inner satisfaction felt by Soviet experts in building permanently and for the people.

'Now who do you suppose could have written those two gems?' said Fred. 'Sara!'

Coolly: 'Yes?'

'I've been looking at your new Coheeze paper.'

'Yes?'

'I've got a new title for it; same alliteration: "Prig and Prattle".'

'Are you being humorous, Father?'

'Not very. When you get a real communist fanatic that's as het up as a prohibition reformer or a censorship maniac, and let him also use machine-guns and firing squads the way he wants to, maybe it sounds humorous, but I don't suppose it is.'

CHAPTER XVI

Her mother had gone to bed; her father, Sara guessed, with just a little uneasiness, had shown unusual powers of keeping his mouth shut and, without any lecture on the subject, had made it clear that he would not contribute to the Coheeze. But that was only part of her troubles, and she said to him coaxingly:

'Sometimes you think I don't appreciate how hard you work, Father, but I do. I've been learning about real work. Not only at the Coheeze . . . I don't suppose you care to talk much about that. But I have so many other activities, too. Did you know I'm going to enter the club tennis tournament this summer?'

'That sounds better.'

'And I'm afraid I'll have to contribute to the courts fund and my allowance is so shamefully overdrawn . . .'

'Ten dollars be enough? . . . No? . . . Fifteen? . . . No? Well, twenty-five, and that's my limit!'

'Oh, I suppose we can get away with that . . .'

'"We"?'

'But if the club were only the end of it! Here I've gone and got myself mixed up with the amateur summer theatre that the Spreadeagle Little Theatre is sponsoring, and they've elected me chairman of the Box Office, Seats, and Ushering Committee--of course it is quite an honour, with Mrs. Channing Pragg and Putnam Staybridge (and how *he* ever came to have a tacky daughter like Annabel I don't know; wait; don't shoot; if Howard and you say she's pretty, I suppose she must be)--and with them on the board of directors, it's quite a social honour, and so of course I'll have to try and raise a fifty- or seventy-five-dollar subscription, somehow or other . . .'

And Fred fired, after keeping his powder so dry so long:

'I know I'm just a clodhopper, that's all, nothing but a clodhopper, just a clown, that's all, nothing but a dumb bunny, but I'll be everlastingly doggoned if I can understand how you can hook up your doggoned Young Men's Anarchist Association with guzzling tea with Sister Pragg and kissing the doggone snobs in the tennis association . . .'

'Yes? Perhaps I might just happen to convert them to socialism.'

'And perhaps you might just happen to not do anything of the kind. You look here, Sara: I've always given you all the allowance I thought I could afford, but now you're proposing to support not only Holy Russia and Holy Joe Stalin but also the white-pants aggregation, and this amateur-dramatics-in-a-barn . . .'

'"Dramatics"!'

'. . . circus, that Sister Pragg would do anything for it except ever come through with a cent, I--well, I'm afraid you'll have to get Comrade Silga to increase your salary--from about ten bucks a week minus to something plus-- and then devote that to these children's games.'

At the end of that scene, as he described it to Hazel in their bathroom, 'She went and got hurt, and then she walked out on me. Oh, I don't want to be mean, but I don't like to see her--yes, or see me--falling for people that just use her for what they can get out of her,' he worried, while Hazel, smoothing his cheek, was worried along with him.

He was the more dependent upon the security of home because he was too busy and doing too well. The Triumph and Houndtooth were prospering; the Duplex Trailer was a sensation; and he had to bounce all over his district, leasing out Duplex rights to sub-agents, and thus getting rid, wherever he could, of responsibility. That he also got rid thus of much of his profits he did not tell his family.

He said nothing about retiring; he did not think about it very clearly; but he kept up his absurdly grave 'training'; and he was giving Paul Popple more experience in accounting and sales.

"F anything ever happened to me, ought to be somebody else could kind of take charge--just temporarily,' he said to Paul.

In one bright idea he had a regrettable failure.

Among the less desirable features of the Triumph shop, along with rats, high insurance rates and a smell of sewer gas, was the continued presence of his near-cousins, Cal and Mac Tillery. Fred had, briefly, been too much of a coward to fire them and to risk receiving the hurt letter which their sire, Cousin Enos, would inevitably write.

He had tried them at cleaning cars, until too many owners complained of wet upholstery, and of running boards abloom with soaked cigarette butts; he had tried them at selling gasoline, until he noticed that with each gallon they donated five minutes of bright backwoods chatter about the weather--'Hot, I'll say it's hot. Oh boy, is it hot to-day--say, it was hot when I woke up this morning--oh boy, was it hot!' Painting did not seem suited to the particular talents of Cal and Mac; they broke spray guns and made the car bodies contrasts of gummy spots with patches entirely bare. At last Fred had put them to packing and toting boxes in the supply department, which they did fairly well, except when they dropped the boxes, lost them or used them as targets for tobacco juice.

In whatever job they might be, they told all colleagues and all customers, 'We're Fred Cornplow's own cousins. He's learned how to get away with it, but say, is that guy a hick! Oh boy!'

Fred begged of them, tenderly, 'Boys, now summer's coming, don't you suppose your dad will need you on his farm?'

'His what?'

'His farm. In West Virginia. From the government.'

'Oh. That. Oh, Dad never got there. He run into a cousin of Ma's, on the way, that's got a wild animal farm, and he and Ma and the kids are staying there to help train the tigers.'

'Well, well, Cal! That's fine, Mac! That must be mighty interesting! Don't you want to join him? I hear tigers make fine pets. I'd be glad to pay your railroad fares.'

'Naw. Dad wrote me a postcard; he said Cousin Albert was an awful tightwad and gives 'em rotten grub. He got so sore he prett' near left Cousin Albert flat. No, we like it all right here, Fred. We'll stick by you.'

By Sara, Fred sent word to Gene Silga that if he could use one or two fine young men, just the sort of real proletarians to whom Gene wished to hand the control of the American government, Fred could supply them, and he might even contribute to the Coheeze.

Eugene sent back jeering word: 'The Soviets and their fellow travellers don't want shiftless bums any more than the capitalists do; in fact, not being sentimental like the soppy American capitalists, the Bolsheviks give slackers a choice between working and losing citizenship.'

It was at that moment that Fred almost joined the communists. And he felt thus for a second time when Howard dragged in his playful friend, Ben Bogey, whose slogan was 'Homes that are nice at lowest price'.

CHAPTER XVII

Having had words with the dean on the matter of tooting his horn in front of Henry Ward Beecher Hall at dawn, Howard came down to Sachem and the Coheeze office to have company during the agony of being solitary and rebellious.

It was all off with Annabel; she had told him that she regarded his well-considered plan of studying finger-prints and becoming a G-man as less than practical; love's labour was lost and Annabel could go to the devil.

There were but two weeks before commencement, but he still had his lamentable senior year to undergo, and he hit on the good new notion that it would be sensible to spend it in Moscow. Gene Silga hadn't exactly said so, but Howard was fairly sure that he remembered hearing somebody say that, in Russia, university students spent most of their time shooting, leaping out of aeroplanes with absolutely safe parachutes, and bathing with lady students who were crazy about Americans.

At a cost in oil, gasoline, depreciation and sustaining hot dogs--to omit the interest and overhead--of approximately seven times what it would have cost to have the envelopes addressed professionally, Howard had come down from Truxon and was sitting now on a small box in front of a big box, addressing

Coheeze letters which informed their 'friends and loyal supporters' that if they could just come through once more, *Protest & Progress* would get along prosperously for ever. Gene was telephoning to the local liberal pastor; Sara was picking out on a portable typewriter an editorial revealing that Kathleen Norris, Andrew Mellon and Dizzy Dean were plotting against the independence of Mexico.

Their happy hour of conspiracy was interrupted by the entrance of a bald but youthful male in spats and a belted coat, who handed to each of them a card:

BEN BUTLER BOGEY
Saringham & Peters
Optimists Bank Bldg.
'Homes That Are Nice
At Lowest Price'

'What would I do with a home?' said Gene.

'Too much home already,' said Sara.

'Can I sell you a subscription to *Protest & Progress?'* said Howard.

'You bet; I'll take a subscription right now!' said Ben.

'Well, I'll be darned . . . How much does one cost?' Howard inquired of Gene.

Ben Bogey cheerfully handed over two dollars and a half, which was more real money than that office had seen for a week; he popped his hat off his head in greeting to Sara; he patted it back on again with a gesture like a vaudeville hoofer's; he sat on the edge of Sara's table and went into action:

'The home I'm thinking of just now isn't for you folks personally. You can kid me, but I'm sure you've got cosy little hideaways of your own. The home I'm thinking about is for your magazine, and your society, this International Workers' whatever-it-is--I forget. My firm is developing a new development on a new principle of developing. It's going to be the first addition in the world that's got culture for a selling point. We don't want to contact brokers or even bankers, but docs and lawyers and advertising men and radio announcers and real intellectuals like that. I can offer you a whole floor in a fine, made-over, old, ancient house, built back in 1890 but with all necessary modern improvements, including electric ice-water cooler, for a mere two hundred dollars a month.

'You'll be taken right into the social and artistic activities of the community. Why, I wouldn't wonder if you'd be invited to a reception-tea by Mrs. Stotes Emery--and there's a real author for you--her husband is the big bond house, and she's had poems published in a bound book that, I know for a fact, has been sent to G. B. Wells and a number of other famous foreign scribes for their criticism, and she'd be tickled to death to advise and inspire you . . .'

'Comrade Bogey!' Gene was smiling; Gene sounded affectionate. 'We're both working the same side of the avenue! I address street meetings myself. I'm afraid you don't understand that our little sheet is entirely subversive. We're what is known as Reds--Radicals--Dangerous Alien Elements; and I'm afraid that

Pansy Park . . . You did say, didn't you, that was the name of your garden suburb?'

'No; it's Lilac Lane. Pansy Park would make a swell name to use, though. Excuse me if I jot it down.'

'Certainly, comrade. What I'm getting at is that your sterling community would throw us out on our ears.'

'That's just where you're off your base. Red Radicalism is the newest, the most fashionable racket there is to-day. Nothing a banker's wife likes so much as to hear that her husband may get stuck up before a firing squad. Say, nothing will get publicity and pack his pews for a liberal clergyman, with a wife and seven children and a mortgage, as much as to say at a society dinner party that family life is going to be abolished. No. You boys come in with us and we'll give you three months' rent free.'

'So kind of you, comrade, but we happen to believe in our "racket". We don't like rich women that give you tea and advice.'

'Good God, who does! I'm not talking about liking it; I'm talking about young fellows trying to get along!'

Not for fifteen minutes did Gene make a real effort to get rid of Ben Bogey, for like all people who work in offices, including magazine offices, publishers' offices and the clangorous offices of latter-day authors, with their lecture and radio and cinema departments, Gene was pleased by anything like an excuse to stop telephoning. When Ben went cheerily out, Howard stuttered, 'S-s-say, could I see you for just a minute, Mr. Bogey? Let's go across the street and have a cuppacoffee.'

At Ye Olde Robin's Egg Rotisserie, Howard confided, 'I'm finishing up college next year, and I've been thinking right along I'd like to go into the real-estate game. Course I've been offered chances in developing television and frog farms and all that sort of bunk, but real estate has always been my one ambition.'

Howard was not lying; he was merely being dramatic and self-convinced, as was Howard's father when he said that he liked writing orders in triplicate.

'I'm not a communist, you understand, Mr. Bogey; I was just in there because I've got a sister works there. Say, I've got a swell idea for a new kind of suburb.'

'Yeah?' cautiously.

'Instead of measly little houses, everybody live in one big skyscraper--go call on your neighbours, winter evenings, not have to get your feet wet--and use all the land for playgrounds and great, big, huge gardens. And grottos, maybe.'

'Yeah?' wearily. 'Listen, brother. In the real-estate game you don't want ideas--you want prospects.'

'But I was thinking--I'm sure I could get my dad to back me--he don't know what to do with all the money he makes, he's such a slave of routine, and with him behind me . . .'

'Who is your dad?'

'F. W. Cornplow, the district agent for the Triumph.'

'Oh yes, sure. I heard him talk once at the Boosters' Club. Great salesman. Great! Wish I could interest him in a new rental. I've got the sweetest proposition for a motor agency in this man's town . . .'

'Let's go and see him. Got your bus here? Shall I give you a lift?'

'Got my coop parked right across. You go ahead and I'll trail you.'

'O.K., Ben.'

'Swell. What do they call you for short, baby?'

Arm in arm, the two swarmed into Fred's office.

'Dad, want you to meet Ben Bogey, the best little real-estate salesman in Sachem, and he's got the slickest proposition for a motor-agency rental in this man's town . . .'

Fred considered Ben's spats, he considered Ben's belted coat, and he was noticeably uncordial. 'I've got a rental!'

Ben Bogey stepped forward and took the limelight away from Howard. 'I know what a busy man you are, Mr. Cornplow . . .'

'I am!'

'. . . and I won't take your time just now, but if you are interested in air, light, space, costs-saving . . .'

'I am not. I loathe all of 'em.'

'I see, but . . .'

Howard laughed. 'You better listen to the old scoundrel, Dad, because Ben and me have just fixed it up to start a real-estate firm.'

'On who? On Ben?'

'Not exactly, Dad. I'm sure that when you hear our plans you'll be able to see your way clear . . .'

'Come back next year, Howard, and we'll talk it over, and now--please--go--*away!'*

Annabel was small and forlorn, at the end of a mahogany couch, pride of the Staybridge Mansion. She peeped at the telephone out in the hall. By now, she thought, the instrument must be so well trained that she would have but to pick up the receiver to be connected with Truxon College.

Why, she thought, did she ever call him up? Howard never said anything on the telephone but 'Ullo, ullo, ullo' in what he considered an English accent. But he was so cheerful and knowable, in contrast to her cultured Parent, whose level voice was always a veil, soaked in ice water, between them.

Forlorn and very small. Actually, Annabel was as tall as her father, who sat in elegant flowing lines at the other end of the drawing-room. But so erect was his pride and self-satisfaction that, beside her, he seemed like an obelisk.

He did not pretend to be reading; frankly he was watching her, everything she did, and she became jerky. She looked away from the telephone. She rose and paced toward the fireplace, airily swinging her hands, trying to think of any reason why she should go to the fireplace. She moved the brass Buddha on the mantelpiece two inches to the right; she felt her father's condemnatory glance scorching her back, and hastily she moved Buddha back again. With a fine fingertip, she smoothed the cool glossy cover of a garden magazine--and peeped at the telephone.

Her fingers wandered through the poems of Yeats; the old edition, with the cross and the mystic rose and falling leaves upon the cover, which her father had brought home from London thirty years ago and which, after her mother's death, he had been wont to read to her until suddenly she had awakened to the charm of the lines, at which he immediately became impatient of them, said they were sentimental, for milk-sick girls, and threw the book on the floor. She had picked it up and defiantly treasured it.

He was half sneering at her now as she read again:

. . . the land of faery
Where nobody gets old and godly and grave,
Where nobody gets old and crafty and wise,
Where nobody gets old and bitter of tongue;
And she is still there, busied with a dance,
Deep in the dewy shadow of a wood,
Or where stars walk upon a mountain-top.

Again she looked toward the telephone, and he spoke suavely, like a man superior to all emotion:

'It would be obvious, wouldn't it, Ann, that you are expecting a telephone call from this bloated young bruiser, Cornplow, this study in the mind of primitive man, whom you have been seeing lately?'

'He isn't bloated. But I am expecting him to phone . . .'

'The word is "telephone".'

'. . . or to drop in.'

'Drop into what? The speech of youth to-day is very picturesque. It lacks only one thing that speech normally should have--an intelligible meaning . . .'

She was screaming.

'Stop, stop, stop, stop! Dear God, I get so sick of your making spider webs of words that choke me! Howard *is* simple! That's one reason I like him! He's like daylight and fresh air, and this place is like a dungeon!'

'I trust you like his family, also--they are certainly on the simple, fresh-airish side.'

'I do! Especially his father. There's such nice wiggly lines beside his eyes, where he laughs. And you dare to patronize him! Oh, I do hate you!'

'Are you quite sure, my dear Ann? I suspect that, at least, my superciliousness will keep you from making a fool of yourself . . .'

And then, astonishingly, Howard was ringing the doorbell. After her father's wry, dark, feline teasing, the young man seemed to Annabel like a jolly St.

Bernard. She clasped his solid chunk of a hand and towed him into the drawing-room.

Mr. Putnam Staybridge was a successful experimenter in moods. He had already dropped the venom and honey, the purr of a cat with a mouse, and he barked like a terrier:

'Good evening, Howard, I daresay you would agree that the weather is warm.'

'Uh . . .'

'I see that we are in accord about the weather.'

'Uh . . .'

'But there is, perhaps, a weightier topic. I don't know whether you have the intelligence to perceive it, but it looks to me as though you either had grossly improper intentions, as they call 'em, toward my daughter, or else you are young idiot enough to think that you could marry her. Which, eh? Which?'

'W-why, I'll tell you, Mr. Staybridge . . .'

'Don't stammer!'

'Well, golly, springing things like that so suddenly--hard for a fellow to answer, right off the bat . . .'

Light fingers on his arm, Annabel had guided Howard to a stiff Colonial settee, and she perched beside him, like a cowbird chaperoning an ox, while he struggled:

'Course, maybe I suppose I ought to finish college before I think about getting married, sir, but I certainly am crazy about Bell, and the minute I get out, I hope to land a good job and be able to support her.'

'It is your notion, then, that all Miss Annabel needs is to be provided with food and lodging? She seems to me to be quite adequately cared for already. Has it occurred to you that it would also be necessary for you to learn her language; the language I've reared her to speak?'

'Her language?'

'Quite! If you see this as in a glass, darkly, Miss Annabel might be willing to explain.'

Mr. Staybridge did not, as usual, embarrass them by snatching up his toys and going home; he embarrassed them more by sitting in easy indifference, reading Baron Corvo. If in the chill of that dry ice Annabel and Howard were too congealed for speech, their touching hands were voluble, and soundlessly they crept into the hall, out to a stiff white bench beside a stiff red plot of roses.

June, moon, tune--roses red and joybells soon; it should all have been a comedy of boy meets girl; but actually the young people were shaken with fear of Putnam Staybridge's contempt, fear of a world where the commonplaces of jobs and rent and food had become as difficult as winning an empire; and most of all, fear of their own overwhelming and illogical love, released now by Putnam's jibes.

Annabel dropped her protective street-corner flipness, all the 'O.K.s' and 'Swells' she had adopted equally from shopgirls and from the elegant Junior Leaguers. Howard was frightened out of his heavy humour. With his arm desperate about her shoulder, he could feel her tremble, her arm and shoulder tremble, as though every muscle were a shaken cord, and he was trembling himself as he struggled:

'G-golly, I g-guess we got to do something about it. I can't stand being away from you any more. All the fellows at Truxon, yellin' and throwing books around, and even drinking gin, and I'm beginning to think gin is awfully bad for your digestion, and the bums, they come bursting into my room any hour, day or night, in those dirty ole sweaters and grey pants, and I want to throw 'em out-- honest, Bell, I guess maybe I'm kind of crazy, but I can see you there standing in the dormitory hall, in a white dress, like a white flower the wind has blown there, and . . . But gosh, I wonder if I'm very intelligent? I don't know if I really care so much for reading, except the comic strips.'

'Dear, my dear, your heart is intelligent . . . I think it is! God help me if it isn't! Oh, it is!'

'Say, I'll settle down and read like the dickens--Tolstoi and biology and all those things.'

'We'll read together. I don't really know anything except what I parrot from Father.'

'You'll have to stand for keeping after me and making me work--be hard on you, but now we can't help it--this love business got so hold of me--feel like I was swimming in some rapids. We'll be married before this week is up!'

'But don't they expel students that marry, at Truxon?'

'Um-huh.'

'But don't you think you have to finish college?'

'We can't go on pretending to be a couple of monks.'

'No. Perhaps not.'

'I'll get a job right away. Dad bellyaches about it, but I can depend on him to find . . .'

'No! Howard! We mustn't depend on anybody! And besides! I have a hunch that Father Cornplow, the darling, is getting pretty fed up on having a bunch of grown-up huskies like you and Sara, and maybe me, hanging on to him as if we were babies with the measles. Be nice if he would give you a job, but . . . He's not like Putnam. That One enjoys having me stick around, so he can nag me and try out all the nifties he heard in Munich and Florence. Father Fred doesn't owe us a thing, not any longer, and he's beginning to suspect it . . .'

'He's *got* to help us! The world and the government and your own folks owe everybody a living.'

'You know: my father--sometimes he's pretty bright, or else he knows what books to steal from--he was saying that there isn't any government; there's nothing but a lot of people that are the government only they don't know it.'

'Maybe, but a fellow's own parents . . . I never asked to be born.'

'I doubt if anybody invited you to, either! No. If Father Fred gets sick of nursing us, I won't blame him. He's not asking us to marry--if we do get married . . .'

'We do!'

'Looks so, from this side. But I want us to economize. I'm crazy to. Honestly, honey, I'd get more kick out of having the nerve to do without things than I ever would getting them. Live in one room, if necessary. And I really am a pretty good cook--Putnam, the old gourmet, has seen to that. Let's live on eighteen dollars a week, if we have to . . .'

'Sure. That's O.K. by me. But before we start, there's a few things we'll have to have, and I'm busted just this minute, so Brother Cornplow will have to come through. We'll need a new radio--I haven't anything but my little portable--and the one in the car, of course--but that's a cinch; I'd be perfectly satisfied with a radio that didn't cost over fifty bucks.'

'Howard!' She was not trembling now, but rigid.

'Think that'd be too much? Well, all right. We could wait to get that--maybe months. But I've simply got to have a new Tuxedo.'

'My child, my child! Good-bye, Mr. Yeats! Goodbye, dove-grey edge of the sea and stormy sunset on doomed ships!' Annabel put on again her mask of country-club vulgarity. 'What a job *I* went and picked out for myself!' She kissed him on the lips. 'Call me ten to-morrow morning, when That One is off to his den,' and she fled into the gloomy house, while he wailed, 'But wait--wait--just minute . . . Aw, Bell, please . . . I'll be doggoned!'

CHAPTER XVIII

Three p.m. A June day. Office of the Triumph Motor Agency, also the Duplex Trailer, the Nation's Movable Home. Mr. Putnam Staybridge calling on Mr. Frederick William Cornplow.

'How d'you do, Mr. Staybridge! What can I do for you to-day? Can I have one of the salesmen show you the mid-year model Triumphs?'

'Thanks, no. Do you mind if I sit down?'

'Why, no.'

'Cornplow, I have ventured on a course, somewhat rare in these complex days--I'm quite old-fashioned, you see--of coming to you and speaking directly. Are you aware that your son and my daughter, mere children both of them, and perhaps neither of them very wise, apparently think they are in love?'

Fred was as angry at the smooth and supercilious tone as he had ever been in his life. Sitting behind his desk, he pressed his fingertips together till his knuckles felt as though they were breaking, but never in his life had he sounded more civil:

'I've noticed something of the kind, Mr.--uh--yes, I have noticed it, Staybridge.'

'You realize that it would be entirely unsuitable for Miss Annabel to marry your son.'

'Possibly.'

Mr. Staybridge waited for wrath, but had to carry on the play without it:

'I suppose your son has no money?'

'Not unless he's been holding out on me!'

'Nor prospects?'

'He tells me he may play in the college team, next autumn.'

'I'm being serious, Cornplow.'

Fred grunted.

'And I think that in other respects they aren't exactly mated,' said Putnam.

'Such as?'

'Oh, need we go into details, my dear fellow?'

Fred tramped the floor for almost a quarter of a minute before he was able to answer with suavity:

'Want me to tell you what you're trying to say, Staybridge? No. I don't suppose you do. But I'll be doggoned if I'm not going to. The idea is that you come from an aristocratic family, and me and the boy from a bunch of plain farmers and blacksmiths. That's the bunk. If it were true, which it doesn't happen to be . . .'

'Aren't you rather assuming . . .'

'. . . as I say, it doesn't happen to *be* true, because there's about six hard-up school teachers or government clerks among the Staybridge gang to one rich one . . .'

'If you *please!*'

'. . . but what of it? We're dealing with to-day. You're the kind of snob, Putnam, that thinks a manufacturer is socially 'way ahead of a wholesaler, and a wholesaler has got it all over a retailer, God knows why, and . . . And it happens that you aren't even a strictly kosher manufacturer--you own in pretty heavily, as a sleeping partner, on the Conqueror Company, which is engaged in peddling cars, same as I am. Oh, Putnam, how could you, my boy!'

Fred had seated himself again, very red; the pearl-pale Putnam had risen, even redder, and was shrieking, 'There happens also to be a question of breeding and manners!'

Quite gallantly Putnam took the risk of turning his back to Fred the Terrier and walking out.

Fred was brooding, 'And now, by golly, I'll be doggoned if I won't go and make those doggoned young idiots go and get married even if they doggoned don't want to! . . . Huh? No, I'm busy. Have Paul Popple talk to him.'

Later: 'But the little rat was right about one thing. Annabel certainly has got better manners than my brat, and I suspect she can read and write.'

Much later: 'What can a parent, that isn't more'n average bright himself, do for his children? Maybe leave them alone? If I only knew! . . . Maybe the poor, conceited little flute player loves his daughter, in his fool fashion. Wants to keep her . . . He's lost her. Do we always lose the people we love; only keep the people that we don't plague with loving? I guess those are the real wars--men against women--parents against children--and not all this monkey business in Europe. I'd like an armistice! I'd like to go off someplace to a valley where there's peace.'

CHAPTER XIX

The first fireflies of the summer beckoned in the garden beside the Staybridge Mansion. There was a smell of rain-wet rhododendrons, and beside the white gate a girl in a white cloak was waiting.

With muted engine, the car crept through the little street of maples and apple trees, stopped with the engine throbbing, and the horn, thrice sounded, was only a whimpering murmur. Annabel rustled through the gate. The right-hand front door was held open for her, and she crept into the car in silence; in silence they slipped away.

Annabel could see that Howard was driving. In the back seat were Sara, Eugene Silga and her brother, Guy.

'Got the licence in my pocket,' muttered Howard.

She patted his arm nervously.

'You're of age, anyway, aren't you, Bell?' said Sara, leaning forward, hands on the back of the front seat.

'Just.'

'Then your father couldn't do anything.'

Annabel sighed. 'You never know what that man might do . . . Howard, did you see your father?'

'Yes. But I didn't say anything about the marriage. Neither did he. He just looked sort of funny.'

'"Marriage!" It sounds so solemn and scary,' said Sara.

'To me it sounds like whiskers and horsehair sofas and whalebone corsets,' sniffed Gene.

Annabel seemed to be talking in sleep: 'Yes. I don't believe we're going to do it. We're putting on an amateur play, and afterwards, pretty soon now, Putnam S. will come back to my dressing-room and say, "Ann, if you had more discipline, if you didn't let the emotion govern you, you wouldn't be a bad actress". Maybe he's right.'

'Him? Never!' from Howard.

'Wasn't he right when he thought me up?'

'Yes, he did have a pretty good idea that time!'

They were coming into the business section, garish with lights from movie theatres. Howard drove scarily, as swiftly as he could, bounding ahead as the lights turned from red to green, till his shaken passengers nodded like Asian gods. Their escape from the stillness beside Putnam Staybridge's garden enlivened them, and they became hysterical:

'Don't forget to stop at the cathedral and pick up the bish and the canon . . .'

'And the trench mortar . . .'

'I've arranged for a hillbilly choir and six Jugoslav maestri playing twelve pianos . . .'

'But how can they . . .'

'With their feet, of course, idiot . . .'

'We can't get the bishop. He's playing poker down at Honest Tom's, and I heard he picked up his skirts and chased the cop on the beat seven blocks with a bung starter . . .'

'Annabel can have a choice of a rabbi, a Mormon missionary, and a Kentucky cardinal . . .'

'That's a bird, my good fool.'

'So is he!'

'Well, all you true-blue Aryan Tories and goyim can have your marriages, but I'd rather learn bezique . . .'

'Howard, for heaven's sake, you're doing fifty-five!'

'Fifty-seven,' said Howard.

Guy Staybridge had been looking through the back window. 'Howard! Ann! I think there's somebody following us. He's been making every turn we make and there's darn little traffic on this Patchin route, so I can pick him out.'

'The road is free, white and twenty-one,' said Howard, contentedly--accelerating.

'The horn sounds to me like my father's Conqueror--I know that horn,' said Guy.

'All right. We'll ditch him. Not that I'm scared of him or nobody,' growled Howard and, after thinking it over thoroughly, 'never!'

But he sped up, turned off on a side street so sharply that they were almost thrown from their seats, missed a station waggon, circled a block and came back on the main road.

'Have we lost him?' Howard demanded.

Guy speculated, 'I think so, but it's hard to figure out--these headlights.'

'Do you mind slowing up?' begged Annabel. 'I'd hate to have "Arrived at her wedding minus seven ribs" on my tombstone.'

'Personally, I'm scared to death,' said Gene.

Guy, still taking sight through the rear window and feeling important in the role of detective on guard, said with fake calm, 'I don't think that was his horn just now. These Conquerors got a whale of a lot of power--more'n your Triumph, I believe.'

Annabel hooted hysterically.

'What's the matter with you?' Howard was stolid and disapproving.

'Oh, darling! Don't you *see?* A curse on both your supply houses! Howardeo Montague Triumph and Annabel Capulet Conqueror!'

'I don't get that. Explain it to me afterwards, when I'm not so busy,' said Howard.

Annabel, with a small sound like a moan, looked closely at him and, no longer speaking, leaned forward, chin in hand.

The parsonage in Patchin, which was half suburb to Sachem and half country village, was a white box, more porch than house.

Sara had imagined aloud: 'The preacher will be a sweet old soul with spectacles, and his wife will be a dumpling, and they'll both be colossal bores. They'll kiss everybody that doesn't skip fast, and tell you two idiots to try to stand for each other, which is plainly unreasonable.'

But the minister and his wife, who came worrying out on to the porch as soon as the car hooted, were a timid, awkward pair, nearly as young as Howard and Annabel, though they possessed a pair of twins, whom they introduced as Abner and Bernice and sent protesting up to bed. They seemed more frightened about the marriage than did the brazen principals, and the pastor's lady begged them all to have 'just a bite to eat--just a little something--maybe some nice fresh doughnuts.'

She did kiss Annabel, and tenderly, but after looking Sara, Guy and Eugene over with anxiety, dismissed them as one of those accidents that just will happen.

The scanty living-room could not have been changed much since 1890. It still displayed a parlour organ and a brocade table-cover with ball fringes. On hanging shelves were the little pastor's books, each volume painstakingly covered with oilcloth.

'This isn't a wedding! Didn't I say it was just a play!' Annabel whispered to Howard, as they lined up.

'Bell, you must stop and realize that this is a very solemn moment in the lives of both of us,' he began, and she cut it short with 'You're telling *me?'* as the little pastor quavered, 'If you please now!'

Hearing an entirely illegitimate sound above them, Annabel looked up and discovered that the pastor's twins were peering down at the enchanted mystery through the hot-air register in the ceiling, vigorously pushing each other and commenting, 'She's kind of a nice-looking lady. I bet she paid anyways five dollars for that hat. What do they want to get married for? Hey, quit shoving me!'

She wanted to laugh, but she grew sober as she understood that the pastor was cutting her off from all the white, shy, maiden life she had known, with the timid solemnity of his question, 'Do you take this man to be your lawful husband?'

After the ceremony, the little pastor said only, 'Dearly beloved, I am not wise, and I don't know much about the rich city you come from, and all I can do is hope and pray you two will be as happy as my wife and I have been in our little house, and help each other the way she helps me every day.'

Annabel wanted to cry, then. She looked at Howard. His mouth was open, his eyes beseeching, and on his nose a tear was absurd and beautiful. But the time when she suddenly did cry, whooping like an indignant baby, was when she looked around to find, standing by the door, unexpected, unexplained, Fred and Hazel Cornplow, holding out to her their plain plump hands.

CHAPTER XX

The initial salary received by Howard Cornplow, a new apprentice at the Triumph Motor Agency, was twenty-five dollars a week, which was eighteen a week as a worker and seven a week as a son. He started in as a salesman, and he liked it. He pictured himself in a silver-and-scarlet automobile, spurting all over the district, crowing over his former fellow prisoners at Truxon College next autumn, and with lush commissions investing in the stock market and becoming a millionaire. He bought a suit of imported Harris tweed and, for no reason that he could ever explain, a pair of binoculars, which he kept in his demonstrator. Meanwhile, on one day at least, he borrowed lunch money from his shaggy second cousin, Cal Tillery.

But he did not sell any cars, not any cars at all, and Fred noticed this more than he did the Harris tweeds. After a week, Fred summoned him to the office, at close of the day's work.

Swinging his foot good-naturedly, Howard chuckled 'Can't take very long, Dad. Bell and I are going out and shoot some golf.'

'Son, I don't want you to think I'm grouchy. But it's time now . . .'

'Oh, golly, Dad, Bell is always saying "it's time now" to do some confounded thing or other!'

'Dry up till I finish! I said it's time for you to settle down to work. No employer is going to pay you for looking handsome--not even Hollywood, because you do have to be on time there, I understand, and in the nine days you've worked here now, you've been on an average of twenty-one minutes late in the morning, and you've taken an average of an hour and twenty-two minutes for lunch.'

'You've checked up on me--spied on me--like that?'

'I have. Any other employer would just have fired you. But your unpunctuality isn't as bad as the fact that you don't know a single thing about automobiles.'

'Now look here, Dad! Fair's fair! I've been driving cars since I was fifteen . . .'

'And you still don't know what all those funny tubes under the hood are for! Before you can sell, you've got to be able to take down a motor. I'm going to put you in the repair shop. I'm going to have Bill Merman teach you how to use a lathe and a hammer and a cold chisel . . .'

'Me work for that greasy, tobacco-spitting roughneck?'

'Maybe chewing tobacco is what makes a good machinist. Maybe you better learn . . . Wait! Excuse me. I didn't mean to get flip. I called you in here so we could get right down to brass tacks and cut out this fencing and covering up that we've always done, all our lives, doggone it! You're no longer a nice kid that I'm responsible for. You're a grown, married man--theoretically--and you're responsible for yourself and for Annabel. So you'll either put on overalls, and really go to work, and maybe some day I may put you to selling again, or else you'll get out and find work somewhere else.'

'And if I can't? With the raw deal Youth is getting . . .'

'Then you'll probably starve.'

Howard struck attitudes by the dozen, heroic ones: 'Oh, I can take it! I can live on handouts! I can sleep in the hay! But what about Annabel? Her father won't speak to her.'

'Your mother and I would be very pleased to have Annabel stay with us while you're sleeping in the hay, but if you come to our house to call on her, please brush off the hayseed . . . Howard! Damn it! Have I got to wake up and find I have a fool for a son? You can get to work or get out, and I've got so now's I don't care which . . . Oh, son, son, don't make me angry! I want to help you. Can't you see that?'

'Oh, all right, Dad. I'll try. I'll spit tobacco juice, if you say so, and pinch every penny . . . Want to drive out with me and meet Bell? I'll buy you a dry martini.'

While Howard and Annabel had been on their honeymoon of a week (which Fred had felt was all he ought, for their own sakes, to give them), he had found for them a three-room flat with appreciable light and air. Three months' rent he paid, and Hazel and he, somewhat timidly, provided electric stove and refrigerator, beds and a few chairs, and painted dining furniture. They called in Sara to approve and were flattered when she found these intrusions tolerable.

When Annabel returned, Fred called her to his office and ventured:

'It'll be a long time before Howard is able to do much more. I want to lend you, uh, lend you personally, Annabel, a thousand dollars, so you can finish the furnishing. I want you to give me your personal note for it--thousand bucks to be paid back in, uh, say ten years, at, uh, shall we say two per cent interest? Oh, it'll be a good investment for me, the way things are!'

'Dad, I don't want to take it. You've already given us enough furniture to scrape along on. I'd rather save, and buy things bit by bit. Howard is sweet, but . . .'

'Doggone it, Annabel, will you stop being so doggone noble? I'm being noble and you're being noble and no wonder Howard goes haywire with everybody forgiving him the whole doggone time, doggone it! Here, you take this thousand bucks and sign this note and get out of here and go buy that furniture, do you hear?'

'O.K., Chief!'

From the sketchiness of the lounge chairs, the couch, the occasional tables, the dressing-table and bureau that she bought, Fred suspected that Annabel had thriftily kept half of the thousand. He came in for coffee or lunch once or twice a week; he found that, as she often asserted, Putnam Staybridge had taught her perfection in making soups and desserts, canapés and salads. But she had never learned to cook roast beef or bread pudding or porridge, she was not precise in bed-making, and she belonged to the school of sweepers who leave rolls of dust under the bureau. She did perceive the sloppiness of her housekeeping, and day after day he saw her trying to remember where she had put the ice pick, trying to clean the ash trays and the glasses which their friends had left on every chair and table at last night's party.

He sighed, 'Dunno how come, but I feel more at home eating sinkers and lukewarm coffee off a soap-box with Annabel than I would having a bottle of champagne with Sara.'

(There were, to him, only five types of wine: champagne wine, sherry wine, red wine, California wine and cowslip wine, of which, as he understood it, only the first was to be drunk for pleasure and not to flatter one's host.)

The third issue of *Protest & Progress* contained two articles which irritated Fred beyond tolerance. He read them on an evening when Sara was away and, despite the sweet vision of sleep, he stayed up, girt for battle.

The first article stated that rarely had there been so persuasive a proof that all Americans were fools as had been seen during the recent visit of General Kynok, of the Soviet Air Corps. Aside from being entertained by the American airmen, invited to lunch by the President, urged to lecture in several cities, and shown all our landing fields and aeroplane factories, he had been ignored.

This curtain lecture was accompanied by a few sound generalizations: (1) It is glorious for a Russian to be a soldier and ready to defend his country. (2) Any American who is ready to defend his country and has become a soldier is either a bloodthirsty fiend or has been misled by the paid hypnotizers of Capitalism. (3) The Russian air fleet is stronger than those of any other three countries combined. (4) America, if she had any sort of nice feeling, would be devoting herself to helping defenceless and aeroplaneless Russia. (5) General Kynok was at once a Wellingtonian commander and a true-blue, tail-wagging Proletarian comrade.

That essay was merely an appetizer for the article in which Gene Silga urged that the Pragg Glassworks, the largest industry in Sachem Falls, be organized forthwith as a closed shop, and since it had been successful in resisting organization, that this be done by violence. He advised the workers to buy rifles, to form classes in marksmanship, to study Georges Sorel.

Fred was raving, when Sara appeared, after midnight.

'Wait a minute,' she said crisply. 'You're just an amateur scold. Look what the professionals have done.'

She gave him an early edition of the Sachem Falls *Recorder*, the morning paper, open at the third page. The right-hand column was filled with a story headed: 'Mayor and Council Denounce Local Red', which announced that one Eugene Silga was a notorious Bolshevik, that his paper was inciting to riot, and that the Board of Aldermen, with the mayor in attendance, would take up, to-morrow, means of ridding the city of Silga and his followers.

'You better get out of town!' agonized Fred.

'No. I can't run away.'

'Yes. That's so. You oughtn't to. But I certainly think you ought to stay away from Gene and your office a few days.'

'I suppose you're ashamed of me! Perhaps it's Mother and you that will want to run away!'

Mildly, rather surprised: 'No--no. I don't have to tell you I don't like what "P. & P." is doing--trying to make the whole country a WPA with unemployability the only test of employability. But of course I want to help you any way I can . . .'

'There is one thing you can do: help straighten up the office accounts. With this beastly attack, I expect all our beastly creditors will be surging into the office to-morrow, clamouring to be paid.'

'They might be. Some business men do like to be paid! I'll step around in the morning.'

'If you'd care to,' she said indifferently, as she started up stairs.

Fred's splendid rage had gone damp. Once more he had discovered that even when you have a sinner exactly where you want him, he still may have something to say; that it is, perhaps, a mistake to rehearse a play without inquiring whether your opposite is going to have some lines also.

He did not long brood on his failure. He knew that his daughter, beneath her icing, must be disheartened. He paddled to the upper hall and, after she should have been asleep, heard her softly thumping about her room. He longed to go in and have what he called a 'real talk with her'. Suddenly, feeling lonely, he saw that not for years had Sara and he talked with easy simplicity. This Coheeze disaster might be a bridge between them.

Did children, afraid to ask their parents for favours, know how often those parents were afraid of seeming ridiculous or bossy, and how they hovered, hesitating, outside bedroom doors?

He knocked.

There was no hearty 'Come in'. Sara evidently burrowed around for a dressing-gown before she opened the door, with an annoyed 'Yes?'

'Nothing, nothing, daughter. Just--well, I wanted you to know I'd help, any way I can.'

'Oh, thanks,' she said bleakly.

Fred had never been in the Coheeze office, and when he climbed to it, at ten the next morning, he felt uncomfortably that he had returned to his early days of canvassing. The unpainted, boxed-in stairs were littered with papers and muddy heelprints, they smelled of yellow soap, and they displayed the signs of an electric healer and of a philanthropist who sold loaded dice 'for scientific purposes only'.

In his one glance about the Coheeze office, Fred rather liked it, reminded of the crazy tents, littered with fishing tackle and old shoes, in which he had camped as a boy. Gene and Sara were sitting on their tables, muttering anxiously.

'Well, Gene, this is kind of hard luck.'

'Eh? Oh, how d'you do, Mr. Cornplow. Hard luck is right. I get all the blame, but how could I guess?'

'You might've known . . .'

'I was following instructions absolutely. Now, I suppose, I won't get a cent more money.'

'You could hardly expect the Channing Praggs to come through when you've jumped on the source of all their cash . . .'

'Praggs? *Praggs?* Oh! Them! We aren't talking about the same thing, Mr. Cornplow.'

Sara said witheringly, 'Of course not!' while the young Fred felt like a calf in the scornful company of these, his elders. Gene condescended:

'I don't mind the Press roasting me, either. That's my job, stirring them up. My trouble is with the C.P.'

'Oh yes. The C.P.?'

'Good heavens, Father!' from Sara. 'The Communist Party, of course.'

'Oh, I see.'

Gene sighed, 'I've just had a long wire from them this morning . . . I'm a good radical, but I never did understand why it is that the harder up a left-wing organization is, the more it sends out hundred-word night letters that could just as well go under a three-cent stamp . . . Happen to notice that in the last "P. & P." I gave quite a boost to the Russian general, Kynok?'

'Um-uhh.'

'The real model for all American soldiers that might want to go revolutionary?'

'Um-huh.'

'Well the Party wires me that Comrade Kynok was secretly arrested in Moscow day before yesterday, as a spy for Japan, and tried last night, and of course he will be shot this morning. Kynok! That stood with Stalin's arm about his shoulders while 175,000 children marched past them, saluting, a month ago! How could I know? Now, I suppose I'm a Jap spy and a Trotskyite, too!'

'But big leader like that, Gene, prob'ly they'll find him innocent.'

Gene turned on his smile, friendly, a little cynical.

'Nope. They don't waste time in Moscow. They don't spend the State's money inquiring whether somebody's innocent unless they can prove he's guilty. It's a new system of justice! Good Lord, I sound like a counter-revolutionary! Sorry. Well, I've got to get to work writing a piece telling how I finally got on to Kynok, the dirty, treacherous rat! The enemies of the Proletarian State must be rooted out ruthlessly! Rat--root--rut'less, that's my tune--my rune--oh hell!'

Gene's typewriter began firing, shooting out flames, the platen turning red hot, the gunner's face grim.

Sara suggested almost civilly, 'You wanted to look over our accounts, Father?'

He indicated that such had been his presumptuous longing.

She led him to a third kitchen table, which the Coheeze office had extravagantly added to its equipment; she pointed to a mess of letters, bills and ten-cent notebooks, and said casually: 'There's our books.'

After half an hour of rustling through papers like a discouraged sparrow scratching up gravel, Fred decided that he was not going to be able to 'straighten up their accounts'. For there were no accounts. Except for transactions during their first week, they had noted down nothing whatever. Uncashed donation cheques were mixed with unpaid bills. On torn slips of paper were such helpful notes as 'Recd cash from J.K., ten.' In one envelope he found a cheque for one hundred dollars from the Southside Marxian and Literary Club and a bill for sixty-five from a stationery firm, and the envelope was from neither party but from the Maplehurst Labour College.

Fred was opening his mouth in wrath at such sacrilege against bookkeeping when the tramp of a dozen heavy feet came from the rickety stairs below them.

CHAPTER XXI

At the tramping on the stairs, the three sprang up, Gene with quivering hand at his lips.

'You scared?' demanded Sara.

'You bet I am! Sounds like the cops. I've been beaten by cops before!'

'They've got no reason to arrest us.'

'They don't arrest you for reason--just for fun!'

Fred took command--not these many years had he dared to command Sara. 'You two get out of this! Hustle up on the roof and hide. I know lots of the cops.' They hesitated, and his voice became military. 'Hear me? Get out! Beat it!'

The two revolutionaries beat it.

He made much of looking as though he had proper business here. He sat squarely at the table, pencil in hand, note-book and bills before him, but he was trembling, and afterward he found that the only entry he had made in the note-book was: 'Scared myself.' He was gravely drawing ballet girls on a blotter when, like pigs bursting out of an opened pen, into the room sprang a police sergeant and five patrolmen, all with clubs in their fists, a couple with hands on pistol holsters.

'What the!' grunted the sergeant.

'Well I'll be!' intelligently commented the others.

'Hello, Sergeant. Afraid you're too late. Your birds have flown the coop,' Fred carolled.

He remained seated; he knew that to be the safest position against a thug not too drunk.

'Who are you? Oh. It's Mr. Cornplow. What you doing here? Where's this anarchist guy?'

'Skipped town, I'm afraid. I'm here representing the creditors. This fellow Silga owes me for a light truck, damn him!'

'What makes you think he's gone?'

'My daughter saw him off at the train.'

'Oh, that's so! She was mixed up in this.'

'She just worked here--she talked it over with my friend, the mayor, before she took the job. She has no responsibility.'

'Well, I don't want her, anyway. Get busy, boys!'

It was appalling to the placid Fred, the gloating frenzy with which the boys 'got busy'. From somewhere out in the hall axes were brought, and they gleefully went to work. There is no greater bliss than to be destructive as hell while being moral as heaven. The guardians of the law smashed tables, threw a typewriter through a closed window, with hysterical laughter. Reporters and news photographers were somehow suddenly there, very cheerful, and it was the glare of a flashlight bulb that startled Fred into action. He rose; he faced the sergeant as he would have faced a chronic dead beat.

'Stop this business or I'll have the whole bunch of you kicked off the force! I represent the creditors, and you have no court order . . .'

'Don't need none.'

'I'll sue you, personally, for every cent of damage! Look, Sergeant--chase all these roughnecks out of here, and I'll explain.'

'Outside youse,' said the sergeant, wiping his hand on the seat of his trousers, that it might be clean to receive the dirty money.

Fred's argument was brief: it consisted entirely in a twenty-dollar bill and the reminder that, already, the sergeant had been photographed enough to ensure publicity.

'I would like to get hold of that there atheist Silga, though. Hate to have the cops in the next town find we let him go without marking him,' mourned the faithful sergeant, as he departed, after giving his inspiring lesson in How to Make Communists.

Fred sat down, unsteadily. As Gene and Sara crept back into the room, he, who had hated all Reds, was positively loving in his address:

'Son, better get going quick--get out of town. They want to beat you. I finagled the cops out, but they might come back.'

Sara said sniffily, 'I suppose you bribed them! I suppose you were humble to them!'

'I certainly was--I bribed and humbled and I lied, you little prig, you Soviet Salvation Army lassie, you . . . Grrrr! Gene, got any compromising papers here? Get 'em out quick.'

'Only the C.P. telegram this morning. I burn 'em.'

That telegram Gene was taking from a telephone book and tucking into his pocket.

'Want to hide out at my house, Gene? Seeing Sara was in this with . . .'

'I do not! I'm leaving town.'

'You probably aren't very flush. Can you use this ten bucks?'

Gene took the bill disdainfully--oh, he took it, just the same!--and without thanks headed for the door.

'Gene!' wailed Sara.

'Well?'

'Can't we help you with your baggage?'

'Baggage? You're very funny, Comrade Cornplow!' Gene snarled. 'My baggage consists of two suitcasefuls--one of them books--which is what I have to show for my twenty-seven years--six of 'em spent in either being beaten by cops, or enduring middle-class females playing at being free souls, like you!'

'Gene!' It slashed Fred's heart to see with what agonized fondness his daughter was looking at the young man.

'But you remind me, Sara,' remarked Gene, and for a second his reckless smile came back. He dialled on the telephone, and murmured, 'Miss Kitz, please . . . Oh, Frieda, this is Gene . . . Yes, they've been here--wrecked everything. I'm hitch-hiking out of town and glad of it. I'll meet you in the old place in Albany, 'bout eight to-night. O.K.? . . . Fine. *Auf Wiedersehen!*'

He turned debonairly on the Cornplows with, 'You see, you needn't worry about my future now, Mr. Cornplow! You wouldn't be a bad sort, if you just had the sense to realize that your good-natured democratic sort of middle-roadishness is plumb finished--or will finish, in front of a stone wall.'

'I suppose you want me to play safe and join the Communist Party!'

Fred believed that he had been chillingly sarcastic, but Gene answered serenely, 'No I'm afraid we wouldn't want you!' and Gene was gone.

Fred turned pitifully to Sara, who was standing mute, hands at her breast. 'Honey, it's what you get if you mix up with folks that are crazy for power. Were you awfully fond of Gene?'

The tornado struck him squarely:

'Gene? You call that little guttersnipe "Gene"? I hate him! I always did! He was just an experiment in psychology to me. "Fond"? Oh, can't you even begin to understand me? . . . I'm going to the tennis club. I've been neglecting my game. I'm going out for it seriously now. But before I play, I'm going to have a Tom Collins and see if I can't wash the taste of all this vulgarity out of my mouth.' She looked indignantly down on the parent who had wished upon her these unpleasantnesses, the Coheeze and *Protest & Progress* and the police. She said, from the doorway, 'It's all very distasteful to me. Bribery! Insisting that I'm such a fool as to like that little rat, Silga. Very--distasteful--indeed!'

Fred was left alone with a mess of unpaid bills.

'I won't pay one cent of 'em,' he stormed--with twenty-five-per-cent honesty.

An hour later, in front of a miraculously straightened table, he added, 'I'd like to get out of this! I suppose I love my grateful son and daughter, but now I know what old man Solomon meant when he said, "Comfort me with apples for I am sick of love!"'

CHAPTER XXII

As an apprentice mechanic at the Triumph Agency, Howard was popular. For a couple of days he sulked at grease and overalls, the time clock and an aching back, but he discovered that the workmen were as individual as the pedigreed young gentlemen he had known in college, and more vigorous in humour. Their stories of jobs and girls and drunks, of the navy, the Pacific Coast, Detroit, seemed to him better than the giggling of young collegians, and it became important to him to be one of the boys.

He learned that nobody will find it out--at least not till the rear-end burns out, months later--if you save your energy by squirting only a quarter enough grease into the differential. He learned to get something very like a nap, after lunch and a couple of Bourbons, by lying under a car and in a friendly manner tapping the springs with a hammer now and then. And the chief mechanic was indulgent when the Son of the Boss got a group about him and taught them 'Three Cheers for Old TruxON'.

Howard perceived that he had been wrong in regarding his second cousin, Cal Tillery, as a lout and a bore. Cal might never achieve life's prime purpose and learn to sell motor cars to bankers; Cal's hair might resemble a ravelled gunnysack; but in the wholesome fastnesses of the Adirondacks, Cal had developed a rustic slyness that to Howard seemed sharper than the book-taught perceptions of Guy Staybridge. He played poker with the tenacity of one who had learned it in the hay-mow; waitresses might laugh at him, but they did walk out with him; and for all city slickers and their rules, Cal had contempt. No scolding from his father could embarrass Howard so much as Cousin Cal's drawling, 'You going to go society on us, are you, Big Boy, and put on the Tuxedo and play bridge whist with the old girls with the red fingernails?'

Cal started by borrowing money from Howard; it ended with Howard's borrowing from Cal and nervously volunteering to his father that Cal was a jewel and they must never lose him.

Fred listened with no comment beyond that of his wrinkling eyebrows.

Fred was calling upon Ben Bogey, 'Homes that are nice at lowest price'.

'Cutting out the bunk, Mr. Bogey, how much chance do you think you'd stand of making a living if you and my son started a firm together?'

'A living? Why, Mr. Cornplow, as sure as I'm sitting here, we'd make twenty per cent on the investment . . .'

'Whoa-up! I asked could you two make a *living?* In my experience, that totals a lot more than the twenty per cent that you boys seem to figure out on some kind of arithmetic different from what I studied. What real prospects you got?'

Mr. Bogey showed letters. Three firms were willing to let him handle their apartment-house rents; another firm congratulated him on 'developing' a cow pasture into a human pasture.

Fred mused, 'Well, now, you take Howard, and what's he got for you?'

'Oh, everything, Mr. Cornplow! Simply everything! I cer'nly understand why you're so proud of that boy. Good looks, nice voice, athletic training--gracious, how the ladies that are looking for suburban homes would fall for that fellow! And fine education and nice dependable manners--why, everything! You don't have to tell me!'

'As matter of fact, I *was* going to tell you a few interesting facts about him. His education is phony. He can mis-spell in three languages. He hasn't just learned the history of the U.S.--no indeed--he's forgotten the dates and names in the history of the whole world. But aside from all this modern education stuff, he's unpunctual, he chatters like a monkey all day long, when he's supposed to be reconditioning cars, he wastes material, he boasts that he's the son of the boss, and he borrows money. Think you could do anything with him?'

'Sure. He's the kind that needs freedom.'

'How much would I have to put up for him, if he went in partnership with you?'

'I figured it would be five thousand dollars.'

'Can't do it possibly. I'll tell you. I'll put up two thousand now. Three months from now, if you two are making a real, honest-to-God beginning, I may put in another two.'

'It's a go!'

So was Howard kicked upstairs; so was the Triumph Agency saved from becoming a glee club; and in the innocent belief that his own overwhelming charm had done it all, Howard began his career as a builder of cities, a king of contracts, a viceroy of choice rentals.

Annabel was hanging the curtains in the bright new three-room office of the bright new firm of Bogey & Cornplow, Realtors. Ben had chosen the city's northern outskirts, a pouncing place for the best suburbs, and for their office chosen the ground floor of a cheerful-looking building filled with doctors and dentists. Already he was out hustling for prospects, while Howard conducted the office, a task which, so far, had consisted in watching Annabel fill flower vases and the girl stenographer type 'The quick brown fox jumped with zest over the gay lady'. He lighted a thin cigar with an air he had never shown in lighter college days, and to Annabel he pontificated:

'This is something like it! Course at the Triumph the trouble was, I was kept back by being the owner's son. Everybody took advantage of it and tried to borrow money . . .'

'Howard! Please! Howard!'

He threw down the cigar; he became serious.

'I know what you're going to say, dear, every word; and most of its true. I was loafing. And I did kinda borrow a little. But what was there ahead, stuck in that dirty shop? Now I'm free! I've got the world by the tail! I'm going to work twenty hours a day, every day, by golly--uh--just soon as there's any customers to work on!'

The Cornplow family had always taken its vacations together, in August or September, at some lakeside hotel. This year, with Howard's marriage, with Sara's revolution, with Coheeze creditors still to be pacified, with the Duplex booming, their vacation plans had been unmade.

Fred sat with Hazel on the screened porch at the side of their house on a late July evening, very hot, conducive to bad tempers and rebellion. It seemed to him that he had been fighting a battle in the fog, with shadows that proved to be armed enemies, and enemies that were mist; and that he could depend only on the fixed cool light that was Hazel.

'Say, uh, Hazel, don't you think we better start thinking about what we're going to do for vacation? Looks like with the boy married, and Sara so doggone busy at the tennis club explaining she never was a communist, just you and I'll go off together. First time in all these years, and will I enjoy it! Let's drive up to the Gaspé. Or how about putting the car on a lake steamer and going out to Duluth? We'll have some adventures, too--no Sara along to highhat the populace! Just us two old bums!'

'It would be nice, Fred, but . . . The children have been talking with me. I know Howard expects to take Annabel and come with us.'

'Now? Just started in business? Just married?'

'He says it would be cheaper . . .'

'I see. He don't so much want a trip with us as on us!'

'And Sara has an idea. She expects to play in a tennis tournament in the South, in October--down at Wormtail Hot Springs . . .'

'That doggone dump? Where the politicians boil out enough alcohol so they can enjoy a fresh filling? If she goes there, she goes by herself, lemme tell you!'

'She feels that after the mistake she made about this fellow Silga's character, she's got to be extra respectable, and she has an idea that if we took a cottage at Wormtail together . . .'

'Of all the . . .'

'I know, Fred, I know, but I also know how Sara is, and if she makes up her mind and starts nagging, we'll give in to her to save trouble. The only way you could handle it would be to run away from her.'

'Well, and what's the matter with running away? Hm! Think I'll take a little walk.'

Hazel stared after him. Fred was excited, and she was afraid of spontaneous combustion.

CHAPTER XXIII

At ten next morning, a dusty and discouraged morning of July, Fred telephoned from the office:

'Oh, Hazel? Sara there?'

'No, she's at the club. Anything I can do?'

'Just something I wanted to ask about.'

'I'll be going down town shopping, in about an hour, Fred.'

'Say, wait for me at the house, will you? Got anything important on for to-day?'

'No, just coffee at Louise Kamerkink's this afternoon.'

'Fine. Wait for me.'

He looked embarrassed, she was puzzled and a little anxious, when he came into the house at this unexampled hour of the day.

'Lookit, Hazel. Grand day, and I'm kind of tired. What say we jump in the car and skip off for two-three days?'

'To-day?'

'Why not?'

'Heavens, you have to make preparations!'

'Don't need any. Gas and oil and a toothbrush and a comb and a nightshirt-- what more do you need? If you have to get a lipstick along the way, prob'ly there are some stores outside Sachem Falls! I brought some cash from the office.'

'If you'd just told me a few days ago. I've made some dates . . .'

'Anything you can't bust?'

'I don't think that would be awfully nice of me.'

'What 'd you do if you stepped off the kerb and got killed by an auto? Wouldn't be able to keep your dates then, would you?'

'Why, what a perfectly awful suggestion!'

'Well, it does happen sometimes, don't it? Hop to it and call 'em off.'

'You're just as arbitrary as Sara.'

'Sure. I inherited it from her. Can do?'

'Oh, I suppose . . .'

'Get at it, then, and pack a bag--just toilet things and some underwear.'

'But where--what . . .'

'Thought maybe we'd run over to Saratoga Springs and see the new buildings there. But the point isn't where we're going; it's the fun of us two running off together.'

'I think I might like it.'

She was already dialling Mrs. Kamerkink.

Fred hurried upstairs and packed one bag--the chief necessity in it, the latest P. G. Wodehouse novel. He telephoned to his secretary, at the office, that it was such a hot day--going take little run to Saratoga--would she call up Mr. Howard and Miss Sara and--tell 'em be back endaweekmiddlanext.

When Howard telephoned, as Howard was certain to, Fred was densely misunderstanding about the overwhelming need of Bogey & Cornplow for his advice on importunate problems. He merely chuckled a little, inanely babbled, 'Yuh, thought I'd check out for couple days--Saratoga', hung up on Howard-- though, to any salesman, hanging up is a crime ranking with malfeasance and conversion--and did not answer the telephone when it rang again. That would be Sara. He knew that Sara would hurry right back to the house, but he also knew that Sara could never hurry right back anywhere without stopping to nag somebody about something, and indeed she did not arrive until five minutes after Fred had set the nickled snout of his Triumph Special Convertible Coupé eastward on Fenimore Cooper Boulevard, with Hazel warm and bewildered beside him.

Though he felt that in his flight into Egypt there were several important principles illustrated, he was thinking less about his boldness in running away from the parental tyranny of his children than about the fact that in the taut grey suit and the small tricorne hat which Hazel had assumed for motoring she looked ten years younger than when, soft and flowing, hinting of the harem, she appeared in an afternoon frock, phony jewellery and household cares. He observed that she was beginning to permit herself the questionable privilege of enjoying life. Could she ever be cured of her servitude to Things, her love of

Possessions and of establishing her secure respectability by showing them off? Could she ever be free of blue china and of lacy mats?

She said cheerfully, 'It'll be interesting to see Saratoga Springs.'

'Yes, I guess maybe it would be, some day.'

'How do you mean? What are you being so mysterious about?'

'You don't know half of it. Listen, honey! I'm the most mysterious guy in this whole length and breadth of Sachem Falls! I'm Frenzied Fred, the Masked Menace. I'm right out of Edgar Wallace. I'm J. G. Reeder, with a dagger in my fountain pen.'

'Idiot! What *are* you . . .'

'I'm the man with three faces--all of 'em prob'ly a mistake.'

'Darling, I thought I heard you sneak downstairs last night and have a little nip.'

'It's worse than liquor, woman. It's the wine of life. It's . . .'

'Please stop trying to be cute, Fred, and tell me what you're up to.'

'Oh, we're merely taking the Golden Road to Samarkand!'

'Well, it may look so to you, but it looks to me like Route 29; and it may be gold, but right along here, there seem to be patches of cement.'

'Don't notice it. Some poor cusses on the WPA came along last night and pinched this stretch of gold. You'll see it again in couple blocks.'

'Fred, dearest, I don't mind, but are you cuckoo?'

'Completely! See that man there?'

'What man, where?'

'Sitting up on the bonnet of the car--the little fellow with the pointed hat and the green whiskers?'

'Oh--yes--well--I can't say I see him very clearly.'

'You will, if you stick around with me long enough. That clears it all up, don't it?'

Not a word more would he say till he had turned at right angles off Fenimore Cooper Boulevard, which led straight to Saratoga. Now, the car was headed south-east.

'Where are we going?' wondered Hazel. But she said it without alarm, for whatever she might think of Fred's capacity as a romantic lover, he was to her the Beethoven of motoring.

'What's trouble?' he droned.

'Why, the car seems headed in the wrong direction.'

'It does? Doggone! We'll just have to go along with it, I guess. Too fast for us to jump.'

'Frederick, will you please stop all this coyness . . .'

'I know. But I feel so cheerful and free--and unusual--and therefore silly!'

'Well, quit it a moment, won't you? I'm sorry, but this is not the road to Saratoga!'

'Whoever said it was?'

'Aren't we going to Saratoga?'

'Whatever made you think we were?'

'I heard you telephoning to Howard . . .'

'Has it ever been your opinion that our darling son is a safe man to trust the truth with?'

'Then where are we going?'

'I think--unless we change my mind--we're going to an inn at Stonefield, Mass., east of Lenox. But does it matter where we land up, as long as nobody can catch us, and we can quit being responsible parents for a few days and see if we're still human beings also? How about it?'

'I--I don't think it's such a bad idea. I do like going with you.'

'Remember one evening I was kind of talking about retiring? I haven't forgotten it. Maybe I'm not so satisfied with what Fred Cornplow has done with life. I want to try and see--just experiment and try and see if there aren't some new things I'm not too old to learn, just for the fun of learning 'em. And then . . . About Sara and Howard. One reason for this running off is, I figure that if I can be plumb away from 'em for a while, where they can't find us and interfere, I'll get over my irritation and quit being so mean to 'em.'

'I didn't think you were so mean.'

'Well, if you didn't, then I missed the target pretty bad, because I certainly set out to be mean. Maybe what I'll get out of this trip will be ability to be a whole lot meaner. Anyway, something interesting is bound to happen to anybody nowadays who has the nerve to buck this Reign of Youth. Rights for the Uptrodden!'

They sat for half an hour on a hilltop of rough upland pasture, loud with insects; they sat on the running board, contentedly saying nothing at all, and his cigarette tasted good.

They had lunch at a farmhouse, under the maples, and he crowed, 'You simply can't get real fried chicken and home-made ice cream like this in the city!' She did not explain that the chicken had undoubtedly come from a can, the ice cream from a renowned creamery in Troy.

They had, in mid-afternoon, an old-fashioned milk shake in a village drugstore and, while Hazel cooed at them to make them feel neighbourly, Fred and the druggist told each other that they had elegant motors, handsome and co-operative children, constructive ideas about the future of the Republican party, and that life was a good idea. Grey-haired, grey-browed, in grey alpaca jacket, his grey hands thin and long, the druggist leaned his elbows on the counter and meditated, 'Nice thing about my business is, grand people like you come in and pass the time of day.'

Fred went out to the car in a one-man parade. He liked to be grand people, reflected Hazel. 'Set that man down in Warsaw or Tokyo', she thought proudly, 'and inside an hour he'd know the names of all the children of the nearest cigar-store man and all the taxi-drivers and the policeman on the block . . . In that, he's like Howard. Maybe some day I'll get my two men together!'

It was not over a hundred and fifty miles from Sachem to Stonefield, and for Fred, normally, that was one-third of a day's driving, but they so happily dawdled, enchanted by deep meadows and thick trees, that at five they were still fifty miles from Stonefield, and filling up with petrol at the Daisy Dell Cabins and Café, All Home Comforts, Flats Fixed.

The Daisy Dell establishment seemed to have been constructed by the carpentry class of a kindergarten. The only reason, Hazel surmised, why no resolute burglar had picked up a couple of the cabins and carried them away was that they would have been of use for nothing but kindling.

With distress she heard Fred cackling, 'Say, I got an idea! What say we spend the night at this dump?'

'But we could be in Stonefield in time for dinner, easy, and I think these cabins look awfully sloppy.'

'Sure. Prob'ly are. But be kinda fun--be a change, camping out.'

'And terrible mattresses. Lumpy.'

'Be good for our souls to not be so dunked in luxury for one night.'

'Well, if you'd like to. But I never did think much of martyrdom if it's going to be uncomfortable.'

'Huh! Think of the lousy camel drivers' huts we'll have to sleep in along the road to Samarkand.'

'And think of what a joke it'll be on us if we wake up in one of those huts and find it's on the wrong road. *However!'*

CHAPTER XXIV

The Daisy Dell Cabins were thin and tall, with a list to leeward; they were of clapboards, once painted white, but the raw pine had soaked up the paint. The yard before them was lined with gravel and cinders and inhabited by a shamefaced dog given to constant scratching. Something more had been done with the 'café', the camp's central building, a four-room shanty with a public room fresh painted a bright yellow and containing chairs and tables in booths, and a counter for five-cent bars of decayed candy, cigarettes, pies, and 'souvenirs' in a way of china ash trays lettered 'Greetings from Butiful Daisy Dell'.

Pa and Ma Stickle were the proprietors. Pa had a moustache apparently made of raw cotton, which needed changing, and the tails of his collarless shirt should have been tucked in oftener, and Ma had smut on her nose. Yet they were friendly as old milk-route horses, and seemed instantly to recognize Fred as one of their own disreputable race of vagabonds.

When Fred had registered--he wrote it down 'Frederick Williams, N.Y.', so that he might not be traced--Pa Stickle whispered, 'Say, neighbour, of course we haven't got a licence here, but a fellow I don't know his name left some applejack and I thought maybe you might be thirsty after driving . . .'

Fred drank, then choked, gurgled, looked around as though wondering who had hit him, and immediately became hilarious. Hazel had a finger of applejack in ginger-ale, hiccupped, murmured, 'Gracious sakes alive!' and began to giggle. When she heard Fred laughing at her, she stared at him with mild bovine disapproval and suddenly became as hilarious as he.

They did not dine till seven, two hours later, but they were enchanted out of the flow of time. They told Pa Stickle all about themselves and listened while Pa narrated that he had been a ship's cook, a vaudeville dancer, an arctic explorer and (since Fred and Hazel seemed to have swallowed all this, as safely as they had the applejack) a trader in the Solomon Isles.

'That's a grand old boy, and I'll bet anyway five per cent of his stories are true,' glowed Fred, as Pa departed to bring their hamburg steak with fried onions.

Hazel was more or less serious. 'But d'you think we ought to start off our journey by associating with such low people?'

'Low? Low? Thank God they're low! After Sara, Pa tastes good to me--like a mutton chop after a diet of cheese soufflé. I love to be low. Like getting back to earth. Provided it ain't Cousin Enos Tillery's earth. Don't want any earth in my ears!'

'Well . . . But I'm sure the hamburgs won't be very good.'

They weren't, but Hazel left unconsumed only one snippet of fried butcher's paper which had got in among the onions.

From the Daisy Dell, only a couple of farmhouses were to be seen, far off, but by eight o'clock the place was filled with rustic versions of Sara and Howard. The café did smell, rather, of frying pans, paraffin, cabbage and Stickles, but it was lively with yellow paint and pink paper doilies and soft-drink posters showing bathing girls, and it crackled now with jokes fresh from the radio. Fred admired one young lady in a silk frock decorated with red poppies, in silk stockings and silver slippers, who sat on a high stool delicately sipping a lemonade into which her escort, a young man with a plaid pullover and an irremovable camel's-hair cap, kept pouring gin.

'Expensive-looking pair,' Fred hinted to Pa Stickle. 'The young lady in silk.'

'Her? Oh yes. Smart girl. She's daughter of Ole Man Bocks, up the road here a piece--the one that's doing time for burning down folks' barns, seems like he just can't keep from it, somehow, and she's got a fine job, working for Doc Onderdonck's folks down in the village--eight dollars a week, yessir, and the washing sent out.' You bet. But that ain't no silk--it's rayon--eleven-fifty for the dress and 'tain't paid for, neither!'

'Oh dear, I'm afraid this place is too fast for conservative people like us,' yawned Hazel. 'I'm going to bed right away.'

'I'm going to hit the hay pretty sudden myself,' agreed Fred.

But at eleven, when Hazel had slipped off to their cottage, Fred was playing poker in the kitchen with Pa Stickle, a brush salesman, the local auctioneer, who was also the local assemblyman, and a hired man, and was losing steadily to all of them and enjoying it. Afterward Ma Stickle invited them to share what she called 'couple sandwiches or something', which proved to consist of beans, brown bread, clam chowder, honey, cold fish and applejack. All of it Fred devoured; he imitated Pa Stickle in lying preposterously about his travels; and he went across the cinder courtyard to bed in his cabin, weaving and inclined to music.

Fred did not look very closely at their cabin at Daisy Dell until he awoke, in the sway-backed bed, on a mattress filled with iron ore and paving stones, at eight in the morning. He had a head, and he knew that Dr. Kamerkink would have been profane about his liver and blood pressure, but he lay and chuckled at his idiocy of the night before.

With slight whimpers as the sutures of his skull cracked open and closed again, he sat on the bed, surveying the caravansary in Samarkand for which they had given up their pink-and-cream bedroom. It was the largest cabin at the Dell; a double one, containing no furniture except the two wiggly iron beds, two straight chairs, a piano lamp minus its shade, a mirror, and a bureau which lacked one drawer. The wall was covered with plaster the colour of withered lettuce, with map-shaped holes where the plaster had fallen, but gloriously, startlingly, on it were hung, by count, nine pictorial calendars, presenting kittens in baskets, cherries in baskets, little girls tormenting little dogs, and a church beside a moonlit lake.

Fred turned to look at Hazel, and she was lying drowsily awake, smiling at him.

'Isn't it lovely--the room,' she said, blessedly making no comment whatever upon his hour of returning last night. 'But what I was thinking was: I never enjoyed a drive in my life as much as yesterday. When we were a young married couple, there were always the children along, bawling and asking questions. Remember how Sara used to say "Why?" . . . "Ma-ma, why is that man ploughing the field?" "So he can plant his seed--now hush, dear." "Why?" "So he can grow crops." "Why?" "So he can sell them." "Why?" "So he can support his family." "Why?"'

'Sensible question, the last one.'

'And ever since, seems like we've always had to get somewhere on time, and then get right back for an "important engagement".'

'I didn't know how you'd feel this morning, when you woke up and had another look at this dump.'

'I don't mind it, because I don't have to worry about whether Hilda will get around to vacuum-cleaning it to-day. Honestly, did I ever worry about things like that? Seems so long ago.'

'Don't it!' What a little wizard he was, Fred exulted. Already he had Hazel half-cured of her slavery to possessions. Then she was firmly remarking:

'Fun here--for a change--for one night. But of course I didn't sleep much. This mattress is like a relief map of the Adirondacks. But it might be nice to have a nice cottage in the country.'

'Yes!'

'But of course we'd want it nice--you know--a swimming pool and a greenhouse, oh, just a little one. But nice. And I do think, mornings when you don't feel so good, it's economy in the long run to have the girl bring you a nice breakfast in bed.'

'Well,' said the diminished Fredk Wm.

CHAPTER XXV

The hills were not so proud as their own Adirondacks, but softer, more feminine, thought Fred, as they came to Stonefield, a dormered and white-spired hamlet in the Berkshires. The tavern, where Fred again craftily registered as Frederick Williams, N.Y., was no Daisy Dell, but a competent grey-shingled inn, and the annex cottages were isolated on the slope of a hillside dark with pines, light with maples, gleaming with a cleared meadow.

In front, the Cornplows' cottage looked from a half-screened wide porch, through the columns of a pine grove, to a meadow, and to a pond which would be silver at dawn, blazing in late afternoon, a shield of rose and black just after sunset. At the back, from a minute brick terrace edged with gloxinia, it looked up to the hills, which led the exploring eye from a mountain ridge to ever higher ridges beyond. There were but three rooms: living-room, double bedroom, and kitchen with dining alcove. The cottagers could prepare their own meals or dine at the tavern.

The rooms were ceiled with soft-stained pine; the only pictures were a few sharply coloured prints; the fireplace was of the simplest--brick with a pine mantel; and everything possible had been built in: bookshelves, bureau, dressing-table, couch. The dishes, Hazel found, gently squealing with domestic fervour, were of the best five-and-ten-cent native pottery, made by handmade machinery; there were, incredibly, enough ash trays, and these devised to hold ashes and butts and not to display reproductions of the higher-class barnyard fauna; the screen doors closed tightly without a bang; and there was a shower as well as a smallish tub.

'It's swell!' said Fred, with an idiotic look of bliss.

He paraded around and around the cottage, as proud as once he had been, years ago, when he had first become an owner of property. That had been one lot, with a four-room yellow house, but every foot was miraculously different from all other earth. Why, its one maple tree had roots and branches and a real bird's-nest, and the sun clung to its trunk, as it never did elsewhere on the block!

He discovered that the name of their cottage was William Tyler Longwhale. Anyway, said Hazel, that was better than naming the cottages Romeo and Portia and Desdemona. They never did find out who the historical William Tyler Longwhale may have been, but Fred insisted on giving their hermitage its full fruity name.

They sat on their porch at dusk. There had been strawberry shortcake for dinner, down at the tavern; they were full of shortcake and humanitarianism. The meadow below them was hysterical with unusually late fireflies; it resembled a still, dark pool reflecting transient stars.

'D'you realize,' marvelled Hazel, 'that this is the first time we've had a house that's entirely our own?'

'I had some such an idee,' said Frederick William.

Not even to a sub-agent who might order fifty cars had Fred ever paid such court as he now was paying to Hazel. He had brought his clubs, and Hazel expected him to spend hours a day golfing, during which time she planned to do a little happy, unnecessary cleaning. But he was irritated at having to do anything, even follow the rules of golf. 'Coupla days, what say we just stroll; not go anywhere in particular,' he proposed to Hazel, and she pondered, 'Why, yes, I suppose we *could!*'

Panting a little, very sweaty, observing that Fred's 'wind' had not been improved by cigarettes, carrying extra sweaters and wishing they hadn't, delighted at the convenience of stopping to see a view without having to find a parking place, they crawled, like two benevolent caterpillars gone vertical, up peaks from which they peered at the placid valley of the Housatonic, into orchards where early apples were afire in the long sweet grass, through pine groves which remembered old German fairy stories. On the multi-coloured stone flagging of the terrace at the King's Arms, the grand hotel of the region, where Austrian counts, their Chicago countesses, and even proud Amherst and Williams students skied all winter, they lazily drank to each other, not to a nervous gang of Sachem citizens determined to be gay and like it.

But Fred's favourite goal was the country store in Stonefield Centre, with its back door opening on forty acres of pasture and sugar maples. Amid the overalls, slabs of dried codfish, patent medicines, and country-auction posters, Hazel and he sat on boxes and listened to the storekeeper's libellous stories about Judge Basser, down the road, of whose housekeeper, who had been with him for twenty-seven years now, people were beginning to suspect the worst.

When they had left this refuge, scented with the molasses sweetness of chewing tobacco, dusty and quiet and serene, Hazel sighed, 'I like going there. Oh dear, I don't suppose there'll be any old-fashioned stores left in ten years--just glass and air-conditioning and telephone.'

'I thought you were the one that liked all these modern improvements--electric kitchens,' he jeered.

'Well, that's different,' she answered in her adequate, wifely way.

Their house in Sachem, he perceived, no longer belonged to them except by the artificial convention of deeds and lawbooks. It belonged to Sara, to Howard, to Annabel, to their friends, to the telephone company and the gas-furnace man and the meter reader, to their maid, and to their maid's sister, sister-in-law, and sister-in-law's sister's son and his large red toy automobile. But William Tyler Longwhale was theirs alone.

Hazel had so zealously taken to housekeeping that she wanted to prepare not only breakfast but lunch and dinner. He caught her just in time to keep her from putting on the hair shirt of domestic discipline. 'That's why we ran away, to avoid fussing.'

'Well, I just thought I'd fix up a bit for lunch--just some cold meat--no real cooking.'

'I see. Just cold meat. And a little soup, maybe?'

'Oh yes, I thought I might make a little hot soup . . .'

'And a couple hot vegetables?'

'No, only one. Honestly. Just some nice peas.'

'And hot potatoes, of course.'

'Oh, of course, *potatoes!*'

'How about dessert?'

'Oh, a tiny bit of prune whip--so light--nothing to make . . .'

'You know, Hazel, you read where women are so much more dependable about bringing up kids and caring for property than men. Fact is, women over-elaborate everything and make life twice as complicated as any normal man ever would, and then they kick because the men don't jump in and kill themselves taking care of things they never wanted in the first place. You can bet no male ever invented dancing schools for children, or lace collars, or sweet little bows to parents, or eating with forks, or saying "please" and "thank you". No man ever invented perfume or round flower beds or service plates or doilies or velvet upholstery or dress suits and boiled shirts--and if some tailor invented 'em, well, he didn't do it; his wife did!'

'In other words, women have been trying to make life a little pleasant and civilized, while men prefer to live in mud dug-outs and never wash,' said Hazel, firmly, as she started to make the prune whip.

CHAPTER XXVI

Men at the dangerous age, between forty-five and sixty, occasionally do land in court and have to writhe over their letters beginning 'Sweetest little earwig', but most of them have not only forgotten how to make love but forgotten that there ever has been so extraordinary a mania as that in which competent young males believe that some run-of-the-mill female, of a physique set forth in the anatomy books without any deception or anything up the sleeve, a young woman with toothaches, freckles, the hives, and admitted ignorance of Bach and bio-chemistry, is a new Helen of Troy.

Fred was of the more fortunate fraction. He exalted Hazel, not as a being of fire, ice and chronic hysteria, but as a companion true as bread and salt.

He had heard that a man sees the ageing of his contemporaries but never sees it in himself. But while he was conscious of his own swelling middle, his violent lack of interest in anything happening after one a.m., and the torture of trying to interest elfin young females skipping about at dances, yet in Hazel he could see no change. Oh yes. She did have grey hair. What of it? Went beautifully with her blue-eyed pinkness. And maybe the least bit more plump? Improved her. Didn't he seem to remember that, thirty years ago, she had been too skinny?

He sang to her 'Ev'ry morn I bring thee vi'lets', but what he actually brought her every morn was fresh eggs. He walked all the way to the King's Arms for chocolate pralines and the New York tabloids, and what could more add to a vagabond vacation than pictures of hammer slayers and punctured gunmen? Every night he kissed her; every morning he patted her hand. He admitted that these attentions might fall short of rapture, but he guessed that if he had done anything more, she would have been justifiably suspicious about his recent private conduct. He knew that in exile she was happy. She smiled at him naturally, and she hummed over the morning ham and eggs.

He was not conscienceless enough to be quite happy in deserting his family. When he walked alone at twilight, or in the tavern lounge he heard the radio play old songs, he remembered the curly-headed, tiny Howard, with a kitten, and the minute Sarah--not Sara, then--who had demanded the string cradles that no one but Daddy could make. The worst thing about real babies and kittens is that they look so much like sentimental chromos of babies and kittens.

In such an hour of grey nostalgia he could not have endured exile without the presence of Hazel. He dashed back to her for protection, and he fretted, while she sat before the rustic dressing-table, her handsome arms upraised to her hair, 'Say, hon, maybe we ought to write the folks now--see how the Duplex and the new-married couple are getting on.'

'Don't you do any such a thing, Fred. Let 'em learn how to get along by themselves for a while.'

'Well, if you think so . . .' he said.

And next morning when Hazel was brisk over the stove, and he came in with an armful of wood, feeling like Paul Bunyan, the god of the lumber-choppers, he crowed, 'Are you happy?'

Once, placidly knitting on the shadow-dancing porch of William Tyler Longwhale, Hazel explained, 'Of course you spoiled both our children. You always were a man to go to extremes. First you encourage 'em to walk over you, and then you fly right to the other extreme and want to run off to Abyssinia to get away from 'em.'

'Maybe. But isn't it the craziest doggone thing in this crazy world to-day, where half the nations are willing to go to war for the right to be slaves, that children have become the bossy parents, now, and the parents scared kids! Say, how did an easy-going couple like me and you ever have such a pair of Japanese waltzing mice for children?'

'Spoiled 'em, I tell you. You *and* me.' Hazel was more placid than ever.

'Maybe.'

'Let's go up to the King's Arms and have a cocktail.'

'Fine. Happy?'

'So happy!'

On the seventh morning of their refuge in Stonefield, Fred awoke at six-thirty, too gay and clearheaded to lie abed. He marched out to the porch, down to the drift of pine needles, in his nightshirt and bare feet. He knew the earth was chilly, yet he did not seem to be chilled. 'Reg'lar grizzly, that's what I am!' he gloated. The ticklish needles felt good to his feet, and the scent of pines and earth and grass and dew was a curtain shutting him away from the odours of gasoline and wet cement.

From inside he could hear the sleepy-headed Hazel grousing, '*What* an hour to be getting up!'

He bellowed that she was to stay in bed. In the kitchen he plugged in the coffee percolator and returned to the porch to loll on a swing couch, violently at peace. He heard Hazel padding about the kitchen; she could not yet believe that a man could master so difficult a domestic task as measuring coffee and water into a percolator. She came out with two cups on a very fine tray which they had bought at the country store for ten cents; she perched beside him and kissed his cheek.

'What say we take William Tyler Longwhale for all summer?' suggested Fred. 'Every couple weeks or so, I could go back to Sachem for maybe one day.'

'Yes. Let's! Oh, good heavens! Oh, *no!*'

A Triumph Special sedan had slid out of the pine grove and up the grassy road to their porch, and out of it were dribbling Sara and Howard.

With suspicious sweetness, Sara commented, 'Oh, Father! Bare feet? How cute!'

Fred glanced down. They looked worse than cute; they looked absurd, those objects called feet which till now he had taken for granted; those flat blobs of flesh, pallid from city living, fringed with imitation fingers. But he flung at Howard, bravely enough, 'How d'you ever find us here?'

'Oh, it took Ben Bogey all of half an hour on the long-distance telephone--he just described you and the car--a cinch, with those red fenders. We've known where you were for three-four days now, but we thought we'd let you enjoy yourselves and imagine you'd made a getaway. But now . . . You promised Ben to let us have some more capital, and we need it pretty bad. And we got a chance for the contract on a new development, Capitola Lodge, but the owners want to talk to you.'

'And the cook has quit--and I swear I don't know why--I gave her so much attention,' said Sara.

'And Annabel is awfully worried about you two getting rheumatism here.'

'And I had to go to the Rochester tournament without any chaperon--oh, that was so thoughtless of you!'

'And Cal Tillery had a run-in with Paul Popple, and he thinks, and so do I, you ought to take a look at the way Popple tries to run things.'

'And Louise Kamerkink says you promised to go to dinner there last Thursday.'

'And Popple's got some papers for you to sign--he's simply going nuts.'

'And everybody's talking--wondering whatever possessed you.'

'And Annabel says that her father says that he knows this dump, and why didn't you go to the King's Arms?'

'And the way I've had to lie to people, and I hate to lie except when it's necessary, and the Coheeze bills are still coming in, and not one word from Gene Silga. The double-crosser! Honestly, I hate to say it, but don't you think it was a little thoughtless of you?'

'And of course, after all, Sara and Bell and I are only kids, and we've done our best to carry on, but . . . I'd never think of trying to tell you your duty, but . . .'

'Well, I would! Honestly, my dears, I wish I could get the picture. What is it? Brave bold pioneers, right out of the movies, returned to the simple days of our forefathers, when men were men and never bathed, and the brats weren't demanding, like Howard and me, but always did what they were told to, and ploughed before breakfast, and walked six miles to the li'l' red schoolhouse and liked it?'

'Grrrrr!' said Fred.

Sara was laughing in quite a well-bred, filial manner as she went on:

'Darlings, I do wish I could see you as tanned and resolute frontiersmen, but I just don't; I see you as pretty pale and overweight, and--do forgive me--in terrible shape for lack of exercise. You'd have done much better, in my humble opinion, if you'd stayed home and seen Dr. Kamerkink and dieted and played golf. And, honestly, I don't think a pre-Civil-War nightshirt is such a romantic garment! And your dear li'l' hide-away--rather damp, isn't it? And *did* they have to go and give it a name like "William Tyler Longwhale"?'

Oh yes, even with her dark Dianic power, that was the most that Sara could do to them: take away all their joy in the adventure; make the still nights they had known, and the placid days, the sight of distant valleys and their sharing of renewed love seem the vain calf sickness of a premature senility. That was all she could do, but such as it was, she accomplished it with the skill she had learned in her diversified training as outlaw communist and polite tennis star.

So Fred and Hazel went back into captivity.

A week after their return to Sachem, Fred applied for their passports. When, or whether, they would ever be used, he did not know.

CHAPTER XXVII

The autumn, no very great season in the selling of motor cars, had become lively with the sale of trailers in which those citizens of Sachem Falls who had retired from the economic struggle, because they had too much money or too little, planned to go to Florida or California for winter. The Duplex had been booming all summer, but in September, Fred's treacherous rivals, the Conqueror Motor Company, dealt the Duplex a nasty blow with its announcement of the Allover Caravan.

The Allover was not a trailer, but built like a bus, with the motor contained in the body. It burst on Sachem with full-page newspaper advertisements which asserted convincingly that the Allover was easier to drive, easier to park, and much easier to handle in passing other cars. As a minor virtue, in this war of transportation with its almost theological disputation, the Allover's furnishings could readily be removed, turning it into a truck.

A sound commercial warrior like Fred would have hated any opposition at all which took money away from him, but in this particular attack, he persuaded himself, there was something malign, for Putnam Staybridge, putative father to Annabel, was known to be part owner of the Conqueror company. And, Fred complained, hadn't he gone and made a fool of himself and thought the Cornplows and the Staybridges were getting on to better terms? For the good Putnam had invited Howard and Annabel for a week at his Adirondack cabin, and Sara for a week-end . . . Everybody except the persons concerned seemed to feel that Fred and Hazel had already had as much vacation as was good for them.

The day after the Allover advertisements appeared, Staybridge invited Fred to call upon him, at the general offices of the Liberty Bell Clock Company. 'Hell with him; let him come here and call on me; I won't go a step,' growled Fred, as he reached for his hat.

Staybridge's office, with its large mahogany table for the directors and the small polished desk for the president, looked like a Colonial dining-room. You could almost smell boiled codfish.

Staybridge was cautiously cordial in his 'How do'.

'Hear you all had a fine time at the cottage, Brother Staybridge.'

'Oh yes. Very agreeable. Your son--uh, Howard, uh--is an excellent swimmer. Really! So sorry we didn't have room to invite Mrs. Cornplow and yourself.'

'Oh, we had our vacation . . . I suppose you might say. And what can I do for you?'

Staybridge looked as though he thought Fred was being rude. Fred was sorry, but he felt rude; in the damp cold air that Staybridge perpetually exuded, he always felt rude. But the gentlemanly assassin of Duplexes was saying graciously:

'No doubt you will have noted the advertisements of the Allover Caravans--the Conqueror company.'

'Good ads! Fine!'

'Kind of you to say so. It just happens that I have some small interest in the Conqueror company.'

'Ur.'

'And I have thought of suggesting to them that they come to some agreement with you, possibly even joint advertising. Since your Duplex is a trailer, and the Allover not, they need not exactly be in competition, and I was thinking that if we--or rather, I should say, they--combined, you might in a way dominate the field together--freeze out the others, I believe it is called.'

'Yes. It's called that. It's also called stifling competition, and ganging up on the other racketeers.'

'Oh? What I was really thinking was that since the Duplex is not made by the Triumph company, you might conceivably try to arrange with the makers to dispose of it to us. Particularly since I understand from your son--uh, from Howard--that you are giving some thought to retiring in four or five years.'

Staybridge's persistent objection to remembering Howard's name would have been enough to irritate Fred handsomely; it wanted only the pinch-nosed patronage with which Staybridge was going on:

'Of course I don't know what you plan to do, if you retire. I shouldn't have thought you were cursed with hobbies, as I am. But no doubt you'll find something with which to busy yourself, more or less. But the point is, if you feel like retiring, just possibly you might not care to face the rather sharp opposition that, I'm afraid, the Conqueror company, with its large resources, is planning to give you. I'm sure you'd be wise to take it easy.'

This to Fred Cornplow, who had never in his life evaded a fight--except with Sara. He exploded up from his chair, but he managed to be fairly calm as he croaked:

'Me? Retire? Where d'you suppose Howard (that's my son) ever got such a foolish idea? Not me! I like a scrap too well. But thanks for the tip. Morning!'

Opposite the large Conqueror agency, Fred hired a vacant lot, and within three days he had installed there a Duplex Trailer display in open air. He had one side ripped off a Duplex, so that its hidden domesticities were revealed. He engaged two men and two young women of a stranded night-club troupe, with a couple of children, and this theatrical family was displayed living the life of Riley in the trailer. They prepared and smackingly devoured large meals; on the roof they drank tea and afterward danced to a radio; they modestly retired, in the several chambers provided when the roof was hoisted; and all one night they remained abed in the Duplex, before a tremendous crowd which stayed up till two a.m. to behold human beings engaged in so very odd a practice as sleeping.

Duplex sales doubled, and Fred's spy in the Conqueror agency reported that salesmen who attempted to demonstrate Allover Caravans were answered with jeers. A week after the opening of Fred's circus, Staybridge telephoned him again, but Fred found himself too busy to call. The next day Annabel came in, and Annabel was near to giggling.

'My father asked me to tell you he thinks your Duplex cabaret is vulgar.'

'Do you think so?'

'Yes.'

'So what?'

'Oh, I like vulgarity. All the interesting things in life are so vulgar, Father Cornplow: birth and death and battles. Have I done my job?'

'Eh?'

'Have I complained properly about the vulgarity?'

'Darling!'

Next night a curious thing happened. A man named Tom McKuffee, a truck farmer who lived nine miles south-east of Sachem, and who had bought an Allover Caravan that afternoon, had an unfortunate accident at or near midnight. In front of the Duplex show lot he tried to park his Allover, but the brakes failed, the Allover dashed in to the lot and was wrecked against a pile of rocks which no one seemed previously to have noticed there. McKuffee, though he could not stop the caravan, had time to jump.

Now he was no hit-and-run driver, even if the object of his solicitude was merely a pile of rocks. He walked to the police station, admitted the accident, and explained that the brakes had failed; explained it so eloquently that a green reporter noted the fact in his story. The detail got past the copyreaders, and in the paper next morning there was an almost libellous statement about the brakes of an Allover.

It was only an item, but the scene of one caravan wrecked, while hard by, in another, night-club ladies were dancing and sipping ginger ale from highball glasses, was too much for the art editor of the evening paper. By this time, the struggle between Duplex and Allover was so familiar to all Sachem motorists that there was no need of a legend to explain what were the makes of the caravans in the newspaper photograph.

All the day after, persons who looked as though they might have trailer money in their pockets stood and admired the cabaret, snickered at the wreck. McKuffee happened, by a coincidence, to be there, and he seemed glad to explain how the accident had occurred, and to point out how flimsy were the smashed and exposed furnishings of the Allover. By another coincidence, Fred Cornplow knew McKuffee, who had once been the Triumph foreman.

'You *are* rubbing it in. Old Putnam will never speak to any of us again,' Sara reproached her father, yet in her he detected admiration.

In another day there were double-page advertisements of the Allover in the papers, but people in limousines, in shops, on street corners laughed at them. The Allover wreck remained there for a week. Then came the chief of police to Fred and offered to cart it away.

'No, you needn't. Glad to accommodate the fellow that owns the thing--what's his name?--McGurrey?--till he raises the money to get it overhauled.'

'There was something funny about this accident,' said the chief darkly and returned to his bezique, after a telephone call.

For a week, not one Allover Caravan was sold. This fact Fred conveyed to Hazel, who protested:

'Why, you absolute pirate! I thought you'd reformed!'

'Look here! I tried to reform. I tried to go off on a pilgrimage and become a better and tenderer man, and my two brats objected. Can I help it?'

Mr. Putnam Staybridge telephoned to Mr. Frederick Cornplow:

'Uh, I thought you might just possibly be interested to know that the Conqueror agency, or so I am informed, intend to reduce their advertising for Allover Caravans to, uh, to approximately the same space used for Duplexes.'

'Thanks,' said Fred. He removed the show trailer, and McKuffee's wreck vanished. But he learned later, all his kindness could not stir up a proper sale of Allovers.

Hazel sighed, 'Well, now you've had another big success, I suppose you've got your teeth in it so firm that you and I'll never be running off together again.'

'You mean it? You'd like to?'

'I *think* so.'

CHAPTER XXVIII

The scene was, for Fred, too fragile and artificial for comfort, yet he admired its gaiety: the club tennis courts, the white cement, the green balls flying, and the young people in white, young men with blue and crimson scarves above white shirts, girls with white shorts and honey-coloured legs, all against hills flamboyant with late September. He particularly liked the tall umpire's chair, now empty. To be perched up there, above the conflict yet close to it and dominating it, would be kingly, he explained to Walter Lindbeck.

'Awful. I knew a fellow got a tennis ball in his eye just when Fred Perry was smacking the hands across the sea,' argued Walter.

Mr. Walter Lindbeck, junior partner by inheritance of the large department store of Swazey & Lindbeck, was fifteen or sixteen years younger than Fred, but he had by chance, on a fishing trip, become one of Fred's intimates. Though he had gone to a large university and spent a year abroad in fruitfully doing nothing, Walter had, in Sachem, the high moral rank of: 'Steady but progressive; a fine, conservative, forward-looking young fella, and got no bad habits even if he is a bachelor.' He belonged to a chess club, but he also rode horseback; he went annually to New York City for the grand opera, but it was said that at the S. & L. Employees' Association he played pool with the elevator men and packers. Altogether, a high type of the youngish captain of commerce, though Sara sniffed that with a man like Mr. Lindbeck, whose thin face, and a black moustache small and neat as a cigarette, looked poetic, it 'made her tired' to see him interested only in sales leaders and invoices.

Fred and Lindbeck had done eighteen holes of golf, and after a quick one, they relaxed by watching Sara play tennis. Fred was proud of her feverish speed-- even prouder than of his new waist-pleated slacks. She was opposing a dull-faced dumpy girl of eighteen who played with the efficiency of a chopping knife. The girl lacked all of Sara's dramatic gestures and elegant backhands; her serves just missed the net and dropped dead before Sara could reach them, though she galloped in like the Light Brigade. In grieved wrath, Sara threw down her racket and screamed, 'Can't you put some fun into the game, Daugherty? We're not digging ditches!'

'Tst! Tst! Tst!' Fred clucked. 'Sara oughtn't to lose her temper that way.'

Walter Lindbeck sounded partisan. 'I don't blame her a bit. I've played that Daugherty girl. She's like lard; just plays to win, while your daughter has so much fire and gracefulness . . . Tell me, Fred, why the dickens did she ever get mixed up with this communist sheet? Doesn't believe all that stuff, does she?'

'I don't think so. But we've got to admit, way things are now, the young folks and the working men are demanding more say, and you can't blame 'em entirely.'

'That's so.'

Both men exhibited almost frightened admiration of their liberalism.

'Tell you, Walter, trouble with Sara is, she hasn't got enough to do, and she's got too much brains and energy to just stick around. She'd like to follow the tennis tournaments to Bermuda and Florida this winter, but I can't afford it. Say, I've got an inspiration! She's got a great eye for colours and all that junk. Why don't you give her a job in your interior-decorating department? If there's any way you could fix it in your accounting, I'd be willing to finance the scheme to the tune of a few hundred bucks, provided she never knew it. She's so doggone proud she wouldn't take a job like that if she found out I'd rigged it.'

'Oh, that wouldn't be necessary. Matter of fact, we do need a little new blood in the decorating department. Old Mrs. Vix is about the period of Edward the Seventh, and I always did think Sara had a lot of dash and go. I'd be glad to try her, if she was interested.'

'She wouldn't touch it, if she thought I'd butted in. You know how touchy all these blasted young people are to-day. If you're interested, too--and I can't tell you how much I appreciate it--let's get her to sell herself to you.'

When Sara had finished her act, Fred beckoned, and she rode up cavalierly to sit between the two ancients. (Lindbeck was thirteen years her senior.)

'Didn't seem to have such a high old time with Miss Daugherty, Sara.'

'Oh, she's the dumbest cluck in the club! It's like playing with a steam roller.'

Lindbeck bubbled, 'I agree.'

Fred chattered, 'I seem to be the only cheerful guy here to-day, in all this lovely autumn weather, with the maples turning. Walter's been kicking because he can't find the right person to put some pep in his foolish furnishing-and-decorating department--somebody that knows the local swells with money to spend and that has got an artistic eye for design. Don't suppose you'd pay real money for the job, Walter?'

'Not at first. Twenty a week for a start, with a small commission. But there wouldn't be any limit on the future, and the right man, or possibly it might be a woman, might work up to ten thousand a year or more. I'm not looking for an ex-charwoman, or on the other hand for some tired lily that thinks he's arty. I'd like to find some college graduate with a knowledge of the history of art and with a lot of energy and sense . . .'

Fred was amused, then a trifle guilty, to see the way in which Sara turned on Lindbeck her full flashlight:

'Funny you should speak of that, Mr. Lindbeck! I've always been so interested in both painting and furniture and, in a modest way of course, I think I know quite a little about them. I have some ideas about decorating . . . It seems to me that people are stupid in just using chromium and red leather and mirrors and rounded corners, so that every room that calls itself "moderne" looks like a café. I think you could take Biedermeyer models and Duncan Phyfe motifs and modernize them so that they'd be original, and do so many unconventional things with concealed lighting . . .'

'Yes, yes, that's so. Would you like to drop into my office to-morrow and talk with Mr. Swazey and myself?'

As they drove back home, Sara babbled to her parent, 'I talked Mr. Lindbeck right into it! He had no idea I was thinking about a job. I just talked about decoration in general, as though I hadn't the slightest notion of going to work, and he, the poor little man, thought it was all his own precious idea, getting me to accept a position. I think I might like it. Decorating, in this dull town--why, I can do it on my head, and please the stupid plutocrats like the Praggs almost to death! Father, my darling, you're always fussing about me, but you wouldn't have thought of a career like this for me in a thousand years, now would you!'

'That's so,' said Fred.

For two weeks he rarely saw her, so absorbed was she in her new job of plotting against every innocent rocker and club chair left in town; for two weeks he had peace; but on a day just after the two weeks' truce, he came home from the office to find Sara, triumphant, and Hazel, very anxious, standing in the hall and looking mysteriously into the living-room.

'What's all the excitement?'

'I tell you, he won't like it!' said Hazel.

'He will as soon as he gets used to it. If my own family can't appreciate creative ideas, how can you expect anybody else to?' said Sara.

'Where's the fire?' said Fred.

'Look at it, and don't blame me . . . It is pretty lovely though . . . I think I'd come to like it a lot,' said Hazel, waving her hand in the direction of the living-room and standing aside.

The room had been magicked. Gone were all the pieces of furniture that to Fred meant home and security; gone was his sacred, rather shabby, rather faded red arm-chair, in which, alone, the evening paper tasted right; gone the couch on which, ritually, Hazel and he had listened to the radio side by side; gone the Maxfield Parrish painting of maidens dancing in twilight; gone the shiftless pile of magazines on a table with dragons' feet clasping glass balls; gone the stuffed head of the deer he had (illegally) shot in Quebec; gone was everything that made home stuffy, ugly and lovable.

Sara had redecorated the room in plum colour and dull gold, rich as mince pie and sombre as the thoughts of a defeated Congressman. The furniture was dethroned Louis Quinze. And on the walls, replacing a nest of cheerful photographs showing Hazel with a watering pot, Fred in wading boots, complete with shotgun, Howard with a toy wagon, and Sara reciting James Whitcomb Riley, was one lone painting of the Towers of Rouen, which towers, taken jointly, resembled a fish fork.

'Isn't it distinguished! Hasn't it real dignity!' bubbled Sara.

'I didn't--I don't . . .' endeavoured Fred.

'It's just on trial, of course.'

'Well, it's certainly swell, but I don't think it quite suits your mother and me.'

'Suits me, all right,' said the treacherous Hazel, all the fanatical love of possessions in her eyes.

'Look, Father; if one's own people don't back you up, how can you expect me to make a career with other people?'

He was warning himself, 'She's got some reason. You were asking for it, Freddie.' He temporized, 'If I did decide I liked the room, when I got used to it, how much would all this set me back?'

'I can do it for nineteen hundred dollars, Father.'

'Ouch!' said Fred, but feebly, as he turned for comfort to Hazel, saw her acquisitive glow and knew that he was sold.

'We-ll, I couldn't possibly pay it all in a lump.' So, for Fredk Wm, his home was turned into a house; and a house was easier to leave than was a home.

CHAPTER XXIX

Cold ham, pineapple-and-cream-cheese salad, scalloped potatoes, tea, beer, vanilla ice cream with caramel sauce--it was a Cornplow family supper again, with Cornplow family food, at Howard's flat.

Before supper, Howard and he had what Fred would have called--would have called? He did call it that!--a heart-to-heart talk, taking refuge in the bedroom from the bustling domesticity of Hazel and Annabel and the stateliness with which Sara sat and read the *New Yorker*.

Not in the four and a half months since the firm of Bogey & Cornplow had been founded had they been out of the red. It was only slightly irritating to Fred to go on contributing, but it was disturbing to have Howard expect advice on every contract, expect him to lure to the Bogey & Cornplow office every prosperous person Fred met in agency or club or church.

Howard was gushing, 'Dad, I think you'll agree with me . . .'

'Rarely!'

'. . . that if I'm going to rent and build swell houses, I've got to prove my standing and show my good taste . . .'

'Your what?'

'. . . by living in a nice house myself, and not in this dump.'

'What d'you mean, "dump"? Wish you could've seen the four-room shack that your mother and I had when we were first married. Only stoves, and no bathroom, just outdoor service. I tell you, in those days a real man was glad to shovel coal and lug the doggone ashes, instead of just moving a lever with one finger. We had oilcloth on the table. And,' Fred added, without great originality, 'guess we were just about as happy as the young folks to-day, that expect to start in where their folks left off!'

'Um--yes. But I want you to look at this as an investment. I know where I can get a dandy, up-to-date modern house, six and a half rooms, for a hundred and ten a month, and then I can take prospects home for dinner. I want you to understand, Dad, I've turned over an entirely new leaf. Golly, Ben Bogey is twice as hard on me as you or Paul Popple ever were. I don't even take a single drink--oh, maybe just a cocktail before dinner . . .'

'Or maybe two?'

'Well, of course, if there's a dividend left in the shaker, there's no sense wasting it . . .'

'Son, if you expect me to put up the hundred and ten a month for your rent, I'm simply not going to do it, do you hear me, won't do it, simply won't do it, do you understand, and that's *flat!*'

Privately, he hoped it was flat.

All through supper Howard seemed to have the hives. He kept winking at Annabel, clucking at her, and once he reached out and tenderly slapped her hand. There seemed to be nothing in the conversation to stir up such fervour. It consisted in Sara's detailed account of wishing a bedroom in powder blue and crocus yellow upon Mrs. Kamerkink, Howard's speculation as to whether he could 'interest' Dr. Kamerkink in a lot at Capitola Lodge, and Annabel's dutiful plea to Hazel for the name of her hairdresser.

Yet Howard was certainly exhilarated, and after the ice cream he pounded the table and gave tongue:

'I've got a very important announcement to make . . . Now, Bell, don't blush!'

'I don't intend to!' said Annabel, blushing.

'Mother and Dad, along about next March, you are going to have your first lovely little grandchild--and you, your first nephew, sister!'

'Oh, Howard--*Annabel!*' said Hazel.

'Heh? Oh. You mean you're going to have a baby? Fine,' said Fred.

'Yessir!' Howard roared. 'And if it's a son, and I've got a good strong hunch it will be, I'm going to name him . . .'

'Heh! I'm in on this, too, aren't I? Won't I be related to the infant?' protested Annabel.

'Why, yes, very much so,' said Howard. He was indulgent about it, too.

'He's going to be called Little Nero, no matter what's entered in the registry. I've always wanted to name a child "Little Nero". It may take the curse off him.'

'Well now, Bell, you just forget that silly idea, and keep your little head clear for action. But Dad and Mother, there's another point to this announcement that I don't want you to forget. Because now, Dad--hard luck, old man, but that's the way life goes!--you'll have to help me make a great place in the world for the little cuss! Your grandson!'

Annabel was snappish: 'I don't see why Father Cornplow should do any such a fool thing! He's not responsible for our having Little Nero . . .'

'I simply do not like that nickname, even joking.'

'. . . and how about your doing a little great-place-making yourself? The Gimme Generation!'

'Annabel, I think this is in the worst possible taste. And at such a moment!' Howard was stern but refined.

'If you couldn't find jobs . . . But, you great, big, darling, beautiful, dumb Greek god, you and all your vintage have the chronic gimmes.'

'That will do, Bell, and if it weren't for your condition . . .'

'Just the gimmes, that's all; just the plain old-fashioned gimmes!'

'Annabel!'

'And that's why I'm going to call him Little Nero, so he won't grow up to have the gimmes too, and expect you to stick at work--I mean, go to work--for him at seventy!'

'I've never heard you talk such beastly nonsense before! What can Father and Mother Cornplow be thinking of you!' Howard turned grandly upon his parents. 'At least, *you're* glad the baby is coming, aren't you, Mammy?'

'Oh, simply delighted, dear. You mustn't mind Annabel's teasing you a little.'

'Just the gimmes,' chirped that lady, so beatifically that Fred wondered if she had sneaked in a couple of drinks before supper. He decided that she had had no such luck. No. The sound of Howard's mellifluous optimism, day by day, would in itself produce spontaneous intoxication accompanied by tremor and slight delirium.

'And you, Dad, you're glad too, aren't you?' insisted Howard.

'Why, of course! Tickled to death. Lit--I mean, our first little grandchild! Gracious!'

'Swell!' said Sara mechanically. 'But you look here, Howard. Don't you go and get the idea you're the only one Father has to look out for. With the good luck I've been having, I wouldn't wonder if I didn't start a decorating shop of my own, and of course it would have to be financed. Of course. But congratulations and all that sort of thing on the baby.'

'You *are* glad about the baby, aren't you?' hinted Hazel, back home.

'What baby?'

'Howard's baby.'

"Tain't Howard's baby. He's just an accident.'

'Well then, our coming grandchild.'

'Oh, I guess so. May be kind of hard on Little Nero himself . . .'

'I *don't* think it's nice . . .'

'. . . but it will amuse Annabel, and it will be swell for Howard. Think of what a chance he'll have now to go swelling around being guide, philosopher and friend to the defenceless kid! There is one thing. You know how often the pendulum swings back to the grandparents. Maybe Little Nero will have some of our independence, and not be a fat-head like his father.'

'Why, Fred! Who ever heard or imagined grandparents not being just pleased to death at the coming of their first grandchild!'

'Well, I am pleased. Don't get me wrong. Only I don't figure on being both granddad and dad. You've read about grandchildren that didn't spend any too much time longing to support their grandparents, haven't you?'

'I suppose so.'

'Why shouldn't it more or less work both ways? You know Howard darned well meant it when he hinted he expected us to drop any personal plans we might have and stick around and nurse the royal heir.'

'Ye-es.'

'And you know, don't you, that if we *do* stick around, he'll probably make us do anything he wants us to--there not being any more powerful influence on God's green earth than the smile that wins, when it's got a bottom layer of good, sticky self-approval. He'll be too strong for us, and too dumb. So we better not stick around. Ain't there something to what I say? Ain't there?'

'Um--anyway, it really is a little too much, expecting you to support four generations.'

'How d' you mean?'

'You helped your father pay off his mortgage when you were a travelling man, didn't you? And you helped your sister start her dressmaking business . . .'

'How that would grind Putnam Staybridge! Aristocratic to wear swell dresses, but low-class to make 'em.'

'And you certainly have always supported your own self since you were a brat--and I'll bet you were a brat, too! No, I don't bet any such thing. I bet you were a cute baby.'

'I don't know about when I was a baby, but 'long 'bout six-seven, I was such a fat, sweet-looking kid, with long curls, that I had to lick the everlastin' daylights out of about one neighbouring kid per day, to keep my standing. Golly--I hope Sara don't come in on us, but that certainly does feel better.'

They were on the new settee in the living-room, the radio turned on so low that it emitted only a background of music, like wind in the trees, but amid all this refinement, Fred had sighingly removed his shoes.

'Well, you and your sister make a second generation you've supported. And you certainly saw Howard and Sara through everything. And now, apparently, Howard expects you to be responsible for this fourth generation--Little Nero. It's a little too much.'

'Maybe that's so,' and Fred looked upon her with such lovelight in his eyes as not even eighteen holes in seventy-five could have set there. 'I wouldn't mind supporting Little Nero. I just hate to think about his being brought up to correct all my breaks.'

'Well, if Little Nero is really *our* sort, he'd rather have a high-stepping, jolly, independent old grandfather than a reservoir!'

That night, remembering Howard's old contention that he was fast in the handcuffs of routine, Fred so far flaunted the ritual of fetishism as to throw his shirt on the floor instead of, as was his compulsion, hanging it smoothly over his coat on the back of the one habitual chair.

Hazel picked it up. She supposed that it was a shirt that had been flung down, and not the strait-jacket of timidity.

CHAPTER XXX

All his life until now, night had been to Frederick William Cornplow only a blank of sleep. Even as a travelling salesman, thirty years ago, waiting at vile junction depots till after midnight or snoozing on bumpy branch trains, though he might have had but six hours' sleep, it had been profound.

Now he took worries to bed with him; they cuddled up beside him when he retired, then laughed and bit him. As long as he tried to lie still, he went tediously over and over his frets:

Howard's extravagance; the probability that he would not support Little Nero and the certainty that he would grieve young Annabel.

Sara's new job, in which she would spare him and his pocketbook no more than she would spare herself.

Hazel's alternation between miserly pride in adornment and a desire to see what the world was like.

Paul Popple's reluctance to take authority at the agency. The wonder whether, if he left them to themselves, Paul and Howard would be forced to become dependable, or simply break.

Always, his own timidity and his meagre learning.

Worst of all, the neighbourhood opinion which kept him a steady and commonplace little citizen: the opinion of Dr. Kamerkink, Ed Appletree, the lawyer, even of Walter Lindbeck, that he would be a fool to do anything save settle inoffensively into old age. He saw that most of us do what most of the people about us mostly expect us to do, become brave or criminal or both, and he knew definite fear of the compulsion upon him to remain safe and dreary, a compulsion which could be escaped only by running away.

Running where? For what?

But when he sprang up from bed, scoffing at the need of sleep, then night became an adventure; sometimes wry, sometimes dismaying, always an excitement. He sat trying not to disturb Hazel, or he crept down to make coffee for himself and to sit brooding at the kitchen table.

He longed for Stonefield and the cottage William Tyler Longwhale. That elopement had proved that he could get along, be amused, without the crutch of daily industriousness which his friends so recommended.

Hazel was conscious of his rebellion and sometimes cocked a drowsy eye at him as he crept out of the room, but she guessed that he wanted to be left alone.

Sara was conscious of it--she was a night prowler herself--but for a time he avoided her probing.

In this unearthly second life he didn't always brood. Sometimes he read, soaked himself in the oddest magazine articles and in books stolen from Sara's shelves: articles about Javanese coffee culture, dialects in Burma, the roof of Ely Cathedral, Cycling in Tanganyika with Notes on Hotels in Dar es Salaam. He laid the magazine down to dream out one-dimensioned pictures woven of coloured cloud: Pike's Peak in the sun, bell towers of Bruges, himself playing the piano in an English cottage, himself chatty at the counter of the general store in Stonefield, with Hazel gaily clattering pans in the kitchen.

Most embarrassing of all were the nights when he did not lie awake, when the worries treacherously let him go to sleep, then woke him jeeringly at three o'clock or four or five.

It was cold downstairs then, even when it wasn't cold.

This November morning, at four-thirty, he knew that he was caught and would not sleep again until an hour at which a responsible man would be brightly awakening.

He bundled himself up grotesquely: sweater as well as dressing-gown, with an old golf stocking about his neck. The house was so still that it was noisy with creeping burglars. He looked out of a window and shivered. The street was bitterly empty; the pavements, and a fire plug that should have been a lively red but was now grey, seemed lonely.

He sat in the kitchen, at the metal-topped table, an illicit cup of coffee and a folder showing the Australian airlines before him. He startled at distant shuffling feet, the creak of the swing door between dining-room and butler's pantry. He beamed with comfort as Sara's face, sharpened with weariness, came peering at him.

She smiled, and she sounded genial:

'Why, you disreputable old tramp! Couldn't you sleep? Neither could I.'

Sara tucked the ridiculous golf stocking in about his neck, she clucked at him and kissed his ear. She seemed more truly his little girl than since she had been a lanky child. She sat opposite him, chin in hand, and said softly, 'This insomnia is the worst idea I ever met. I've got some little pills for it. Don't you want some?'

'No indeed.'

'But you've got to sleep!'

'Why? What's the difference, as long as you get rest? The need for sleep is kind of a superstition. I enjoy breaking up my old routine. And besides, I don't want to get this little pill habit.'

'Mine aren't habit-forming, not a bit.'

'But the habit of taking them, of depending on taking anything at all to make you sleep, is habit-forming. Don't get to depend on it, sweetie.'

The whole hour, the empty hour that was neither night nor day, seemed to him strange as Sara's abnormal kindness. He was too listless for self-defence, and thus was he betrayed into honesty.

Sara hinted, a little more sharply:

'Curious, you, of all people, can't sleep. Worried, Father?'

'No, not exactly.'

'I noticed you were reading a lot of travel stuff . . . Do you still want to retire and go places?'

'Maybe. Sort of.'

'But you wouldn't really go to Europe, would you, or some other place far off from us?'

'Well, thunder, if you're going to make a break, might's well make a good one. No particular novelty for me, going out to the club for golf!'

'It'd be fierce for me if you did go away, Father; especially if Mother went, too.'

'Why?'

'Oh, Howard would think he was head of the family and the boss, then, and he's such a dope! I suppose Annabel is all right, but Howard's one of these curly-headed boys. He's the kind that reads books about How to Sell, and gets so busy rushing out and selling that he never takes time to find out what he's going to sell.'

'But why do you worry so? You're smart enough. You're making a go of this decoration thing.'

'But if I start my own shop, I'd never get away with it without your help.'

'Then why start it? You got a good boss in Walter Lindbeck.'

'Yes, he's kind of a nice little man. But . . . Probably I wouldn't bare my throbbing little heart if it weren't such an ungodly hour, but I don't always want to be a lone spinster, and between us, as man to man, I don't seem to click with the boys, except rootless freaks like Gene Silga, curse him!'

'I suppose Gene was sort of on the free-love side.'

'And how! And theoretically, I agree. I never did think much of getting caged up with a man you've hardly been introduced to! But practically, I guess I've got too much Cornplow and Jenkins in me, doggone it . . . Heavens! I'm talking just like you!'

'What's the matter with talking like me? I always do!'

'Not always, darling. Sometimes you forget yourself and become quite literate.'

'Well, I did more or less go to college, and recent years, I've been brought up on luncheon-club oratory: "Fellow members, real and enduring prosperity lies in the abandonment of the antiquated ethic of every guy for himself." I have got some vocabulary, but mostly I leave it up in the attic, with the trunks.'

'Of course you have. But, Father, I wonder if you're really and truly quite on to yourself? If you'd still like to go off and be a hobo . . .'

'I would!'

'But why don't you face it as you would a business problem? Suppose you were in a European hotel, where almost every guest was a globe-trotter. You'd feel as out of place as a stray pup. Oh, I know you have worries; you've always worked so hard. In fact, I have an idea you're more exhausted than Mother or even you suspect. You don't know how I've been watching you. But it wouldn't be any remedy to go roaming. That's hard work for anybody that isn't used to it. I wish you'd just relax and rest. I wish you'd get help from somebody who understands these things. I wish you'd get well!'

'Now what the . . . Get well from *what?* What's supposed to be my fatal sickness?'

'This insomnia. All this fretting about Howard and me. And--do let me say it, Father, in all friendliness--this crazy restlessness. The idea that you'd enjoy wandering, or taking up some hobby that you're too old to start on. Please! I don't think you're selfish in being willing to leave us flat--not entirely selfish, at least; I won't even say it's utterly absurd; but I do think you fool yourself. If instead of riding off in all directions at once, like Leacock's hero, you would relax and go to some place where the doctors are accustomed to advise people and help them to get into shape . . .'

Fred was angry now:

'"Get in shape"! "Get well"! Good Lord, girl! I've been told there are wives who believe that any husband who doesn't absolutely slave himself to death for the little woman is a dirty traitor, and ought to have his head examined by the docs. Now looks as though wives are getting over that notion, and the children are taking it up. By golly, I thought the younger generation during Prohibition was bad enough--the generation of Flaming Gin--but I swear they were better than the present Youth, that despise their folks if they forget a quotation they haven't looked at these thirty years, or if they think they got just as much right to travel and buy clothes with their own money as their kids have and . . . I couldn't get your switching from Red Radicalism to Society Upholstering, but now I see you're consistent: in both cases, you think that the world was born in 1917, and everything we thought we knew or we thought we were doing before then was idiotic. Well, let me tell you . . .'

'Father, have you had a drink of liquor this morning?'

It was almost a knockout, but he rallied.

'I have not, and you know it.'

'Well, certainly you'd never talk in such a wild, senseless, exaggerated way if you really were *well.* And this insomnia of yours . . .'

'Got it yourself, ain't you?'

'With me, it's different. I'm a creative artist.'

'And I suppose I'm just a pedlar!'

'You used the word, dear! I didn't!'

'Oh, Sara, don't let's scrap! You almost seemed like my girl, to-night, when you came in first. You're too young to understand that old codgers like me can change, too--a few of us--and push out old habits with a set of new ones--same as when I get to humming a tune till it bores me, I start another tune to chase it out.'

'That's curious! That's practically what Dr. George Janissary says--you know, the famous psychiatrist--I met him once at dinner, when I lived in New York. You sounded like him--for a moment, I mean.'

'Huh! These mind doctors, like Friend Janissary, haven't patented psychology and mental hygiene, have they? I guess Ben Franklin and Voltaire and Dickens must have known something!'

'Father, you wouldn't think I was too rude . . .'

'Prob'ly would!'

'. . . if I pointed out that you're not Franklin or Voltaire? Honestly, the help a man like Dr. Janissary could give you in re-education, by constructive personal conferences . . .'

'I don't know the gent. Maybe he might re-educate me into being some kind of a tabby cat I wouldn't want to be. Yes, there's something I am getting well from, all right: from crawling along through life and being doped by routine. But Howard and you never thought that was a disease. You thought it was pretty convenient for you!'

'Oh, Father, to talk like that--if Dr. Janissary heard you!--to make us out monsters . . .'

'You're not, of course. But neither am I. We're just normal people, up to the oldest trick in the world: nagging your relatives for nagging you. I didn't want to be rude, girl. But get right over this idea you can coax me out of my idea of turning myself from a Parent into a Human Being. Good night--uh--good morning!'

So Fred clumped up to bed, with the intention of lying awake to lick his parental wounds, and went to sleep blissfully and at once.

Belowstairs, Sara was still in the kitchen, vowing, 'His idea of leaving us in the lurch--it's insane--it's beastly--and now I've got to do something about it!'

CHAPTER XXXI

There is no way in which a normally stubborn husband can more fruitfully surprise and annoy his loved ones than by being a 'good patient', which means a man who brightly agrees with the family doctor even when the doctor isn't sure that he agrees with himself.

Another technical phrase that goes along with 'good patient' is 'worried about his health', and it happened to Fredk Wm now that his wife decided to be worried about his health.

'Don't you think you ought to go to Dr. Kamerkink and have a general physical overhauling?' she said, on a beautifully Saraless evening.

He had watched her nervously approaching this bold position by way of chatter about a respected neighbour who, at eighty-one, probably from gross over-use of coffee, alcohol, tobacco and attendance on baseball games, had astounded the community by popping off. So Fred was ready for the attack and able to be genial:

'Why?'

'Oh, no special reason. I just think everybody past fifty ought to look after his health.'

'But not before fifty?'

'Wellofcoursebutimean . . .'

'My state of health been bothering anybody lately?'

'No, but . . .'

'Pains in the back, dizziness, sudden loss of memory, B.O., athlete's foot? Do they laugh when I say I can speak French? Won't my best friends tell me? Delusions of persecution? Violent and unexpected assault on man believed to be income-tax collector?'

'Don't be so silly!'

'Comrade Sara been hinting I'm losing grip--unable to see smart decorator's shop as an investment?'

'Well, she is a little worried. So am I!'

'What's the matter with old Fred?'

'You know you don't sleep right.'

'If I can get along without sleep--and all through the ages people been kicking because that's the worst waste of time there is--then I must be in swell shape!'

'I wish you would have Lafe Kamerkink look you over. Please do.'

'All right. I will.'

'When?'

'Next Saturday.'

'I'll be hanged!' she said, unprophetically but with the most gratifying astonishment.

After the usual assaults and embarrassments which doctors call an examination, Dr. Kamerkink illustrated the advance of medicine, and proved that he had kept up, by grunting:

'You'll have to take a basal-metabolism test, and I want a blood count.'

'All right.'

Kamerkink looked suspicious. He was certain that Fred had something up his sleeve.

'I said I want a B.M.R.'

'Whatever it is, I'm for it.'

'For a B.M.R., I want to have it taken after twelve-fourteen hours' complete rest, without food and even without your smoking a cigarette.'

'O.K.'

'I wouldn't trust you to do that at home.'

'Neither would I.'

'So you'll have to spend a night in a hospital.'

'O.K.'

Dr. Kamerkink was overwhelmed. Was Fred concealing a flask, or drugs, or a revolver? Never in these years of acquaintanceship had Fred given him any reason to suppose that he could be so abnormal as to act like a sane and normal patient. Doubtfully, wondering when he would find the trick in it, Dr. Kamerkink telephoned to engage Fred's room in the hospital and lighted a cigarette, prefatory to telling Fred about cutting down the cigarettes.

Fred liked his hospital room. He had declined Hazel's company and all offers of flowers and depressingly cheerful bedside books. It was refreshing to have, without the penalty of pain, this simple room that was pictureless, pinkless and candlewick-spreadless, and that falsely seemed to get itself cleaned with none of the horrors of hiring maids, seeing that they were transported to the movies and otherwise entertained, and listening to the whine of their vacuum cleaners. The better rooms in heaven must be automatic cells like this, he thought.

They did let him undress himself and get into his fine small high bed without tender helping hands. The one thing he had feared, in contemplating this adventure, had been that with mocking jeers some pretty young nurse would snatch his protective clothes away and show him up as just a skinned rabbit. But he certainly had no intention, he assured himself, of missing any of his opportunity to be waited on.

Hazel was fond enough of him, but Hazel wouldn't think at all well of bringing him cooling fruit juices all evening, and extra pillows, of smoothing the bedclothes if he was such a fool as to keep on violently turning over, or of listening to his oldest jokes, as did the floor nurse who--usually--answered the bell this evening.

He thought it was a splendid idea to have a call bell on the end of a cord, hanging beside his head. He wanted to introduce it at home, though he had the sanity to admit that he didn't know what would happen if he pressed it with any idea that it would influence Hedgar the Hun.

He had heard (though he was to discover that the tale was false, and told only to make the narrator seem heroic) that in taking a basal-metabolism test he would find it difficult to breathe, and he had every intention of enjoying himself by lying awake and worrying about it. But in the pleasure of not having to wonder whether Howard would call up, late, or wonder at what time Sara would be coming home, he forgot about being insomniac, fell sweetly asleep at ten and awoke in daylight to find a keen young woman in white wheeling into his room what resembled a trench mortar polished up for the use of the crown prince.

The floor nurse was chirping at Fred with the sugared cheerfulness reserved for children, manic-depressives and patients, 'This is the technician.'

Fred had time only to note that he ought to look into this fact that all hospital technicians were beautiful before the lady pinched his nose with a glorified clothespin and fitted over his amazed and protesting mouth a rubber apparatus through which, she told him coolly, he was to breathe.

That breathing, it seemed, caused a polished plunger to rise up and down in the trench mortar. Instantly scared, but resolved to be gallant, he enjoyed fighting against choking, his body tense, his breath labouring. But he discovered that he was merely making things hard for himself. He quit being gallant and energetic, and therewith the breathing was as natural as though he stood on a hilltop, free of rubber gadgets and hospital beds.

'Good man! That's fine,' said the technician.

He was to treasure that commendation along with the highest distinctions he had known in life; with the letter from the president of the Duplex company saying that his agency had the best credit in the East; with the admission of the golf professional that he had a fairly accurate swing; with the sigh of a very young Hazel that he had been so nice to her father; with his election as vice-president of the Boosters' Club; and with the remark of his professor of rhetoric, back in Truxon, that his essay on The Character of Portia hadn't been bad at all.

He was still in the glow of this honour, and the rubber mask had been removed, when the technician, taking his hand tenderly, turned savage and jabbed into his finger a needle stuck in a cork.

'Ouch!' he wailed in protest.

It was true that it hadn't hurt, but he felt that the principle was very bad. Then he was asleep, before he could do anything about it; and he awoke to a tray of ham and eggs, and to Dr. Kamerkink by the bed, saying suspiciously, 'Why, there doesn't seem to be one darn thing the matter with you!'

'But did they look at your teeth and tonsils, too?' said Sara when, at home, Fred crowed over his superiority.

CHAPTER XXXII

In all innocence and glee, Fred was playing poker at the residence of his friend and lawyer, Edward McTavish Appletree, and the conversation was hearty with humour:

'By me.' 'I'll whoop you two.' Knock, knock. 'What're you trying to do with that hooch, Ed--save it for your grandchildren?'

But he was also present, though not physically, in his own house, where Hazel, Sara, Howard, Annabel and Dr. Kamerkink were sitting as comfortably as possible, which wasn't very comfortably, on Louis Quinze. Sara was holding forth:

'You may think I'm absolutely silly, maybe a little melodramatic, in asking you to meet, but we've really got to be serious and practical. I don't mean Father is the least bit insane, of course, but I do feel he's got some pretty queer ideas that might make him do things that, afterward, he'd be the first to regret.'

'Oh, come down to cases. What's so queer?' fretted Hazel.

'These ideas about going off and being some kind of a John Ruskin, wandering around Europe studying art. Father's one of the dearest, most dependable men living--or at least he has been--but even you, Mother, have got to admit that he can never be anything except a completely unimaginative small-city merchant; and with all affection, we ought to keep him from making himself ridiculous.'

They spoke together:

'Only one of the whole lot of us that *has* imagination!' from Annabel.

'I think there's a lot to what Sara says,' from Howard.

'He's never even pretended he wanted to go Ruskin-ing around Europe,' from Hazel.

'His euphoria does kind of puzzle me,' from Dr. Kamerkink.

'His what? Is that one of these things you take this to your druggist now and he'll fill it, take three times daily just before meals?' from Annabel.

'Euphoria. State of gaiety and well-being. I don't,' said the doctor resentfully, 'see what the dickens Fred has got to be cheerful about!'

Sara took over the debate again:

'I don't want to be an alarmist. I suppose Father is perfectly all right, really. But you all know of cases where a man who has been a reliable husband and father has suddenly gone haywire, and at just about Father's age, and started gambling or drinking or chasing women, and left his family . . .'

('With all their gimmes,' murmured Annabel.)

'. . . unprovided for. Of course Father has built up a good business, but you know what can happen to any business, these days, if the responsible head starts neglecting it. So far as I know, the only real safeguard any of his family has is Father's fifty-thousand-dollar life insurance. Now I'm the last person in the world to be grasping or dependent. I belong to the new race of women who want to carve out their own destinies, but at the same time, I have to make a start. It's not my fault if I have to have lots more training before I can achieve a great position and get my own shop. I'm simply not going to let Father let me down! Considering that we are, after all, the only people that Father depends on, if we stick together, he'll just have to give up any ideas of ditching us . . . And of course Howard's career also, I suppose, and your child coming, Annabel.'

('Howard, is this true? Why didn't you tell me?')

('Oh, shut up, Bell.')

('Do you belong to the new race of men, beautiful?')

'Now I'm sure Dr. Kamerkink will back me up in saying that the comparatively new science of psychiatry has developed to a point where they can cure a twisted mind just as they cure a twisted foot, and I happen to know slightly the most wonderful psychiatrist in New York: Dr. George Janissary. His patients look up to him with absolute reverence--and, mind you, they're not a bunch of hysterical spinsters, but a lot of them are brokers and engineers and college professors and doctors, too. Why, ever so many of them come back to him every year.'

Annabel snorted: 'If a doctor cured my twisted foot but I had to go back every year, I'd think he was a bum untwister.'

'For heaven's sake, Annabel, will you please permit *me,* at least, to be serious?'

('Butting in again . . . Gimmes.' Annabel's mutter was like the muted bark of a small dog that has been told to dry up.)

'I ventured to talk over all this with Dr. Janissary when I was in New York on my last buying trip, and he says it would be a cinch--very common psychosis, mild delusions of grandeur--and he says he can easily guide Father into getting well.'

Through it all, though she had not glibly interrupted like Annabel, Hazel had looked shocked. She stammered now, 'B-but did this doctor make a diagnosis just from what you told him?'

'After all, a daughter, and living right in the same house with her father, ought to understand him, if she's reasonably intelligent.'

('If!' from Annabel.)

Hazel struggled on, 'I'm perfectly certain you're wrong. I've never known your father clearer-headed.'

'But you'll admit, Mother, it wouldn't hurt Father to *see* Dr. Janissary? Weren't you glad when he had his general physical examination?'

'Ye-es . . . though he did crow so, afterwards!'

'And what do you think, Doctor?'

Dr. Kamerkink said benignly, 'Well, I don't suppose it would hurt Fred any, though I certainly don't see any need,' but he barely got it out, so vigorously did Hazel take over the conference:

'Sara! Listen to me for a moment--even if I am only your mother! Strikes me this all comes down to how honest a man your Janissary person is. I'm not so behind-the-times that I don't know that psychiatry, or however you pronounce it, does do wonders; helps ever so many people get straight what it is that's worrying them. But to a lot of folks, and I confess I'm one of 'em, it still seems a little like magic, and if they depended on a psychiatrist that was money-grabbing, and if they thought he was an all-powerful medicine man, wouldn't it be dangerous? Seems to me I have heard about American women going to Europe and getting into the clutches of fancy psychologists . . .'

('With whiskers!')

'. . . that got them all confused and milked 'em.'

'Foreigners? Yes, possibly. Foreigners are often crooked. But Dr. Janissary is a real American. And he speaks five languages and plays the violin and goes trout fishing.'

'The fishing part sounds fine,' said Dr. Kamerkink.

CHAPTER XXXIII

Fred was flattered to a point of grinning when Sara invited him to accompany her to New York City on a buying trip for Swazey & Lindbeck. He accepted with zeal and with the notion that he would show the little girl a thing or two: the best restaurant in New York, and how a real salesman could order. He swallowed her statement that she wanted the aid of his common sense in buying furniture for game rooms--those assemblages of pool tables, card tables, private bars, and grills for cooking chops which were decidedly the thing in Sachem domestic architecture. But on the train she so buttered his good taste that, remembering the Louis Quinze into whose chill lap he had been enticed, he became suspicious.

In the city he was so lulled by the toe-tapping music of 'Kiss Me Quick', so youthfully enchanted by an Italian café and by memories of the Paris boulevards which he had never seen, that he trusted her as though she were not a relative, and he agreed gaily, next morning, when she invited, 'Come along with me, will you? I want you to meet such a nice man.'

Their taxicab stopped at an uptown apartment house. A chaste bronze sign in the lobby announced that the Janissary Sanatorium occupied Floors 7-10 Incl. & Roof. Still was he gullible . . . Some pleasant man living upstairs whom Sara had known in New York days, or met in this decoration game? . . . Would he be married? Oh, surely . . . Would he have a handsome flat? . . . Would he offer Fred a drink, and would Fred take it, so early in the day? . . . Probably!

They entered a room which didn't in the least suggest a friendly flat, nor yet a drink. At first, indeed, it suggested nothing whatever to Fred except quantities of money. It seemed to be a combination of a baronial hall in the North Riding, an operating room, and a beauty parlour in Hollywood. On either side of a high oak Tudor fireplace were oak thrones, but at one end of the room, modestly, was a young woman in a white uniform at a desk of white-enamelled metal, with a glass top, uncomfortably hinting of surgical knives. And the lulling voice with which she sang 'Your names, *if* you please!' wafted the sweet fumes of ether.

They waited ten minutes.

'What the deuce are you up to?' protested the aroused Fredk Wm.

'I wanted you to meet Dr. George Janissary, the psychiatrist--the grandest man--you'll love him.'

'I doubt it. Somehow this shack he's got here don't seem to rouse any stirrings of love. Psychiatrist? Mind doc?'

'You appreciate them, don't you?'

'Of course. For those that need 'em. I don't. I also don't need a chiropodist or an aviator.'

They argued in the most spirited manner, those ten minutes. Sara asserted that it was handy for almost anybody to drop in on his psychiatrist now and then, and find out what phobias, schizophrenic reactions, paranoid behaviours, or obsessive-compulsive neuroses he might have developed this past week. Fred said that, in his experience, if your carburetor is working right, don't let any mechanic monkey with it.

He could not have been expected to know that, in a psychologist's or a psychiatrist's office, the only person who is ever permitted to say 'in my experience' is the healer.

They were admitted then to the friendly presence of George Carlyon Janissary, B.A., M.A., M.D., L.H.D.; and Fred, who had come to expect a point-headed wizard in a black gown sprinkled with crimson stars, was relieved. Dr. Janissary was a jolly, tweedish, sporting, lanky gentleman, with a long red moustache and sun-browned hands. He smelled of heather, good pipe tobacco and the best soap; he shook hands merrily and spoke in baritone:

'I don't really know why you're here, Brother Cornplow, but Miss Sara seems to have some kind of an idea that I might be able to advise you on how to get the most fun out of your retiring--great idea, retiring; majority of us keep our noses to the grindstone too long. Just as you might advise me about buying an automobile.'

This was fine.

Fred beamed. Sara beamed. Dr. Janissary beamed more than twice as much as both of them put together. But he somewhat less suggested golf courses and the fishing camp on the Ouareau River as he reached for a handful of filing cards and demanded: 'What was the date of your birth?'

'What was the calling of your father--his father--his mother's father--their financial condition?'

'What do you believe to be your ambition in life?'

'Do you usually consider yourself passionate or frigid by nature?'

'Have you any hobby--any interest outside of making money and caring for your family?'

Till this point, Fred had been too hypnotized to do anything but answer meekly, and inadequately, but he shook himself loose:

'Say, what's the idea of all this, anyway? Sara, have you signed up for my giving a lecture on my life and adventures? And who pays who for it?'

Dr. Janissary did not think this was in the least funny--for that matter, Fred didn't think it was so very funny himself.

The doctor was grave and warning:

'Mr. Cornplow, from what Sara has told me and from what I have already observed, it is clear that you have lost grip--oh, just the least bit; nothing that can't readily be corrected by psychobiologic re-education. Lost grip on your personal affairs. Don't be frightened.'

'I'm not!'

'That's splendid. It happens to the most competent men of affairs, sometimes, from exhaustion and worry. I'm quite sure that your hallucination about being an explorer is temporary. Quite a satisfactory prognosis, I should think. Your only real danger is the practical one that in your state . . .'

'My state?'

'. . . you might be led into extravagances that would dissipate your entire small fortune. But of course, my dear fellow, you're not even sure that you want us to do our modest best for you, as yet. Do let me show you our place here--our "plant" you would no doubt call it.'

Fred had swung between amusement and exasperation till now, but he found nothing amusing at all in the four floors and roof which made up the sanatorium. The bedrooms, though small, were bright enough with red-and-yellow upholstery, and there were no bars on the windows, but the corridors smelled of drugs, and he saw a male attendant, a shaved gorilla, standing in a niche, watchfully looking up and down a corridor--up and down, with surly slowness. His forearms, revealed by the cut-off sleeves of his white jacket, were strong and horribly well scrubbed.

Half a floor was given over to the workshop activities which Dr. Janissary called Occupational Therapy, Dr. Kamerkink called Hobbies, and the untutored Fred Cornplow called Tinkering. There was apparatus for basket making, model-boat making, carpentry and knitting, and there, most busily knitting, was, to Fred's embarrassment, an aged gentleman with a white beard.

'Knitting?' said Fred.

'Yes, it's so soothing. Very recreational. Last year we had an ex-United States senator here, seventy years old, and he knitted a sweater for his wife.'

'What she do with it? Give it to her gigolo or to the Salvation Army?' said Fred.

In the light of Sara's look of affliction, Janissary's look of pain, he warned himself he was nothing but an upstate hick and mustn't annoy these sophisticates with his rustic American jeers. He wanted to, but didn't, ask whether men patients got well because they knitted, or got sick in the first place because they were the kind that would knit.

He fell into low humour once more when Dr. Janissary had showed them the roof of the building, which he called the 'recreational garden'. As a garden, it wasn't so much, thought Fred. Besides the gravelled roofing, parallel bars and a few deck-chairs, forlorn under December sky, it exhibited no entertaining features save a view of the Hudson and a brewery across it, and a high woven-wire fence. Before Fred could check his unfortunate humour, he had demanded, 'What's fence for? Keep the nuts from jumping off?'

Dr. Janissary did not answer, but so queerly did he glance at Sara that Fred felt boorish. He looked about the roof, trying to think of something agreeable to say.

A few feet behind him, the same male attendant was standing, rigid, his arms folded.

(Now the truth is that the attendant was not following Fred. He had sneaked up to the roof for an illegal cigarette. But it is a principle known to soldiers that it is as bad to be frightened to death as it is to be killed.)

As they descended from the roof, Sara said, and her tone was infuriatingly kind and maternal. 'Now don't you think that's a lovely fresh-air nook?'

'A *nook!'* was all that Fred could get out.

He really spoke up when they were back in Dr. Janissary's office:

'Well, Doctor, I'm glad to have seen your shop. I'm sure you could do a lot for people who are disturbed and puzzled. But I hope you don't think any of this is for me! Nosir! Well, Sara, let's skip back to the hotel.'

But Dr. Janissary would not let him go. Presumably there was no law by which he could force Fred to sit there, sweating, yet Fred felt as though a couple of deputies stood behind his chair, ready to spring, while the doctor said amiably:

'I'm afraid you're not entirely original or unusual, Mr. Cornplow, in thinking that while we could do something for the other fellow, you're too clear-headed and self-analytical for us to do anything for *you*. What we strive for here chiefly, perhaps, is to train our friends to understand themselves. People have so many blind spots in their mental steering vision.'

Bluntly, 'You got any blind spots, too, Doc?'

He felt slightly astonished that Janissary neither hit him nor called for handcuffs, but merely hesitated, 'Oh yes--yes, of course.'

'So we can call it quits, eh, Doc?' (Within, 'Why can't you be refined with these highbrows, Fred, and not try to jolly 'em the way you would Cal Tillery?') 'Because I certainly hope neither you nor Sara have any idea I'd ever let myself be cooped up here and have somebody try to "do some constructive psychiatric work" with me, as I believe you call it.'

Dr. Janissary did not, thereafter, sound so tolerant as one would have expected in a teacher of toleration:

'About your condition, my dear Mr. Cornplow . . .' ('I'll be everlastingly doggoned if I'll let any doggone man say I've got a "condition"!') '. . . there can be no question whatever. You are suffering from disassociation and a toxic condition probably due to drug escapism. And, to scotch one of the commonest lay errors, no one can do anything permanent by the use of his own so-called "will power". You need the help of trained experts.'

'You mean nobody at all can get in shape by his own will power?'

'Oh, there are apparent exceptions.'

'And maybe I'm an exception! And maybe there's more'n you think. Because sensible people don't worry too much about worrying. And maybe a lot of 'em steer clear of you. So, Sara, let's beat it.'

'Mr. Cornplow, let me say, in this amiable parting, that in a way I agree with you in your own diagnosis.'

'Eh? What's wrong with it, then?'

'I wouldn't consider taking your case useless I had complete authority--which I'm afraid you wouldn't agree to, as you suffer from the very common complaint of thinking you know as much as the doctor!--unless you agreed to stay under control for, at the least, six months.'

'Six . . . Sara! We're going.'

He had no farewell for the doctor. In the reception room, the white-clad secretary said tenderly, 'It will be one hundred dollars for the consultation, please, and if you don't mind, with new cases the doctor would prefer cash.'

Fred choked a little before chuckling (and it was his only chuckle of the day), 'This young lady will pay. She brought the Case here. He can't. He has a Condition!'

At the lower door of the apartment house, he said, 'Get this straight, Sara. I don't blame Janissary. I blame you and whatever you've been telling him. You take a taxi. I'm going to walk. And I shan't see you in New York again. I'm taking the noon train to Sachem . . . Shan't see you again. No!'

CHAPTER XXXIV

On the noon train to Sachem there was a celebrated lecturer who beguiled the tedium by analysing the people he saw along the way. He devoted only one glance to Fred Cornplow, sitting in dumpy stiffness in his Pullman chair. There he was, merely a round little man with a round little head and half-round little moustache and round little hands, his fingers tapping with slow regularity on the side of a folded magazine, his glance straight ahead and uncommunicative.

Obviously a petty business man, too unimaginative, too regimented, too incapable of strange sorrows and of fierce achievement, to be worthy the contemplation of a celebrated lecturer who, only eight hours from now, would be explaining to an audience with nice clean shirts and nice earnest smiles that life would be ever so much more amusing if you trained your eyes.

Fred had heard, as something that might happen to people whom you never met, that there had been cases in which entirely sane persons had been forced into private institutions, that were really private insane asylums, by relatives who were grasping or simply stupid. They had been penned in for years, and the more they protested, the more they had been considered dangerous, until they had sunk into the belief that they really were cracked.

He did not know whether these stories were ever true. He did know that Hazel and Annabel, certainly, Dr. Kamerkink and Walter Lindbeck and Lawyer Appletree, probably, would not find anything unsound in his sudden protest at being a combination of mint and treadmill. But he also knew that a whole world of easy-going people can be swayed by such single-track, demanding minds as Sara's. And he believed, perhaps foolishly, that a week at such a hospital as Janissary's, with that skilled finger hooking out of him the quirks and crankinesses all of us possess, would really make him unwell. It wouldn't be anything so melodramatic as padded cells and strait-jackets; it would be just the spying, pitying, incessant care that would turn him feeble-minded.

Didn't he know, Fred insisted to himself, in terror--at the moment when the skilled lecturer was dismissing him as a human polyp--that sound fellows, competent enough in their professions and their homes, when they were drafted into an army often appeared as clumsy plodders scorned by every boneheaded sergeant, or even as quivering, yelping cowards? Why shouldn't a sanatorium be as black with magic as an army?

Fred half opened his magazine, closed it and went to tapping it again.

He drove out his nagging thoughts and began swiftly to scheme what he would do. Absorbed though he was in planning, he was sensitive to every smell, every sound, as he had never been since boyhood, when he had gone off to college in a grimy day coach and everything had been new and promising and terrifying and beautiful. His senses were heightened to ecstasy. (Dr. Janissary would probably have smirked and called him 'hypomanic'.)

This was not a familiar Pullman chair car, such as he took forty times a year; it was a coloured jungle swaying in an earthquake. He smelled the plush of the seat, the metal and leather of his bag beside him, the gasoline-washed gloves of the woman across the way, the cellared grey air from the vestibule. He heard the steady bang of chains between the cars. He was conscious of the dustiness in his throat, and in imagination he tasted the thin, vintage coolness of a glass of ice water which had ripened till the ice had almost melted.

He was emotionally aware of fellow passengers whom normally he would never have seen. He hated the bushy-haired, vellum-faced man with a cord on his eyeglasses. (It was the celebrated lecturer.) He loved the powdery-cheeked old woman who sat so primly, soft old hands quietly folded. He was agitated by the sharp-nosed thin man far down the car . . . Could he be a shadow, sent by Sara to spy on him? Why did the man watch him so? Hell with him!

At a station stop he heard a radio, in a standing taxi, blatting 'Coming Round the Mountain', cloying as eggnog, and he wanted to weep. 'Oh, stop it, you sentimental old hen!' he jeered at himself, but that liquid oozing sweetness made him yearn over everything tender and banal: church bells on a June morning, babies laughing on a lawn, sunset over a lake, the cottage William Tyler Longwhale, and Hazel polishing glasses.

He was aware of the stream of life on which he was floating, and aware of himself as not being, any longer, merely Our Mr. Cornplow, Sr., a suit of clothes sitting at a desk, but a separate and exciting soul, a little different from any other. He rejoiced in his self, selfishness, self-consciousness. Why, he demanded, shouldn't he be as gloriously self-conscious as any of the great souls of which he had read: Napoleon or St. Francis or Philip Sidney? Perhaps a part of their greatness had been an unwillingness to be cogs.

He had only this one life to live; on this side Jordan, he still had, at most, some thirty years for seeing all the hills and headlands and bright rivers, and he must hasten about his business of seeing.

Perhaps he would yet walk up the Champs-Elysées.

He was in Sachem Falls a little after four. With no telephoning, he took a taxi to the Triumph agency. He cut short the greetings. He summoned Paul Popple, his aide.

'Paul, I want you to stick around till you hear from me. It may be about six o'clock. It may not be till late evening. Now send me in Cal and Mac Tillery. When I get through with 'em, give 'em each a month's salary and make sure, you personally, that they're out of this place before six.'

Cal and Mac ranged in, looking slyly confident.

'You boys are fired. You're no good. You'll get a month's pay.'

'Say, Cousin Freddie, I think you're making a big mistake. Mac and me are always watching out for your interests. The mechanics you got out there are no good.'

'For once, I'm not going to argue. I don't want any long song and dance. Let's admit you're related to me. So is Judas Iscariot, if you carry it far enough. You two pose as the simple country boys that get done by the city slickers. Fact is, you're wolves. They're rustic, too! Your only idea of a job is that it's a fight between you and the boss, and every minute you can loaf, every time you can duck a piece of work, is just one skirmish you've won. It's never occurred to you there could ever be anything but hatred between you and the man you've consented to work for. You're fired, and you might write this to your father: When he comes around to ask me, "You can't let your own relatives starve, can you?" I'll tell him, "With pleasure." Now get out!'

They fled.

The grim little round man at the desk was saying within himself, 'I don't know how long I can keep up this hard-boiled attitude. I better work quick, while it lasts . . . Don't it prove Dr. Janissary *is* good? One hour with him, this morning, and I'm re-educated already.'

He telephoned to the house, then to a series of half a dozen other numbers, found Hazel at a hat shop, and demanded, 'Be home in half an hour, could you? Something important I want to tell you'.

He telephoned to a tourist agency in Sachem and to one in Boston.

He telephoned to Lawyer Appletree.

When he left the office, he did not look back.

He took a taxicab home. In it, over and over, without quite knowing it, he repeated:

'For to admire an' for to see,
For to be'old this world so wide--
It never done no good to me,
But I can't drop it if I tried.'

He became conscious of what he was quoting, and laughed at himself--not bitterly, now.

'Old Freddie, the International Bum! Remember that time we met the tea planter at the Shanghai Club bar and went up the Wing Wang Wong in a catamaran--now what the deuce *is* a catamaran, I wonder?'

Hazel was at home. Before he could attack, she kissed him, unexcitedly, and said, 'Howard has been trying to get you on the phone. I couldn't quite make out what he wanted: something about Sara telephoning from New York, about how you met a Dr. Janissary and liked him so much, and Sara thinks we ought to get this doctor to come to Sachem and look you over some more. Is anything the matter with you?'

'Not any more! Not ever again! Hazel, I don't want to take a lot of time explaining, but Sara is bound and determined to keep me from retiring, or even taking a year's layoff.'

'But how could she keep you?'

'I don't know. But she's a smart girl and awfully determined--and if you don't believe it, look at this doggone inhuman furniture that somehow, I swear I don't know how, she wished on to me. Hazel, I'm leaving for Europe . . .'

'Europe?'

'. . . to-night, and I want . . .'

'To-night?'

'. . . you to go with me. I won't stop to explain why I want to get out and get out quick. Let's say it's just for the fun of it. That's really the best reason, anyway, I'm *going*. To-night. Are you with me or against me?'

'Why . . .'

'Are you?'

'Why, yes, of course, though . . . I'd love to go to Europe with you. I think it would be lovely. But start to-night? It's crazy.'

'Certainly. So am I. At least, I'm doggone serious, and seems that's the same as being insane. Coming?'

'You're joking. We'd have to have two weeks, at the very least, to get ready.'
'What ready?'
'Clothes.'
'You'd be surprised, but they sell clothes in Europe, too. And I'll bet anything, maybe you could buy toothbrushes there.'
'But why . . .'
'Because Howard and Sara will gang up on me, on us, and if they get us to delay our leaving--call it our sneaking off like cowards, if you want to--we never will make a break. They'll put up such an argument about my having to stay here and get them started standing on their own feet--keep on for the next twenty years getting 'em started. Oh, Sara wouldn't ever let us go.'
'Don't be silly! How could she prevent it?'
'Oh, maybe she couldn't absolutely prevent it, if we kicked and screamed, but I'll tell you what she doggone well could do: she'd sneer so and jeer so that she'd spoil the whole thing, same as she spoiled William Tyler Longwhale and our second honeymoon; she'd manage to take all the fun out of it and make us feel we were irresponsible old fools if we ever did anything except sit and knit.*Knitting!* We either go quick, and go secret, and go to-night, or we never go at all. And I'm going. Are you going with me? Are you my wife?'
'I--I think I am, Fred. What time do we leave?'
'Before midnight.'
'I'll start packing . . . Will you want your winter underwear?'
'Yes--no--I don't know--and if Howard calls up again, stall him off.'

To Lawyer Appletree's considerable indignation, Fred insisted that they stop only for a sandwich, instead of dinner, before they set to work, at Appletree's house.

A bank cashier, who on the telephone had even more indignantly complained, 'But what's all the hurry?' went wearily into the closed bank and met Fred at Appletree's with twenty-five hundred dollars in travellers' cheques.

Paul Popple arrived at Appletree's with Fred's car, which Paul himself had been greasing and inspecting. To Appletree and Paul, Fred stated, with a refusal to argue:

'Paul is left in charge of the agency, entirely, for the next three months, possibly much longer. Ed, I want you to draw up some kind of a fancy power of attorney for him, showing he's the boss. He is to receive his present salary, plus fifteen per cent of all profits. The rest are to be deposited to my account in the Grangers' National.

'Against that account, you are to pay Howard fifteen hundred dollars to-morrow, and Sara five hundred, and thereafter, a thousand a year to each of them, except that if Sara marries, which don't look any too doggone probable, she gets only five hundred. She is to stay in our house, meanwhile, and you are to pay the servants and taxes and insurance--I'll give you a list of all those items-

-but if I send you word at the end of three months, you are to let the place furnished.

'Now you, Ed--you have a complete power of attorney, and all I ask you to do is not follow my example and begin enjoying yourself. Because, as you are about to tell me--I'll admit it's a dirty trick to spoil your speech--sane, normal, honest-to-God citizens with a stake in the community don't do anything so crazy as pull up stakes and hike out for no reason except they merely want to. No indeed! They sit around and think it over and make preparations for going so carefully that when they're ready to go--they don't go!'

CHAPTER XXXV

Not till ten minutes before midnight were they off for Boston, which Fred had chosen as a safer port than New York, where Saras and Janissarys lurked in every alley.

When he returned from Appletree's, Hazel had begun to pack, but had not finished. She was sitting on the floor of a closet, whimpering like a baby, her wet face wrinkled like a baby's, as she pawed over a box filled with the shabby treasures of lost youth. Silently she held up to him a report card of Howard from the fourth grade--Deportment was Fair; Drawing and Language, Excellent; Arithmetic, Geography and the rest were Poor.

Fred chuckled, 'He used to draw curlicues, and he said they were smoke from a chimney, but I'd turn the house into a pig!'

She held up the gilt-lettered invitation to Sara's first public dance, the High School Assembly, when she had been fifteen. He remembered Sara in the preposterously short skirt of the day, her legs so long and reedy: remembered that her hair had been short and choppy and uncombable as a boy's. Such a gallant little tike she had been.

Hazel was sobbing, 'Oh, Fred, must we . . . They're so sweet. And they're all we have.'

Just then the one thing in the world he wanted to do was not to do the intemperate thing that was the one thing in the world he wanted to do. As desperately as a man who has got himself into a fight that is too big for him, he wished that he had never started the commotion. He struggled:

'I know. But we'll mean all the more to them if they see us as something besides a couple of stand-bys that they can take for granted.'

He helped her finish packing. She had brilliantly foreseen that they mustn't take anything they didn't indisputably need; they kept the luggage down to eight bags, and perhaps a canvas roll and a few odd bundles; and in all of them, later, they found nothing unnecessary except, possibly: A large framed photograph of Sara aged eleven and Howard aged four; photographs of the same ones, two, five and nine years later; a handsome binocular case which proved to contain not the binoculars but shells for a sixteen-gauge shotgun; a map of New England; volume two of *Tom Jones*--neither of them had read volume one; a guidebook of Austro-Hungary dated 1913; half pair gent's alligator-hide slippers; a bar of almond chocolate; an extra hairbrush, which each of them had thought belonged to the other; four sheets of letter paper headed 'Olympia Hotel, East Utica'; a pair of round golf garters; nail tint, which Hazel never used; an empty box for digestive pills; and a magnificent, transparent, purple waterproof, which proved to be split down the back.

Their bags were all in the Triumph coupé; they sat outside, in a forbidding world of frost, looking up at their home. It seemed kind and secure, built not of bricks but of hopes. The street before them was a corridor of forbidding steel.

She gasped, resolutely turning her face from the house, 'Oh, go, go quick--while we can.'

It was miles afterward that she asked, 'Do you happen to know what ship we're going on, what port we're going to? I don't suppose it matters, really, now that we've given up everything we've loved and trusted, but it might be interesting!'

He stopped the car. 'Sure. It's hard. We can go back, of course. It all comes down to--and I'm not so doggone certain I've got a right to ask it--but it's a question of do you trust me?'

She rubbed her left forefinger, in its knitted glove, on the seat between them; she hesitated; and said, a little doubtfully, 'Yes, I . . .' Then, strongly, almost gaily, *'Yes!'*

From Sachem to Boston the distance was two hundred and forty-two miles, and they drove it in seven hours and forty minutes, with Hazel cautiously deputing at the wheel for seventy miles of the way, while Fred leaned his cheek on his fist and tried to sleep.

They seemed to be slipping through no living world at all, but through unending cemetery aisles lined with pale tombstones. The car fled smooth and effortless as the passage of a ghost. Between the tombs, now and then, were lights that might have been villages, but they passed so quickly that Fred could not be certain that he had seen them. Only when a bridge bumbled quickly under the car, or they heard the swishing that marked their rush through a narrow defile between hills, was he sure that he had not really died, but was actually going forward to more life.

Then around and in front of them was Albany, a cauldron that bewildered and frightened them, and they stopped hastily, climbed stiffly out, to demand coffee and to gulp its scorching bitterness. Again they drank coffee in a sleeping

Pittsfield, and he thought of Stonefield near by, of William Tyler Longwhale, and the happy evening carelessness in which, decades and decades ago, Hazel and he had lounged on the porch there and tried to sing 'Seeing Nellie Home'.

He tried to hum it now, as they creaked on, flipped around a corner and shot straight ahead, but it died on the dead air inside the car.

Hazel was intimidatingly silent and withdrawn beside him. But once, beyond Stonefield, she fondly touched his arm, and he was moved to crow, 'The golden road to Samarkand--we're on the way--the golden road!'

He was certain, presently, that she had gone to sleep, and he could drive as fast as he wanted. It lulled his nostalgia to watch the needle of the illuminated speedometer, only spot of light in the gloomy car, flicker up to fifty-five, sixty, sixty-five. Hills arose before him, as dark mounds beyond the headlights, and he flung the car at them with joyful viciousness. Flats spread beside them; he imagined that--in snowy December--he could hear frog choruses, and he pushed the wheels into eating up the level road. Village lights came up at him and he scorched by them, ever faster, so that they slipped past like clusters of fireflies.

He felt sleepiness parching his eyes and, as a veteran driver, stopped by the road, let Hazel jolt awake in the motion of stopped motion, turned the wheel over to her and tried to doze off.

He startled as he remembered that on his desk at home he had left a marked list of sailings from Boston.

Would it lead Howard or Sara to him? Would their complaints, their drugging appeals to his sense of duty, paralyse him again and at the last moment prevent his going?

No. They'd never find it till morning. And so indirect were the flying routes that they would not be able to catch him even by plane.

He gave up sleep. When he lighted a cigarette, in the glow of the match he saw Hazel's face tense. 'Lemme drive again,' he grunted, with no shadings from the tenderness he felt.

The route nicked off only a corner of Worcester, and instantly they were again in the graveyard lane. But at Waltham there was a shivering hint of daylight, and he suddenly felt strong and gay. Almost in Boston! Almost on a ship! Almost bucking the winter ocean! So he cheerfully slowed up for the first traffic, after their dash across one wide state and half another, and decorously he slipped up to a hotel on Beacon Street, in winter daylight.

The doorman yawned, 'Like your car garaged for all day?'

Fred slightly alarmed him by sighing, 'I want to pay in advance for storing it, dead, for three months,' and by sentimentally smoothing the hot cheeks of its bonnet.

Would he ever drive a Triumph again?

He slept for two hours; Hazel, so far as he knew, till noon. He hastened to the tourist agency to which he had telephoned from Sachem and bought two tickets from Boston to Constantinople (Constantinople!), on the *Aranjuna Queen*, a cargo ship which carried some twenty passengers and which was headed for Channel ports, Lisbon, Gibraltar and clear round the Mediterranean. (But he did not call it a 'cargo ship' as yet; not till he had been baptized with salt water and the chief officer's salty jeers would he know how land-lubberly he had once been in calling the *Aranjuna* a 'freight boat'.)

He galloped about Boston, being polylingual to the extent of always saying 'Jah' for 'Yes,' and timidly demanded visas for Great Britain, Portugal, Jugoslavia and other patently fictional lands. He bought a book called *A Satchel Guide to Europe,* and a small motion-picture camera with which he hoped to snap Hazel walking in front of the pyramids, Hazel feeding pigeons at St. Mark's, Hazel fishing in a Norwegian fjord.

And he bought for her six winter roses--very expensive.

At two o'clock that afternoon they stood amidships on the S.S. *Aranjuna Queen,* looking down on the freight-littered pier. From the bridge, they heard the captain shouting to the chief officer, up on the forecastle head, 'Single up, fore and aft,' and the bosun bellowing to the sailors, 'Heave the gangway aboard.'

Hazel clutched his arm. 'Our last link with shore! In a minute, it'll be too late!'

'Yes, too late,' he croaked.

The gangway was slid up and flopped on the deck.

The last lines were let go. The captain, above them, cried to the third mate, at the engine-room telegraph, 'Slow astern.' They were incredibly moving; going, for the first time in either of their lives, from the security of land to the savage unknown. They held each other like terrified children as the whistle burst into obscene blatting.

Just then two people galloped along the pier below them, screaming.

'Good Lord! It's Howard and Annabel! How'd they ever know? Can they grab us and make us come back now? No! We're safe!' rattled Fred.

Out on the perilous edge of wharf beside the dock-house ran the little couple. Annabel was crying, 'Take me with you! Please! Take me along!'

Hazel sobbed. The ship was quivering now and moving more swiftly. Howard had been waving imploringly. Now, as the black side of the ship drew definitely away, he stopped waving, and his whole face puckered with weeping.

'My boy--my little boy that we're deserting! He's so unformed yet. He can't take care of himself,' whimpered Hazel.

The *Aranjuna Queen* snorted regally again and drew out into the harbour, and they could see their children only as doll-like figures, faithfully waving to the last.

'How did we ever get here on this boat?' marvelled the completely astonished Fredk Wm.

CHAPTER XXXVI

'Poor kid! I know--I know! Howard, the poor kid, he's never had to take anything seriously, not even his marriage. I guess it does jar him to see us running out on him. I've got a hunch it's been our fault; we never worked much at teaching him to stand on his own feet. Maybe he'll learn now. And then someday he'll want to get a little acquainted with himself, too, and maybe he'll have to run away from Little Nero!'

He had been trying to comfort Hazel, down in their stateroom, but out of all his chatter nothing was distinct except 'Poor kid'. In a few days, he assured her, they would forget Howard and enjoy being wrecked on the mobile desert island that is a ship.

'I'm going to hate it! I'll want to come back the minute we land! I'll see poor Howard crying there, all the time,' she bawled, while Fred mechanically tapped her back . . . and, no longer listening much, over her shoulder surveyed their first stateroom . . . He carefully did not tell her that there was such a thing as returning to Boston on the pilot boat.

The room, rather humble, delighted him more than a rosewood-and-tapestry suite on any cruising hotel would have done. Its stripped neatness belonged to ships. There were two beds, as promised by the travel circulars on which he had become such an authority, and between them was a bedside table with electric reading lamp, but the chairs were straight and small, the wash-bowl was of the tricky, delightful, old-fashioned sort that folded up like a shelf, and one side of the stateroom, of white-daubed bolts and steel plates curving up to an honest porthole, was frankly the side of the vessel.

'I'm sure enough on a ship!' he exulted.

That moment the ship rolled heavily, and his stomach did not exult.

'Guess better guppon deck get li'l' fresh air,' he panted.

They struggled, step by swaying step, up the forward stairs, and in the beginnings of distress Hazel began to neglect being homesick. Astern they saw a grey bank--she did not know whether it was fog or land, but she decided on land, so that she could agonize over leaving it.

'Take a last look. Snow and ice. Next land we see--golly, think!--it'll be foreign land!--a strange country!--and I reckon it'll be all green,' he said with false buoyancy.

'By the way, Fred, where are you going?'

'How do you mean? I showed you the ticket--all these different countries--whole slew of 'em!'

'But what port, what country, do we touch first of all? Where are we *going?*'

'Golly, I was so busy getting away, I forgot to ask!'

It was to Hull, in Yorkshire, that they were going, said the purser.

'Oh yes, that's what I thought,' said Fred.

Never, not even in William Tyler Longwhale, had they been so lured to each other as in the three days, out of a ten-day crossing, when they idled in the stateroom, never getting out of dressing-gowns, always in the not too disagreeable state between seasickness and a bounding health that would have compelled them to go up and be athletic and social. In the Cornplow home, meals had been brought up to bedrooms on trays only in case of definite illnesses, and with increasing sense of power and travelled sophistication they enjoyed ringing for the steward and for tea and toast and orange juice all day long.

'I just can't face the thought of leaving our nice little room and meeting a lot of strangers,' Hazel sighed. 'I'm sorry, Fred, but I can see now I'm not going to be any good as a traveller. I'm too shy of new people and new ways. But you'll be grand at it, you old mixer, and I'll just stick along . . . till you get tired of it and want to trot back home.'

So all day, contentedly, for hours at a time forgetting that they had shamefully deserted their helpless brood, they talked of themselves; recalled, with snorts or giggles, old, far-off, unhappy things and battles long ago, such as the quarrel, comic now but devastating then, when he had been discovered, during a stately ball, shooting craps with a bunch of chauffeurs in the basement, with his dress coat hung on a coal shovel, and on his proud shirt front a skull and bones drawn in lipstick.

Never had Hazel found out what female serpent had drawn it . . . Neither had Fred.

They first emerged from their cave for dinner in the saloon. Hazel wailed, 'I'm going to be embarrassed to death--all those people staring at me.' So she was embarrassed by nobody's staring at all. The company didn't even cackle at her having failed to show up. They had been sufficiently seasick themselves.

The eighteen passengers were divided among four tables in the saloon. As members of the wholesale-selling, or knightly, caste, Fred and Hazel were seated at the captain's table, where they found no one more intimidating than a Mr. and Mrs. Alphen, of Joliet, and Miss Pablum, a school teacher from Minneapolis, all three of whom seemed to have no particular reason in going abroad except to inspect things, to be found only in Europe, called Culture, Castles, Napoleon Brandy, and Points of Historical Interest.

The captain was a very good captain, and as such his chief interest was in real-estate investment in Mount Vernon, New York, where he resided. He was tall and thin, he told jokes about nagging wives, and he played the piano.

Mrs. Alphen showed the Cornplows, at the very first meal, pictures of her grandchildren. Miss Pablum lent them a lively book called*In the Footsteps of British Bards*. As for Mr. Alphen, he was that vestigial remain, a State Patriot. He asserted, touchily, that Illinois air was tastier than Wisconsin air, Illinois taxes lower than New York taxes, Illinois Swedes more Swedish than Minnesota Swedes, and Joliet penitentiary more flourishing than Sing Sing.

'Why, they're all nice, friendly people, just like home,' said Hazel.

There was a good deal of merry jesting between table and table; each insisting that it possessed more wit, more skill in bridge playing, than the others. But, complained Hazel, the other passengers seemed even shyer than herself; they did not 'get together in social activities'.

It was she who organized them.

In company with the purser, who pleased her very much indeed by insisting that she must have 'crossed' at least ten or twelve times, Hazel got up a bridge tournament, a backgammon tournament, a shuffle-board tournament, a masquerade ball, and a Reading, by Miss Pablum, who led them plodding from footstep to footstep of the bards.

On vacations Fred had noticed that Hazel took cheerfully to new people and to those extraordinary games by which adults escaped sitting and thinking, but he had explained it as a few days' excitement in getting away from domestic chores. He perceived, now, that she had more talent than he for liking strangers and strange ways and for being noisy and jokey with them. She became, indeed, Queen of the Ship, and it was she whom the other passengers asked about the day and hour of their arrival in Hull, the amount to tip, the name of the what-is-it that swings out the boats, the rules for deck tennis and the latitude of Spitzbergen.

Fred was merely her Prince Consort.

He had pictured, as a chief joy of travelling, greater than ancient abbeys and beards on the Boulevard, being intimate with ever so many new wandering gentlemen. Was he not the trained salesman, the jolly good fellow, who could enter an unfamiliar hotel lobby and be calling five men by their first names within ten minutes?

But, released from having to be any particular sort of person, he found that he wanted to get acquainted only with himself. Brother Alphen, he admitted, was a swell fellow; but somehow, he marvelled to Hazel, he didn't want to hear anything more about the New Deal or the convenience of oil furnaces. He had had to listen to so many hearty citizens, for so many years, at the Triumph Agency, and to Hazel and Sara at home afterward. He thought it queer in himself; he wondered what Dr. Janissary would have said; but he enjoyed silence. Doc Kamerkink would have ridiculed the notion that the breezy and back-slapping Fred was actually an introvert, interested only in the forms and colours of his hidden little soul; and Hazel an extrovert, and not at all the inward-looking sensitive plant that the seclusion of domesticity made her appear. But a great deal of the ten days Fred spent in circling the deck by himself, or in standing at the forward rail, while Hazel was in the lounge, playing contract.

Mrs. Alphen, from her deck-chair, would call at him brightly, 'Aren't you ashamed of yourself, being so selfish and neglecting us ladies and all!' and she would gesture at the deck-chair beside her, but he would only smile and scuttle away, realizing that he was asocial and a scoundrel.

Hour-long, as the ship rolled, he watched the forward derrick sway against the seas rushing at him. In the power of the waves he felt freedom; in the bows, tenderly swelling to a piercing point, he felt speed; and in the pendulum of the derrick, a rhythm of security . . . Perhaps in wandering he could be minutely great, as in room-bound labour he had, these years, been greatly small.

Toward the end of the passage, Hazel spoke of home and of Howard and Sara barely once a day, as if merely by habit. Her homesickness, and his, was acute only at Christmas, which they spent on the *Aranjuna Queen* in the English Channel, with a dim sight of Margate and the mouth of the Thames.

'B-but anyway, we aren't any homesicker than the others, I guess!' she sobbed gallantly.

Indeed, the more the *Aranjuna's* passengers tried to be festive and bear in the garlands and the Yule log, the more veiled and timid were their eyes. They had a Christmas tree in the lounge, and the captain swore it was a damn fine tree, for hadn't he brought it himself from Mount Vernon? The head steward rather mechanically produced silver cord and crimson glass balls, and rather mechanically the passengers dressed the tree. They cleared out the cubbyhole which was the 'souvenir shop' of the barber-bath-steward, and gave one another souvenir handkerchiefs and tin toy automobiles and ten-cent boxes of candy; they had a large dinner, with goose and turkey and anguished paper hats, and afterwards they danced.

But every time Miss Pablum danced awkwardly past the tree, she looked away. Her mother had died on the first of December.

In mid afternoon they had their Christmas radiogram:

MERRY XMAS HAPPY NEW YEAR EXQUISITE EASTER MUCH LOVE DONT FORGET LOVING KIDS SARA HOWARD ANNABEL LILNERO

Then Hazel wept, and watered the sacred rose of Christmas.

'They're grand children. They'll be perfect, now they see they can't run over us!' swore Fred. 'Say! Do you still feel you want to go right back, soon as we land in Hull--just take couple days in London, maybe, and then sail . . .'

Hazel was judicious:

'Well, now we're here, seems to me it 'd be an awful waste of good money not to take advantage of it. Katie Alphen says we'll just love the Riviera. But we certainly won't want to stay long . . . Look, Fred. If we just happened to still be here next summer, just happened to decide to stay on, I mean, do you think we'd enjoy having a country cottage in England? Minnie Pablum says we'd adore Rural England . . . Not that she's been there.'

'Well,' said Fred.

They drank a toast to home, in the smoking-room, which wasn't a smoking-room but an alcove off the lounge.

'Let's drink an extra one to Annabel--best of the lot,' proposed Fred.

Hazel giggled. 'You're so funny! You don't know yourself one single bit? You're half in love with that girl, and you have no idea of it!'

'You think so? Ha, ha!' he said.

It made his voyage of discovery of himself curiously easier to travel with a pleasant person who did not embarrass him by understanding him.

CHAPTER XXXVII

The Villa Sophie, at Belfayol, on the Côte d'Azur between Hyères and St. Tropez, was a smart little pension, a respectable pension, a white pension streaked with purple bougainvillaea, on the beach, overlooking the fishing boats, with the tiny casino only two blocks away, and with victorias, in which no one ever seemed to drive, always standing in front of it. It had a tidy salon with Spanish arm-chairs, yellow marble-topped tables, grey marble floor, and gold-coloured curtains. Tea could be had in an arbour in the rose garden. And though the bedrooms were small, their long windows, opening like doors, gave on tiny iron balconies facing the full brilliance of the tideless sea.

At the Villa Sophie, in late April, Frederick William Cornplow & wfe, as it was stated in the pension register, were living the life of international culture de luxe, all modern improvements, lowest rates.

They had seen perhaps one half per cent of London (on the 'side trip' from Hull), of Rotterdam and Brest, of a Lisbon hysterical with the waxing Spanish revolution, of Capri by way of Naples, of divine Venice, of Ragusa, Athens and at last of Istanbul. (They blushed that they had ever called it 'Constantinople'. Which name they went right on calling it, whenever they weren't careful.)

At Istanbul, Fred was embarrassingly near to the golden road to Samarkand, and at Istanbul he was uncomfortable to a point of terror. He didn't understand what they sold in these crazy littered shops; he didn't know how to get a hot bath; he saw no Triumph cars nor ever heard a meaty American voice. He was a Heck Centre pup lost on Hester Street.

Though they had not known there was such a thing as a Jugoslavian steamer, a particularly trim and slim and black-and-nickel Jugoslavian craft had taken them back to Villefranche, whence they timidly drove to Belfayol.

In Ragusa they had received, and in the shadow of its old walls they had re-re-read, the cable from Sara saying that she had just been married to Walter Lindbeck, her boss, and could they rent the Cornplow home?

Yes, they could, Fred cabled, though he felt that with the den of their wolf cubs thus gone, and with Hazel daily more sprightly about the joys of Europe and the Great World, he would never be able to return now to the one place in the world he longed to see.

Early in March they had the cable from Howard that Little Nero had been born, that Little Nero's name was Franklin R. Cornplow, and that 'mother son self oke'.

So when they came, weary and eyesore and foot-aching, to the Villa Sophie, in April, they were for a certain time glad to feel they had found a new fixed home.

The guests of the Villa were very cosmopolitan, considered Fred and Hazel. They included a Belgian count, a Russian colonel and lady, a professor who, unlike most professors, looked like a professor, a Swedish sculptor who never seemed to do anything to rocks and whose favourite daily joke was that he was there 'studying villasophie', a mysterious lady in black who had nothing to recommend her except her mysteriousness, a fat Englishwoman called Lady Jaxon, five respectable but indistinguishable women, and a fat retired Irish contractor from Omaha, also with lady. The contractor was cheery and became Fred's best friend and worst pest: his wife spoke of art and was studying French--as, suddenly, amazingly, Hazel seemed also to be doing.

In this international musical comedy troupe Hazel could not star as she had on the steamer, but she fitted, she loved their wan references to ancestral wealth; she became smarter and rosier, and daily keener about the pension's communal sports: meals, swimming, anticipation of meals, *boule* at the casino, reminiscences about meals, shopping, and picnics with hot meals and bottles of white Bordeaux, on top of Mont Nid . . . Fred noticed that the fat contractor, the fat Lady Jaxon and his own plump self were invariably favoured with the bills for these picnics.

Hazel had first been awed at the be-titled company but within a month she was muttering to Fred, 'Oh, these are nothing but small-time pension tramps. I'm looking forward to Monte Carlo and Paris, and then our cottage in England. Lady Jaxon--she really is top-drawer--she says we can get a perfectly ducky cottage near her Place in Devon. Would you like that?'

'Uh--oh yes--sure--I guess so.'

'Happy?'

'Oh yes--sure!'

'Oh, *be* happy!'

But daily he felt more out of it, out of everything. In this alien land, with its funny language, nothing, not politics nor business nor manners nor food, was any of his affair. He was an outsider, merely tolerated, and without very definitely longing for home he wanted to be back where he could exercise the citizen's precious privilege of kicking about the way everybody ran everything.

It seemed to be one of Fred's typical mornings in this suburb of Samarkand.

He had successfully begged off from a morning's motor trip to Bandol with Hazel, Lady Jaxon and the contractress. Hazel was so exceptional among American women that she understood that he might, without viciousness or secret plans of dissipation, want to escape so feminized an expedition. She didn't suspect him of having an engagement with a Provençal enchantress. In this, unfortunately, she was right.

He sat alone, feeling alone and lost, drinking coffee at a café on the plaza, with the sea in front, the casino on one side, and on the other, the plaster railway station. If on the steamer he had been glad to avoid noisy inquiries about the state of his family, now he would have rejoiced if someone he had known long ago, almost anyone he had ever known, had come up behind him, assaulted his back and bellowed, 'Well, you old so-and-so! What you doing here?'

He tried to read the last crop of American newspapers.

What was all this about this new labour organization called the Committee on Industrial Organization? He wasn't sure what he could do about it, but he felt that he ought to dash right over to Michigan and show the boys, on both sides, how to act nicely. He puzzled over the President's proposal to change the Supreme Court. He could do nothing here in Belfayol; these foreigners, these Frenchman, didn't seem to think he was an authority on their politics; but if he were back in America, where he belonged, he'd certainly have something to say that would help the President.

In Belfayol, not so far from Spain, there was a backwash of the great rebellion; now and then he saw refugees, bewildered with bundles, but he had already discovered the queer fact of how little a world calamity changes streets and customs.

As he always did, when he was here alone, he studied the tramway passengers debarking at their end of the line. He saw a young couple, American by their voices, and longed to pick them up, but they were too worldly for him: the girl in slacks and sweater, the man in beret, flappy blue trousers, espadrilles. No. Prob'ly they had a villa up the mountain; prob'ly been coming here for years; prob'ly think he was only a vulgar tourist. Well, and maybe he was. But doggone it, in Sachem they didn't think he was just a tourist.

More dramatic than the tramway was the railway station, at which the Paris train was now due. Sometimes whole squads of Americans got out. Once he had gloriously seen, coming from the train, a Kansas City man he had met at a Triumph convention in Atlantic City! The coachmen before the station were waking up; their horses were shaking off flies. The porters were streaming inside, yelling at one another as though war had started. The sellers of oranges were gathered. From the station straggled the passengers. Suppose there should again be a man from Kansas City! Or even from incomparable Sachem!

Fred watched the doorway like a trysting lover. He noticed a young woman in clothes that he guessed were American. She was carrying a very young baby and looking feverishly back at the porter, ahead at the carriages, shaking her head over the crowd's volubility, comforting the howling baby--altogether clean flustered.

'Wonder if I could help her any way?' thought Fred, not much concerned.

Then he saw that the young woman was his daughter-in-law, Annabel.

CHAPTER XXXVIII

Returning from her bland and chatty drive to Bandol, Hazel climbed out of the mildewed limousine, calling to Lady Jaxon, 'Such a pleasant trip, and indeed I will look into the Cotswolds.'

She revolved and saw, entering the Villa Sophie, a procession consisting of her husband, looking agitated, of Annabel Staybridge Cornplow, who was, of course, not here at all, but in Sachem Falls, U.S.A., of her first grandchild, F. Roosevelt Cornplow, who didn't exist, except as a sentence in a cablegram and a few gushing pages in a letter, a porter, with bags that seemed familiar, and a furious *cocher,* who had not received his fare.

'Good heavens and earth!' said Hazel.

Her slight jealousy of Annabel vanished in joy of this dear, customary face; she swooped on the girl, kissed her, kissed the baby and babbled, 'Bell--Bell--and the baby--but only six weeks old--how could you come--where is Howard--what's it all mean--Bell--I couldn't believe my eyes--I can't!'

Fred mumbled, 'Oh yes you can. It just means Howard has gone to pieces, and I've got to sail from Havre to-morrow afternoon and yank him out of it.'

Annabel's room in the Villa Sophie, where the baby was asleep in a crib improvised from a bureau drawer, a room with clattering composition stone floor, high panelled plastered walls, and frigid pink-and-gilt ceiling, seemed unfriendly to them, these lost Americans, and to Annabel's sorrows.

'Now what is it, dear? Where's Howard?' said Hazel.

'Back home. He didn't want me to come. But he was drunk. He couldn't prevent my coming. Father gave me the money. But Father wouldn't go see Howard. He just laughed at me. He talked about giving me a trip to Reno as a belated wedding present, Father did . . . I don't just know why I came here. I just felt so lonely in our flat, with Howard lying drunk.'

'Honey, I don't know what I can say that's very comforting. But let's see if there's anything I can do. What about Howard's business--Bogey & Cornplow?' said Fred.

'Howard said Ben cheated him. Ben said Howard hurt their business--not booze so much as he didn't keep dates. They quarrelled. At the flat. I grabbed Howard's arm and kept him from hitting Ben. Ben bought him out--for five hundred dollars. He's living on that, and the money Judge Appletree sends him from you. But I don't think it will last. He keeps giving it to Cal Tillery . . .'

'Cal? Cousin Cal?' Fred was appalled.

'Yes. Howard says Cal is his only friend. Cal doesn't nag him. Cal's brother, Mac, got fed up with them and actually went to work. He was so surprised to find he liked it! Now, Howard and Cal have bought a garage together--that is, Howard gives Cal the money, and Cal *says* he's paying for it, on time. Howard never goes near the place. Mostly he stays in the flat. And Cal brings him in booze. Cal laughed at me.'

'Cal's scum! He's a cousin-by-accident!'

'And once Cal tried to kiss me. That's what made me run away--and I was afraid what might happen to Baby--oh, Howard was always sweet to the baby, even when he was drunk, but he was so shaky--once he almost dropped the baby on the floor, when he was trying to dress it--and I didn't want it to grow up listening to Howard and Cal sing "The Old Oaken Bucket"!'

'But Annabel, dear,' said Hazel, 'what's Howard going to do, now he's out of the firm?'

'Oh, he has a hundred new plans a day: he's going to join the army and learn flying. He's going to Hollywood and be a star--but oh, his face is changing so; it almost seems as if it was getting coarse already . . . Oh, my darlings, I don't like to talk this way about him!'

'Go on! You're as much our child as he is,' Fred vowed.

Hazel looked only a little doubtful.

'And then he talks about going to Alaska--he thinks he can get a free farm there--he says it's the only place where "a young fellow has a chance". And he talks about making millions selling cotton-stripping machines. And the latest I heard, he was going to be a tree doctor! But no matter what he says, I feel he's just given up. Completely discouraged. He's only part to blame, maybe . . .'

Fred groaned, 'I'm to blame! Me and my insisting on running away.'

'No. Your going isn't to blame. But maybe your putting it off so long is. Sara and Howard thought you'd always be there and nurse them.'

'Annabel! What about Sara? Does she seem happy?' demanded Hazel.

'Darling, Sara has now been married to her Walter for fifty years, and she just can't understand why Howard doesn't obey me the way Walter has obeyed her, these sixty-seven years they've been married . . . She made him put on a sale of surrealist paintings in the store; they already have two pictures in it; one of them was done by a bookkeeper in Schenectady, and one by a Frenchman, who wanted to come over, but they wouldn't let him out of the asylum.'

Fred interrupted, 'Sweet child, I love you, but we must get going . . . Hazel, I find I have to take an evening train, to catch the *Sovereign* at Havre, tomorrow . . . I'll be in New York in six and a half days!'

'But you want us to come along--me, anyway?' said Hazel.

She was a little reluctant.

'No. Stay here. Show the Riviera to Annabel. Take her to Paris. I want two people in this doggone family to do what they want to do for once. If you can pull *that* off, the Associated Press will put it on the wire, and it'll go down in history as the one big event of the year!'

He might be fond of Annabel, but he wanted his last half-hour in Belfayol alone with Hazel. He lured her to their best café; not the historic castle cave but the tiny new bar where the wall bench was so bright and red, the iron tables such shining green, the awning over the sidewalk so sunshine-like a yellow. Embedded in the glass of the windows was wire in the shape of stalks and flowers.

'Lord, I hate to skip off and leave you, girl. Will we ever sit in a foreign saloon again?'

'Oh, we will, and be so close to each other. I regret every second I've spent away from you; like running off to Bandol with those silly women this morning.'

'No. Less friction, when we don't tag each other. And now you just forget me for a while.'

'Maybe.'

'Well . . . By golly, we pulled it off. Didn't we!'

'Yes . . . We did see Europe. Didn't we!'

'Yes . . . And I didn't do so bad. Did I! I wasn't too bad a greenhorn. Was I!' Fred seemed not too sure about it.'

'Never . . . And I was a good sport. The old folks showed they could run off together. And I did learn to like Burgundy. Didn't I!'

'Yes, you bet . . . Golly!'

'Happy?'

'Yes.'

'Oh, be happy!'

So absorbed was he in Hazel, their last half-hour, that when the young American couple whom he had always wanted to pick up went swinging by, he nodded to them casually and wasn't even flattered by their pleased bow in answer.

On the R.M.S. *Sovereign's* five-day falcon flight to New York, Fred spoke to no one but stewards and the inescapable stranger who interrupted his vigil, again at the forward rail of the promenade deck, by inquiring, 'Well, how do you like this weather?'

He was a veteran of travel now; he could have produced seasoned remarks to the effect that he 'liked it a little rough like this; then you know you're at sea.' But he barely saw the friendly greeter, for wavering between them were Howard, Sara, Hazel, Annabel, Cal Tillery.

He grunted, 'All right, I guess,' and let it go at that. Beyond the bobbing spectral faces he saw, on the midsea horizon, a quivering dark bank that must be the Long Island shore, that must be America.

Standing at the rail, he tried to work out a philosophy of The Family. He saw it in sharp-coloured little motion pictures rather than in definite words, but they might have been translated thus:

Women have for decades been revolting against the restrictions of men and the home. Votes. Jobs. Uniforms in 1914-18. Cocktails they didn't appreciate enough and cigarettes they appreciated too much. Now the children were revolting; thought their parents were convenient bores at best, tyrants at worst; children not, as for centuries past, claiming merely their own just rights in the household, but domination over it.

Perhaps next would come, perhaps there was already coming, secret and dangerous, the Revolt of the Men; they would admit how sick they were of the soft and scented cushions of women, of women's nervous reminders that pipe ashes didn't belong on the floor; perhaps they would go off to monasteries and fishing camps (much the same thing) and leave their wives and children flat.

If the institution of The Family was to survive at all, if it possibly could survive, parents would have to stop expecting children to accept their ideas (but that was a warning even older than Bernard Shaw). Men and women must expect nothing, nothing whatever, from each other as of vested right (but that was an ancient battle, too, though still as little won as when Ibsen was new and shocking). But beginning about 1914, and each year since then more violent, there was a growing revolt of parents against the growing revolt of Youth; a demand that the young Saras and Howards should regard their parents' houses as something more than places in which to change clothes before dashing off in motor cars (dressing-rooms, clothes and cars all provided free, by the courtesy of the management) to places more interesting.

But Fred didn't at all advocate the Fascist-Nazi-Bolshevik system, the naively new and wearisomely antiquated system of belief that everybody ought to sacrifice himself for everybody else. He had the opposite faith: that nobody ought to expect any sacrifice from anybody else, and that (in merely another ten thousand years or so, if the luck and weather held good) thus might be ended for ever the old structure, equally practised by small circles of relatives and by monstrously great nations, whereby A sacrificed his honest desires on behalf of B, and B sacrificed for C, and C sacrificed himself violently but complainingly, all day long, for A, and everybody resented the whole business and chanted, 'How loyal and unselfish we all are--curse it!'

The sight of the Statue of Liberty was not his chief thrill on arriving in New York, but rather his first American 'cuppacoffee, slabapie, à la mode, please, Sister.'

When he trudged out of the railroad station in Sachem, he was astonished to see that after this lifetime of five months, in which the entire world had been changed, Harriman Square seemed exactly the same. Apparently the cigar stores had unfeelingly gone on selling cigars without his aid; and the familiar corner loafers looked at him without interest.

He had telegraphed to Sara--Mrs. Walter Lindbeck--but not to Howard.

He went up the sandstone steps of what had been his home. But his tread sounded different on the stones; the doorbell sounded different and unwelcoming; and the door was opened by a strange maid who, when he sighed, 'Is Mrs. Lindbeck in?--I'm Mr. Cornplow,' snapped at him, 'Whajah say your name was?'

In the hallway a new and echoing mirror had replaced the reproduction of Whistlers' 'Mother'.

But Sara came downstairs affably enough.

'Well, well! Mrs. Lindbeck, by golly!'

She didn't frown.

'Glad to see me, Sara?'

She was placid in her: 'But of course, dear.'

'Forgiven me for sneaking off like that?'

'But you don't need any forgiveness. You were quite right. We were all getting on your nerves, and your going away was good both for you and for us--I trust. Oh, I've settled down, and I hope I've acquired some sense, since I married.'

'Like it?'

'Immensely. Walter is the Rock of Gibraltar, and what's more important, he's amusing. I do think we're a quite unusually rational and understanding pair . . . Oh, Inga!' This, sharply and confidently as a section-gang boss, to the maid, lolloping about the adjacent dining-room with some notions about dusting. 'Will you kindly be more quiet?'

'Still keeping up your interior-decoration job?'

'But naturally! . . . I mean: I've laid it aside just temporarily.'

'Now give me the low-down on Howard. I haven't seen him yet.'

Then did she lose her disciplinary serenity.

'Father! I never want to see him again! After what we did to get him started! I can't believe he's my brother. He's drunk all the time, and associating with that disgusting clodhopper, Cal Tillery. Walter and I did everything we could for him. We gave him all sorts of good advice, and Walter even offered to take him into the store, if he'd sign a promise not to drink. We've had to wash our hands of him. But cheer up, Father dear. You have *one* child who's quit boiling and begun to set!'

'Yes--yes--that's fine--that certainly is--it's fine to know you're happy--certainly is fine--but I feel I ought to try my hand with Howard.'

'Of course.' She laughed then: 'The only thing I can't figure out is who's who in your new version of the Fable of the Prodigal. You're Prodigal Son, obviously, with Mother as Assistant Prodigal, and I'm the forgiving parents, and I'm afraid Howard is the swine, with Cal for husks, but who's the fatted calf, and who's the elder son that got sore?'

He was wincing at her complacent humour. Trying to be conversational, he interrupted:

'Ever hear from this fellow Silga?'

'Silga?'

'Yes. Sure. You remember. Gene.'

'Oh, *him!* That rat! I understand he was mixed up in some auto strike in the West and got arrested, and now he's doing time. Serves him right.'

'Now, Sara! I don't think that's nice! I never had any reason to love him, but you got to admire an enemy that's got nerve.'

'Do you? I wouldn't know. But just as you like, my dear!'

With considerable awkwardness he got himself away from the assured and masterful Mrs. Lindbeck. He refused her invitation to stay at the house--his own house, from which he had fled, to which apparently he could never return--with the lying explanation that he had arranged to sleep on a couch at Howard's.

Well, he persuaded himself in the taxicab, for good or ill, this one child had been set on the way. But there was another child that needed him, needed him urgently . . . he hoped.

CHAPTER XXXIX

Howard's flat was a 'second-story walk-up'. The first flight of the stairs was clean and waxy; the second, littered with cigarette butts, mud and a dozen milk bottles, some empty and tumbled on their sides, some full of milk turned sour.

When Fred knocked, from within came a voice, apparently Cal Tillery's, bawling, 'Ah gwan, beat it!'

Fred walked in. The living-room, which Annabel had kept sweet as a new moon, was like a junk shop. Middle of the floor lay a glass lamp, smashed, with its vellum shade dented, and beside it, Annabel's volume of Yeats, with the cover torn off. Cal Tillery, in undershirt and trousers, happily waving a cigarette, lay on Annabel's chaise-longue, upon a woolly afghan (she had knitted it). Beside Cal was a highball on a low maple table, in the middle of which a cigarette had burned itself out. The charred paper and ashes still outlined its corpse.

Nailed to the wall with an ice pick was a photograph of Annabel's father, the beard daubed red with a coloured pencil.

Cal looked up cheerfully. 'Hello, Cousin Freddie! Who let you out? So they wouldn't keep you in Europe heh?'

Fred took an appreciable time in walking over to him. His voice was low. 'Get out. Quick.'

'What's your hurry? Have a drink?'

Fred's voice was not so low now. 'Quick, I said!'

'Give a fellow time to put his shoes on, can't you?'

Fred looked about for the shoes. They had been placed, carefully ranged side by side, on Annabel's baby-grand piano, which her mother had given to her when she was ten. Cal's straw hat and coat were dumped on the floor. Fred picked up shoes, hat, coat, and threw them out into the hall.

He was thirty years older than Cal, and small and fat and unexercised. He stooped over Cal, his plump hands making clawing motions. He must have looked mad.

'I said--quick!'

'All right--all right--keep your shirt on--Freddie!' But Cal was staggering out, as he said it.

Howard could be heard groaning, 'Oh, what's all racket?' from the bedroom.

Before Fred went to him, he looked over the kitchen-dining-room. There was not one plate or glass left in the cupboard; a pile of dishes, smeared with egg yolk, bacon grease and burned toast crumbs, tottered on the dish slide. In the sink were a dishpan full of greasy water, the smashed ruin of a glass coffee percolator and the slowly perishing shred of a cake of expensive hand-soap. The roller towel, behind the door, was streaked with black.

Fred marched into the bedroom. Howard, in pyjamas, the top unbuttoned over his woolly red chest, lay flat on the bed, groaning, trying to stroke his wet and blazing forehead. A whisky bottle was snugly tilted on the pillow beside his cheek.

With pain he lifted his reeking, tousled head and stared.

'Oh, hello. It's Dad, ain't it? I know! You came back from Europe!' His drivelling triumph at this recognition he interrupted with the surly demand: 'Where's Cal?'

'He's gone out.'

Howard wept with self-pity. 'You get him back, ri' 'way. Cal's best of the wholy cranky lot. Only one that never asks me to do anything don't want to. Family always after me to hustle an' do something. Howard--wash your fool neck! Howard--don't ever stop on the street and be nice to folks, because you got to be in the repair shop at eight sharp! Howard--curse you, now appreciate this highbrow music I'm playing! Howard--quit laughing and get busy and make a million dollars, even if you don't want a million dollars! Howard--don't smoke, don't drink, don't play poker, don't kiss that hat-check girl, don't skip dumb classes, don't drive over thirty miles an hour, don't ever laugh! . . . Cal's the only one lets me be a roustabout, which what--what--that's what naturally am! Only one lets me be!'

He closed his eyes, exhausted by his oration.

Fred stood by him, unspeaking. With a shock he realized that there was much to what the boy had said.

Howard reared up, looking ugly, and scolding, 'You send Cal in now! I don't want to talk to you. I won't talk to you till Cal comes in . . . Cal! Oh, Cal! Hey! Come on in here!'

'Howard, for a start, I'm afraid you'll have to get used to doing without Cal. I've chased him out of here--for keeps.'

'You did? Well, blast and damn you, then! And you can chase yourself out, too. Get out and stay out!'

Feverishly Howard had bundled himself out of bed. He loomed far above his father. He swayed, but his eyes--not his eyes, but the eyes of the evil leering thing within him--were murderous. He reached back, stooping a little, and fumbled for the whisky bottle on the pillow. As he shakily raised it, Fred hit him, clean and hard, on the point of the chin.

Howard tumbled on the bed, threshed, tried to rise again, whimpered like a little hurt dog and passed out.

Fred drew up a chair and sat watching him, too profoundly troubled to think anything tangible. Presently he rose, creakingly, and began to bustle.

In the bathroom there wasn't a clean towel. Fred rinsed out a soiled one and carefully wiped Howard's sweating forehead, the back of his neck, his wrists.

Howard slept on.

Fred began on the kitchen. Swiftly, not very competently, he scraped the dirty dishes into the garbage pail, washed them, put them away. Meantime he had telephoned to a laundry, to a clothes presser, and when the runners came, he gave out all of Howard's garments that he could round up, for cleaning by special twelve-hour service.

He telephoned for coffee, cream, eggs, a percolator. He scrubbed the kitchen floor, painfully down on his plump knees, the small of his back stinging. By now he was in shirt sleeves, his hair tousled, his cheeks smutty, and when the messengers came in answer to his telephoning, they looked as suspiciously at him as he had looked at his son.

When he heard Howard groaning he shambled in to give the boy hot black coffee and aspirin; shaved him as well as he could; combed his hair. He said nothing at all the while. Howard looked at him gratefully, got out a hoarse 'Sorry, Dad,' and went back to sleep.

Fred telephoned a cable (deferred!) to Hazel:

HOWARD OKAY PLANNING JOB FOR HIM AM WRITING LOVE YOU HAPPY QUESTION

He had just sent it when Sara telephoned:

'Father? I was so nasty about Howard when you were here. Please forgive me. Kind of upset about him, and I guess I was trying to hide it or something. It was a dirty mean trick of me to take it out on you, darling!'

Then Fred rejoiced, 'Hallelujah! Now let's see what a dumb worker can do with the other child.'

Wearily he began to clean the living-room.

Whether many of the things he did for Howard were wise, is not to be known. One was intelligent; as soon as the flat was clean enough so that the Cornplows could face the world, he sent out for a cook, a powerful coloured woman, and began to feed the young man.

Since Howard was no old and conditioned alcoholic, Fred guessed (as he set up in rivalry to Dr. Janissary as domestic psychiatrist) that it would be injurious to fix his attention too much on alcohol by drastically forbidding it. He let him have three or four, later one or two, drinks a day, and with no great pleasure shared them with him.

For three days Howard slept most of the time between meals, in the secure feeling that his father was there, not going to nag him, ready to give anything and forgive everything.

Not even on the two steamers, since there he had by his tension been helping push them forward to a destination, had Fred devoted so many unclocked, eternal-seeming hours to meditation on the one question that is of moment: Why are we here in life? What is its purpose?

He persuaded himself that he had to know something of the answer before he could do anything for Howard; before he could determine whether it was his business, or merely an impertinence, to 'do anything' for Howard at all.

Like every other philosopher since time was, greybeard in a hermitage of old, or parachute-jumper with two seconds for contemplation before pulling the rip cord, he gave up trying to master the question entire. But he did work out a comforting notion or two, and the first was that he had in all his life done nothing so important as to cease completely the bustling which had given him his little distinction as a citizen, and let life itself work on him.

If it be doubted that a Fred Cornplow would evolve a philosophy, it may be answered that the Fred Cornplows are great men, but most of them do not have the disastrous good fortune of sitting for many quiet hours beside a heartsick son, after having for five months sat, ineffectual and alone, by café tables in strange lands, and do not, thus, often ask: what is a Fred Cornplow that he too should live, along with such divine creatures as the humming-bird and the shark?

He perceived that his purpose in life had not been, as usually he had believed, to sell motor cars or handy household gadgets. Yet such selling was not, as the professors and communists would have it, trivial. It had demanded diplomacy, patience, ingenuity, faith that cars are worth having.

He worked away, also, at another notion:

Howard had been reared to demand, not that he be permitted to train his eyes and memory and chest muscles, but that he have, without passionate struggle, all the material richness of a medieval emperor: a palace small but luxuriously heated, a chariot which could gallop at eighty miles an hour, a magic device whereby he could talk to fellow potentates five thousand miles away.

Could he teach himself, then teach Howard, a vision of self-mastery?

Fred came out of his dreaming with a dismaying snap.

'Can any father do much of anything--that is, permanently--for any son? Golly! Not even sure I can make him see he's got to start at the bottom and build, because if I did have the gift of gab, like Doc Janissary, when I got all through my lecture, Howard would say, "Sure, I get you, but fellow has to show some class and be up to date, these days, hasn't he?" But anyway, even if I can't actually help him much, maybe by trying to I can keep my own doggone self from withering too much.'

What, definitely, ought he to do with Howard till the boy was ready to run on his own feet?

The normal thing, free of all fancy romantic ideas, would be to start him off in the Triumph agency again. But a new world would for a little while, suggest new thoughts. In strange lands, Fred hoped he himself had at least learned to be alone and lonely without whimpering.

Take Howard with him to Europe? No; let Annabel rest there. And it looked now, in all the news from Russia, Spain, Germany, Italy, as though the wise old nations of Europe that so despised America's rawness were going to devote their ten thousand years of culture to butchering one another again.

He thought of the Whitefall River, in Canada, where he had once gone fishing. Even if it did nothing to turn Howard from an easy-going young gentleman into a stalwart hero, so dependable that he might some day become assistant to the assistant to the first vice-president of a chewing-gum factory, at least the sweating on the hot trail through the pines, the cold searing plunge afterward, and the chill still nights would in themselves be glorious living.

CHAPTER XL

Howard laughed. Of late he had been more given to laughing. They were making the last portage, about Little Run Rapids, before returning to their permanent camp on the river and to the supper for which they had been longing this past hour. The portage was a gash between thick spruce, close as a closet, hot, lively with mosquitoes which jabbed at the sun-sore backs of their necks. The edges of the upturned canoe bit into their unaccustomed shoulders as they toted it, and their arms ached with the burden of blankets, paddles and cooking kit.

When they came out again on the river bank, with the sun glaring on rippling river, the sand flies pounced on them.

So Howard laughed. 'Certainly a swell idea to come three hundred miles to get your neck chewed and have your shoulders feel like they'd been through a clothes wringer!'

'Like it?' grunted Fred.

'Sure. As Mother would say: "Happy!"'

Their tent awaited them on the river bank, at the edge of an unknown country of jack pine, spruce and birch, through which the only highway was the Whitefall; it was not three hundred but three thousand miles removed from the clatter and contacts of Sachem. The world well lost, thought Fred. His son was ruddy again, and confident, and for three weeks now had lived in company with a whisky flask, without touching it.

Fred was certain now that the boy was neither an alcoholic nor cruel, but the victim of confused marriage and confused jobs in a confused world.

Fred was camp cook, and he celebrated their return that evening, by not merely frying bacon, but with steaks of the lake trout and muskallonge they had caught at Lake Dead Man, but adding the inexpressible luxury of prunes. They gobbled; silent, content.

Howard stretched out luxuriously afterward, his head against a stump, droning:

'You ought to be head of the Boy Scouts. You sure were a great little inspiration this afternoon.'

'Well, what's the daily insult now?'

'Funny enough, I mean it! Seeing an old coot like you, the way you sweat at paddling and didn't give up when you looked ready to drop, I got ashamed of how lazy I am.'

'Thinking about starting in with the Triumph Agency again?'

'I'd like to. I'd like to really learn it, so some day, possibly, I might succeed you . . . if you thought, then, I'd made good.'

'Fine. Like to look at my book on internal-combustion engines now?'

'Be glad to.'

That was all there was of the camp meeting and the mourners' bench.

In the tent, by candlelight, sitting on his folded sleeping bag with a suit-case on his knees for desk, Fred was trying to answer Hazel's anxious query from Paris:

Aren't you coming back to join me, or shall I sail for home, whichever you think best. This is a lovely city, we would enjoy it so much here and Annabel is the nicest companion but not without you. Your loving Hazel.

For half an hour he had been inspired, and he had reached the climactic point in composition where almost everything he had written had been crossed out. He was not used to letters like this. Most of his epistles home, all these years, had confined themselves to: business good, hope you are all well, as is Yrs Truly.

But now he had painfully achieved:

You stay in Europe, see some more of London as well as Paris, etc. etc., as long as you want to. In this family we never did have much compulsion, us over the kids, you and me over each other, and if maybe it has not entirely worked out O.K. always I think children beginning to appreciate it and everything going to be swell. And hope you and I will start off again some day. But now it don't seem to matter like it did when I used to talk about golden road to Samarkand and when we got near there, Istanbul, etc. etc., wasn't the smell fierce in that market place! It seems to me now that it isn't going where you want to that is freedom, but knowing that you can go.

That was all the high creative effort he could endure for the time. He wiped his brow, said, 'Whew,' killed a mosquito and crawled out through the netting to squat beside his son.

Howard observed, 'Do you hear something like an outboard motor, 'way off down the river? Wonder why they got one. Must be fierce job to tote it round the rapids.'

Yes. Fred could hear, like a rapidly beaten carpet, the exhaust of the motor. What tenderfoot would use it in these waters? He listened nervously. He felt that, unexplainably, it was coming for him.

The canoe, a big nineteen-foot freighter, had rounded a bend. Its small headlight, probably a camp flashlight fastened to the bow, illuminated the wrinkled, tumbling brown water, the wash of current about rocks sticking out of the river like the backs of seals, and ashore, the fallen and rotted log-cabin of a trapper, in a grove of willow and scrub pine. It seemed to be heading for their camp fire.

The two men by the tent muttered, 'What's the idea?' and 'Don't believe there's any bad Indians left along the river, but maybe if they'd got hold of some liquor . . .'

The canoe darted in to shore, well guided. They could make out a tall Indian in the bow, and behind him, nothing but a blurry mass. The blurry mass arose, crawled forward, edged past the Indian, stepped cautiously ashore. And the blurry mass was Hazel Cornplow, plus two blankets and man's felt hat.

'But where is Annabel? Where? Where?' begged Howard.

'I left her in Paris, dear, to study a little there. She's such a darling. I've become so fond of her. Imagine! Once I was almost jealous of her! Silly. And the baby seems to be thriving. It's the huskiest little mite you ever saw. My! He grabs your finger and almost breaks it in two. And his smile, I declare, it's exactly like yours when you were a little tad, Howard.'

'But Annabel! Is she coming back? I want her!'

'I thought--it's hard to say, Howard, but I thought she ought to stay away until you earn her.'

'Hm. Man earn his own wife? Well, maybe it isn't such a sour idea. It'll be something to work for!'

Later Hazel purred, 'My, I didn't know we three would all be together again, sitting cosy on a blanket and eating bacon! Isn't it nice here! No telephones ringing.'

'Practically never,' Fred assured her.

'And Fred: I don't want to be too light-footed, but some day would you like to go travelling again? I would so like to see Scandinavia, if they don't manage to have a war in Europe, and--oh, not make a business of wandering, like these silly restless tourists, but just see a *few* places, say like Brazil and Egypt and Cairo and Java and Iceland and so on. What do you think, Fred?'

'I don't know yet. Say, here's a hot one! Right there in the tent I've got a letter about it that I was writing to you. Yessir, by golly, just this minute. I'll tell you, dear. Just now I feel like I ought to stick around a while and . . .'

Then Howard took charge; the Howard of old, cocky and omniscient, yet more affectionate than the old Howard had ever been:

'Now you're not looking at it right, Dad. Way I see it, you old codgers ought to get out more and learn how the world is changing. I tell you, you haven't any idea what the young fellows are doing, these days, Dad. There's nobody like you for steadiness, but you ought to take a chance once in a while.'

'Indeed you ought to,' said Hazel.

'I see,' said Frederick William Cornplow. 'Say! In Brazil we ought to get doggone good coffee. Well, you can sit up and talk till sunrise if you want to, but the old man's going to turn in. I hear where there's good coffee in Egypt, too. We'll see. Good night--good night!'

CPSIA information can be obtained
at www.ICGtesting.com
Printed in the USA
LVHW081113251020
669749LV00018B/2735